Dadgummit

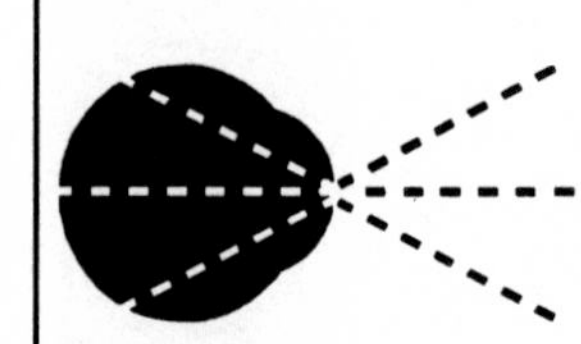

A DREAMWALKER MYSTERY

DADGUMMIT

MAGGIE TOUSSAINT

THORNDIKE PRESS
A part of Gale, a Cengage Company

Farmington Hills, Mich • San Francisco • New York • Waterville, Maine
Meriden, Conn • Mason, Ohio • Chicago

Thorndike Press, a part of Gale, a Cengage Company.

Thorndike Press® Large Print Clean Reads.
The text of this Large Print edition is unabridged.
Other aspects of the book may vary from the original edition.
Set in 16 pt. Plantin.

**LIBRARY OF CONGRESS CIP DATA ON FILE.
CATALOGUING IN PUBLICATION FOR THIS BOOK
IS AVAILABLE FROM THE LIBRARY OF CONGRESS**

ISBN-13: 978-1-4328-4785-2 (hardcover)
ISBN-10: 1-4328-4785-6 (hardcover)

Published in 2018 by arrangement with Camel Press

Printed in the United States of America
1 2 3 4 5 6 7 22 21 20 19 18

This one's for Annaliese.

ACKNOWLEDGMENTS

Special thanks go to Holly McClure, who provided information about the mythology and spirits of Native American culture. Critique partner Polly Iyer and friend Gordon Aalborg helped sharpen this manuscript. Any errors made with the information are mine.

Chapter One

The campfire's flames soothed my soul after the eight-hour, three-hundred-fifty-mile drive from the coast. We had six glorious days in the Georgia mountains before jobs and the start of school demanded our return.

Should have done this months ago. Should've packed up the people I loved and hit the road for a vacation at the start of summer. But between dreamwalking and police consulting — two new jobs I'd added seven months ago — and my Pets and Plants business, I'd barely had time to catch my breath this year. Now we'd nearly run out of August. It was the last Tuesday of the month, and I had until Sunday to relax, unwind, and recharge with my favorite people.

I'm Baxley Powell, and apparently I'm a workaholic. People say I look a bit like Emma Watson from Harry Potter fame, but other than the shoulder-length brown hair, cocoa-colored eyes, lean body, and extra abilities, I don't see it. At five-six, I'm taller than the actress and shun the spotlight. And then there's my dreamwalking, which melds several psychic abilities, as opposed to her character's fictional magic.

Mom cleared her throat, drawing me back to the campsite. My folks were the last wave of baby boomers, but their style of dress remained true to the 1960s. Both sported tie-dye T-shirts and wore their long gray hair in braids. My mom was dressed in a denim jumper, my dad in denim shorts and flip-flops. In age, they were nearing sixty, but I'd never known anyone more ageless and agile.

After the Army declared my soldier husband dead, I'd moved home to the house I'd inherited from my grandmother in Sinclair County, an hour south of Savannah, Georgia. My parents lived about ten minutes from me. They were a constant source of inspiration, encouragement, and child-care. Between my mother's affinity with crystals and my father's ability to talk to the dead, I had a built-in support team for dreamwalking.

"Tab and I are headed over to my friend Luanne's farm first thing in the morning,"

Mom said. "We're helping her put up pickles. Her brother is there and he offered to teach Tab how to whittle. Everyone is welcome to join us."

"No thanks. I plan to veg in the sun," Charlotte said, firelight glinting off her glasses. My friend's outgoing personality, ambition, and her love of bold colors and chunky jewelry made some folks wary, or maybe it was the heavy makeup that stood out in our small town. Honest to God, she never had a stray hair in her auburn bob or bangs, while my hair constantly stuck out in every direction.

We'd been best friends since Sinclair County Elementary School, and she was the closest thing I had to a sister. Plus, she was three months older than me, so I got to tease her every year about being an older woman. Right now, she was twenty-nine to my twenty-eight.

For months Charlotte had been vying for top dog at our local paper, but the constant friction had worn her down. She'd leapt at the chance to get away.

"I don't want to think about deadlines or careers," Charlotte continued. "Last time I visited Annabelle's place in the mountains, I was a teenager. I plan to relive my glory days of being a slug."

Charlotte's cousin, Annabelle Kinsey, owned this property at Stony Creek Lake in north Georgia where we'd parked our borrowed RVs. When we'd asked Annabelle to recommend a campsite, she insisted we stay on her land. Three years ago, a friend of hers had sprung for electricity and water, installing it in the nearby pavilion along with an outdoor shower, thus creating the ideal temporary getaway. Annabelle said we'd be doing her a favor by making sure everything worked.

Her kind offer plus the campers we'd borrowed made this an inexpensive vacation. My tag-along style camper was a loaner from one of my Pets and Plants clients, and my folks were using their friend Running Bear's small motorhome. They'd towed their sub-compact sedan behind it for scooting around in the mountains. We'd already connected both campers to water and power, so camping was going to be even easier than we thought.

"Sounds like we can accommodate everyone's wishes," I said. "The forecast is for blue skies and low eighties. A perfect day to be outdoors. Fishing in the morning for me, and paddleboarding in the afternoon for Larissa."

As one, the dogs lifted their heads. Maddy,

our black lab, bolted to her feet, her hackles raised. A deep rumble sounded in her throat, a menacing sound I'd never heard her make. Elvis and Muffin, our Chihuahua and Shih-poo, stood at attention behind her, their gazes riveted on the same spot in the woods.

Something was out there. Unfortunately, my Beretta was in the camper under my pillow. As concerned as the dogs were, I wouldn't have enough time to grab the gun from inside and protect my family.

Swallowing my fear, I stood to face the threat. "Who's there?"

The unmistakable sound of a shotgun racking echoed through the meadow where we'd camped. What had we gotten ourselves into? *Priorities.* My-ten-year-old daughter's safety came first. Without turning, I said, "Larissa. In the camper. Now. Lock the door."

She scrambled to her feet and darted inside. A small measure of relief washed over me. I called out again, "Who's there?"

My parents and Charlotte inched toward me. Not a good idea. If we clustered together, a single shotgun blast could get all of us. "Separate and take cover. Charlotte, call the police."

Charlotte dug her phone out of her

pocket, but in her haste, fumbled it. She shrieked and fell to her knees. All three dogs barked their heads off. A shot echoed through the woods. A branch fell from a pine between us and the lake.

I dropped to the ground to make myself a smaller target, hoping and praying everyone I loved was safe. A quick glance around showed my parents and Charlotte were uninjured, though their faces were ghostly pale. Both cats had vanished. Between the barking dogs and my racing heart, I could barely hear myself think. This couldn't be happening. After all I'd been through, after I'd finally achieved financial security through the Army Survivor Benefit Program and my police consulting work, would some mountain wacko with a gun end my life?

It had to be a mistake. That was the only thing that made sense. I summoned my courage. "Don't shoot. We're unarmed."

"No phone calls," a man yelled from the shadows. "You're trespassing on private property. You've got five minutes to clear out."

Fear had rendered me stupid. I'd forgotten to use all the tools at my disposal. Quickly, I slid into my extra senses to check the perimeter for life signs. Only one heat signature, so only one guy out there. We weren't surrounded by a band of militia or a rogue motorcycle gang. Even so, a single shooter could inflict a lot of damage.

I gathered my nerve and spoke loud enough to be heard in distant Atlanta. "We have permission from Annabelle Kinsey to camp here. Please put down your weapon."

The man marched out of the shadows. As he neared, I noticed his camouflage attire from the brim of his ball cap to the heel of his sturdy boots. My late husband had served in Afghanistan and worn those same camies. This guy carried himself with the soldier-straight posture of former military.

Annabelle's last-minute caution surfaced in my head. A neighbor of hers was hypervigilant. When Annabelle had given me the safe words in case I encountered this guy, I'd dismissed them. But the conversation came back to me in a blinding flash.

"Blue marmalade," I said over the yapping dogs. The man kept advancing, so I shouted the phrase again. "Blue marmalade."

The man halted ten feet from me, his weapon aimed at the ground near his feet. In the firelight, his angular, blackened face barely reflected any light. I couldn't see his eyes at all under the brim of the cap. His thick neck ended abruptly in square, solid shoulders. A heavy, gear-laden belt circled his trim hips. This guy expected serious trouble.

His teeth flashed pearly white as he replied, "Roger, Red Rover. The enemy is wily. New targets appear daily."

His response gave me the courage to sit up. I quieted the small dogs and called Maddy to my side. Elvis and Muffin followed their leader. According to Annabelle, her neighbor needed a second confirmation code, another color response to completely disengage. The answer would fit a pattern. Blue marmalade and red rover. Blue and red. What went with them? The answer unfurled like a flag. Red, white, and blue. The colors of patriotism.

"Copy that, White Duck. This grid is clear."

He nodded. With another quartering glance at the perimeter, he tipped his cap to me. "Evening, ma'am. Burl Sayer. I look after Mrs. Kinsey's property."

"I see that you do." I took a deep breath. We were all right. It had been a misunderstanding. Though my pulse still thrummed, I stood. "I'm Baxley Powell. My daughter Larissa is in the camper. We're camping here all week with my parents, Tab and Lacey Nesbitt, and my friend Charlotte Ambrose.

Charlotte and Annabelle are cousins."

"Sorry to have rousted you, but a soldier's job is to patrol and question those he encounters. Now that I know who you are, I won't bother you again."

Sayer obviously had a few issues, but at least he wasn't keen on shooting us anymore. What was the protocol for receiving a gun-toting vigilante in the night? "Would you like some supper?" I asked.

He refused with a twitch of the head. "Don't eat on patrol. Slows me down. Gotta keep watch for the invasion."

Sayer seemed to be suffering from post-traumatic stress disorder. Several of my husband's friends returned from the war changed forever, so I recognized some of their traits in Sayer. The restlessness, the extreme watchfulness, the armament in a civilian zone. Was he harmless or a time bomb waiting to go off? PTSD victims covered the full spectrum.

They lived in two realities at once.

Heck, most people said that about me, and I had no plans to kill anyone.

I nodded toward the forest. "You see any signs of activity?"

"Not in this sector," Sayer admitted. "Spotted an incursion the other night through my scope, but the enemy quickly moved on."

Unsure what that meant, I offered up a bland reply. "I see. Well, then, thank you for your vigilance. I'm sure Mrs. Kinsey appreciates it as much as we do."

Sayer gave a curt nod and shouldered his weapon. "Guard your flank. The dogs will sound the alarm if the enemy approaches. I have miles to go before night is done." With that, he melted soundlessly into the shadows.

The camper door opened, and Larissa bolted out to join us. She glommed onto my waist. I could feel the pounding beat of her heart through our clothes.

"Oh my God." Charlotte bear-hugged me from behind. "You've got guts, girlfriend. You just defused a crazy man."

My knees trembled, but I'd rather keep my adrenaline overload to myself. I disentangled myself from my friend's awkward embrace. Bravery came at a steep cost. "I didn't believe he was a threat after he came forward. Different and weird, yes. He's got problems, but as I watched how he moved, how he scanned constantly for danger, I kept thinking one thing. . . ."

My parents crowded close for hugs. I gave up on trying to project a façade of calm and savored their familiar comfort.

"That you should call the cops?" Charlotte prompted.

I shot her a quelling look. "Not hardly. Wartime broke a lot of men, including my Roland. I know my guy's supposed to be dead, but I can't help thinking he could be a lot like this guy. Fried but functioning off the grid in survival mode."

My parents nodded encouragingly. Larissa squeezed me again. That she wanted her dad to be alive went without saying.

Charlotte looked at me with pity. "Oh, Baxley, don't torture yourself with false hope. Roland's dead. The Army said so."

My chin shot up. "The Army has no proof. They declared him dead. They never found his body. Dad and I have searched repeatedly for him among the dead. He isn't there. That leaves one possible answer: Roland's alive."

Charlotte's face fell. She patted my shoulder. "You should've taken a vacation years ago, Baxley. Getting your hopes up like this sets you up for an even bigger disappointment. The chances of him being like Burl Sayer are slim to none."

"A single chance is all I need."

My dad moved between us and kissed me on the cheek. "That's enough excitement for me tonight. I want to be up early to watch the sunrise over the lake. "I'm off to bed."

"Me, too," Mom said with another loving touch.

"I'm ready to call it a night," I announced, not wanting to argue about my mental health status or Roland's whereabouts with Charlotte.

After dousing the fire, we all turned in, but sleep wouldn't come. Automatically, I expanded my extra senses, letting them quest out as they did every night. Burl Sayer was long gone. We were blessedly alone.

But Charlotte's certainty about Roland's fate kept churning my thoughts. I wouldn't accept his death. I couldn't. As long his spirit wasn't among the dead, logic and emotion dictated he had to be alive. He would come back to me. I couldn't allow anyone, even someone as well-meaning as Charlotte, to dampen my hope.

Roland was alive.

Chapter Two

I stood beside the lake and flicked my line out again, enjoying the sunshine sparkling across the water's surface. Charlotte sighed happily from the blanket where she drowsed in the warm, golden sunlight. Her glasses lay beside her. Without them, her freckles stood out and she looked radiant. Coming to the mountains had already invigorated her. I hoped the time off would give her clarity about her journalism career as well.

My parents had gone over to Luanne's farm, promising to return early afternoon in time for the paddleboard excursion. Sayer's intrusion last night made me wary. But I wouldn't be caught flatfooted again on this vacation. This morning I'd stuffed my handgun in my back waistband as a precaution.

Larissa lounged beside my friend, head propped on a fat roll of beach towels, reading something on her tablet. I bit my tongue to keep from scolding her about tuning out. We all relieved stress in different ways. Reading suited my daughter.

Everything seemed peaceful at the lakeside, except for a mechanical whine in the distance. Someone was enjoying a boat ride, I supposed. I reeled the line back, cast it out again. So far, no luck with the lake trout. I hoped they weren't on vacation.

"You miss him, don't you?" Charlotte asked.

There had been only one "him" in my life — Roland Powell. "Only every night and every day."

Charlotte's heavy sigh sounded epic and moody. "At least you had a husband and a family. Time's running out for me."

"I still have both, though we should agree to disagree on that point. I'm concerned, though . . . for you."

"You should be. I've been getting a weird vibe from Bernard at the office. I think he might ask me out."

Charlotte had spent the last year railing about her rival getting the plum assignments, while she'd been on the jumbo vegetable circuit. "Oh? Say he followed through. What would you do?"

"I'm not interested in him romantically. There's no spark. He's like the annoying brother I never had." She hesitated. "But there's a small voice in my head that says he's interested in me. That says I'm not the fat girl nobody looks twice at. You know what I want more than anything? I want to be part of a couple. I hate being alone."

I was dismayed to hear her voice break, but she'd push me away if I offered her more than consolation. My plus-sized friend blamed her weight for her lack of dating prospects. Anyone who couldn't look past a few pounds at what a wonderful person she was didn't deserve her.

"You're not alone, Char," I said. "You have us."

"Thanks, but I want what you had with Roland. Someone I can snuggle with at night. Someone who'll keep the boogeyman away. I thought I'd have kids by now. I'm still the girl in town people look right through. The one who never went anywhere or did anything."

"No one sees you that way."

"Just the same, I'd rather have a hunk to light up my world."

"Your guy will come." My fishing line snagged on something. I tugged it to the side, and the pressure eased. "You need to announce your request to the universe."

"You daring me?"

"If that's what it takes."

"Okay." Charlotte pushed up to a seated position, cupped her hands around her lips and yelled. "I need a hero." She lay back down, still smirking. "Satisfied?"

"Quite."

I tightened my line, then released the slack. The rumble of an engine became more pronounced. Definitely a small craft motoring our way.

"You hear something?" Charlotte asked.

"Sounds like a boat to me."

"Relax," Charlotte said. "You just squared your shoulders like the sheriff back home does when he expects trouble. Boats are common in lakes. Relax and enjoy the scenery."

Easy for her to say. I was already aware of one crazy person running loose in these parts. Who knew how many crazies we had up here?

An inflatable craft in the lake's center made a course correction, heading straight toward us. I reeled in my line. "Looks like we're about to have company."

Charlotte sat up, donned her glasses, and shaded her brow with her hand. A second later she beamed and fluffed her chin-length hair. "I should've announced my desire for a hero to the universe years ago. Two hunks dead ahead. Proceed with shameless flirtation."

Chapter Three

"Good morning," Hunk Number One said, his voice deep and rough as sandpaper. He stepped out of the beached craft, planted an anchor on the shore, and took our measure. The name plate on his navy-blue uniform said "Duncan." He moved his wraparound sunglasses to his ball cap.

I returned the scrutiny, noting this white male's shiny shoes, crisply pleated sheriff's department uniform, close-cropped hair, and sharp blue eyes. Hunk Number Two, a lanky African American also in uniform and armed, seemed concerned with scanning the tree line around us. According to his uniform ID tag, his surname was Loggins.

Larissa shushed the barking dogs, scooped up Muffin and Elvis, then came to stand by me at the water's edge. Charlotte stood on the blanket, her bare feet pale against the bright pink fleece. Larissa's black lab leaned against my leg, while the two cats scurried to the nearest bush. Something about the intense way these deputies studied us made me wish I could skulk away and hide with the cats.

"Morning," Charlotte said, waggling her fingers in greeting.

"Good morning," Hunk Number One said. "I'm Deputy Duncan, and this is my partner Deputy Loggins. We're checking on folks using the lake. Please give us your names."

Charlotte looked at me. I motioned for her to continue being our spokesperson. "I'm Charlotte Ambrose. We're visiting from the coast."

"And that would be . . . ?"

"Marion. We're nearly halfway between Savannah and Jacksonville."

"This is private property," Deputy Duncan said in a stern tone.

"It belongs to my cousin, Annabelle Kinsey. We have her permission to camp here. Would you like me to call her so you can confirm our right to be here?"

"That won't be necessary." He turned to me. "And you, ma'am?"

I swallowed thickly. "Baxley Powell. This is my daughter, Larissa. The three of us drove up from the coast yesterday, along with my parents. They went to visit their friend Luanne Sweet's farm today." I searched their faces. "What's this all about?"

"There was a disturbance nearby," Duncan said, writing quickly on a small notepad. "We're making sure everyone else is all right, and at the same time compiling a list of people in the area. We're searching by water and by land to make sure we don't overlook anyone. You're the first folks we've spotted by the lake."

On the boat, Loggins tapped rapidly on an electronic tablet. I gulped. With today's technology, they could instantly run a background check on all of us. I hoped Charlotte didn't have any outstanding parking tickets. Even so, I felt queasy at being investigated. Was this about our visitor last night?

"Are you aware of anyone else staying in the vicinity?" Duncan asked.

"We've only met one individual so far," I said.

"And that would be?"

Was I getting a vet in trouble? Too late now. "Burl Sayer. He stopped by and introduced himself last night."

"Sayer? No one's seen him in months. We thought he'd moved on."

"Nope. He's alive and well and very much here."

Duncan stilled. "He can be confrontational. No incident to report?"

"We sorted everything out right away," I hurriedly added before Charlotte blabbed about the shotgun. Sayer would not do well in police custody.

Duncan glanced over his shoulder at his partner. "Sayer can be a bit much. Was he in his Army duds?"

"Yes."

"We need to find him," Duncan said. "Put out an APB."

I chewed my lip, wishing they weren't intent on finding Sayer. Couldn't they give a vet a break? Maybe Sayer's skills would keep him from harm during this manhunt.

"On it." Loggins fiddled with the tablet, then picked up a radio from the dash. "Be on the lookout for suspect male Burl Sayer." As he gave Burl's height and weight and other identifying features, I reached a stomach-knotting conclusion. An incident had occurred at the lake. These cops thought Burl might be responsible.

I heard the unmistakable yet distant wail of a police siren from somewhere behind us, way uphill and distant. If I was a suspicious sort, and I was, I would think they were sending cars to move us somewhere. I edged closer to my daughter. What kind of disturbance happened nearby? Were we in danger?

Loggins' tablet beeped. He was fully absorbed by whatever had popped up on that screen. If I hadn't been watching him, I'd have missed the slight flaring of his eyes as he caught his partner's gaze.

Suddenly the air felt wrong in this tranquil setting, as if it was too heavy to draw into my lungs. These cops were searching for a suspect. *Not my problem.* Except I had a sinking feeling it would become my problem.

All three dogs howled at the siren, and Larissa, bless her, tried to quiet them.

Loggins scowled and stepped off the boat toward Charlotte, tablet tucked under his arm. He was taller than me and looked former-professional-athlete solid.

I felt a tug on my elbow and jumped.

Deputy Duncan gestured toward the path leading back to our camp. "Come with me, ma'am. We have cruisers meeting us at your campsite for transport."

My feet grew roots. The fishing rod bobbled in my hands. "I'm not leaving my daughter or my friend. We're traveling together. If you need someone to vouch for my character, call Sheriff Wayne Thompson down in Marion."

"You're in our database as his consultant, and we've already got a call in to him. This is a routine precaution. For your safety as well as ours —"

"Gun," Deputy Loggins yelled from behind me. "She's got a handgun in her waistband."

"Hands in the air," Duncan said, weapon drawn. "Now."

"But I can explain."

"Hands up."

A millisecond later, my Beretta was gone, my pockets emptied, and my arms were tightly clenched behind me. In the second before I totally locked down my extra senses, I got an inkling of the cop's mental state. *Neutralize the threat. Protect my partner. Assess the danger level. Contain the situation.*

Fear threaded through his laser-focused thoughts, along with excitement. I needed to do some fast talking before the situation escalated further. "I can explain the gun," I began again, twisting around to search Deputy Duncan's face. "Sayer's visit last night spooked me. I didn't want to be unarmed if he strolled by today. I have a carry permit."

Maddy charged the deputy, barking like she'd cornered an armadillo in the yard. In slow motion, flecks of dog spittle flew everywhere — on me, on the deputy. The man behind me shifted his weight onto the balls of his feet. Was he reaching for his gun again?

"Mom!" Larissa shouted.

"No!" I yelled at the deputy, who had drawn his weapon. "Don't shoot!"

Chapter Four

Sirens wailing, dogs barking, females screaming, big guy behind me channeling two-hundred-proof adrenaline — this misunderstanding needed to be turned around before someone got hurt. I sent Larissa an urgent telepathic message, *Calm Maddy right now, or the cops will shoot her.*

"Maddy!" Larissa shrilled. "Heel. Maddy. Come. Maddy. Here, girl."

The Labrador stopped barking, but she didn't cede an inch of territory. Her protest turned to a deep-seated growl. I'd never heard this dog take offense before, but she sounded like a hellhound about to go for the jugular. I didn't need my extra senses to feel the man's fear behind me. He telegraphed it in waves.

Deputy Loggins motioned Charlotte and Larissa away from the fray. I saw the tight set of my daughter's mouth, the militant jut of her chin. But I also saw the shudder that coursed through her body. I didn't know what she was thinking, but I needed to ensure her safety. "Do what he says, Larissa."

Deputy Duncan put me between him and the growling dog. "Call off the hound, lady. You don't want me to take care of it."

"Maddy, it's okay." I used my most soothing voice. The dog shook her head, flopping her ears. I repeated the phrase several times until she heard me. The dog stopped and cocked her head, confused. She whined softly. I tried again with a quiet voice. "Easy. Easy does it. That's a good girl. That's a good dog."

I glanced over at the tree where the rest of my party and Deputy Loggins huddled. Charlotte's red cheeks and stiff posture spoke volumes, as did the fierce expression on my daughter's face. "Call her now, Larissa," I said. "She'll come this time."

"Leash the dog," Deputy Duncan ordered once the Labrador padded over to my daughter.

Larissa handed Muffin and Elvis to Charlotte, then she clipped a leash on Maddy.

Duncan released me, and I finally felt like I could take a full breath. "Thank you." I rubbed my wrists and glared at him. "I'm not accustomed to being treated as a suspect."

"Sheriff Blair treats everyone as suspects until she proves otherwise. I didn't mean to frighten you, but you should have declared your weapon from the start."

Heat flooded off my face. He was right. "Sorry. I forgot."

Deputy Loggins' tablet beeped. He glanced at it, then nodded to Deputy Duncan. "We need to remove your party from the area," Duncan said.

"What incident happened nearby?" I asked.

"I'm not at liberty to say, ma'am. Please, if you'll walk up to the campsite, all will be explained soon."

My daughter's questioning look asked, *What now?* I responded via our one-way telepathic link.

Do what they say, even if we get separated. This situation is temporary, and we've done nothing wrong. Keep calm.

She nodded, so I felt like I could count on her to cooperate with the authorities. Charlotte, I wasn't so sure about. She looked like she was ready to whip out her Press Club pass and demand to know what was going on.

"You can't violate our civil rights like

this," Charlotte said.

"Loggins, give us five, then follow us to the campsite," Duncan said. He latched onto my arm again. "Let's go."

"What about our stuff? And our cats."

"Since this lake frontage is Ms. Kinsey's private property, and since we saw no other boats or people on the lake, your belongings should be secure for the time being. And long ago I learned you can't make a cat do anything it doesn't want to do."

Deputy Duncan kept a steady pressure on my arm as we marched away from the others. *Great.* We were in the divide-and-conquer portion of our encounter. "You may have a point." Other than the cops freaking out about my gun, they had been fair with us. But something had them wired to the gills. "Do you arrest every visitor to your county?"

"You're not under arrest, ma'am, just detained until we get further clarification of your role from both sheriffs."

If only I weren't moving, I'd risk a dreamwalk with this guy's thoughts. But the circumstances weren't dire enough for the potential consequences of me appearing to lose consciousness. I could wake up in a hospital full of IVs and drugs. An involuntary shudder ripped through me. Not going to happen.

We walked in silence along the wooded path. My curiosity flared at their interest in us. "Were y'all looking for someone in particular?"

The path narrowed, and he released his grip on my arm. "Can't talk about the case, ma'am."

The case. So there was a case. I sighed. Just my luck to go on vacation and land in the middle of an investigation. Sinclair County's Sheriff Wayne Thompson would love this. He was probably laughing his head off right now. Heck, to spite me he might even tell them to lock me up and throw away the key.

"How'd you do that with the dog, ma'am, if you don't mind me asking?" Deputy Duncan asked.

Ah. My hopes flared. Had this guy decided I wasn't a criminal? My dreamwalker skill set included truth detection, touch readings, and talking to the dead in the spirit world. I was certain he'd never met a person like me before. "In addition to my police consulting work, I have a pet and plant care business. I understand animals, at least dogs and cats."

Twigs crunched underfoot. The shadows around us quivered as a breeze ruffled the tree canopy. I didn't need ESP to tell me this man was deep in thought.

Finally, he spoke, his gravelly voice tinged with wonder. "I've never seen a dog quiet from a mad like that. You train dogs?"

"Some."

"Huh." We walked on a bit. "How much you charge for your services?"

I bit back a smile. "Depends on how long it takes to get the dog's attention and to retrain the pet owner."

"You saying my dog's bad behavior is because of me?"

My cheek twitched. "Every situation is unique. Just like this one. You could extend some professional courtesy and tell me what's going on and why I'm separated from my daughter and friend."

"You're being detained at the request of our sheriff, ma'am."

I glanced over my shoulder and pinned him with a glare. "You're serious? I'm a stranger to these parts. No way I could've done whatever is wrong."

He had the decency to blush. "Procedure, ma'am. I'm doing my job."

Crap. He'd use the p-word. I trudged in silence, ever upward toward the meadow where my truck and the campers were parked. I'd seen Wayne round up suspects time and again. He exercised every means he had to make the suspects realize he was in charge so they'd hurry up and level with him.

The divide-and-conquer strategy was effective in this instance. I didn't want my daughter to go through an interrogation. I didn't want her spending a second of her vacation in an interview room, or worse, worrying about her mom going to jail.

As we approached the campsite, the filtered daylight turned emergency-light blue from the two cop cars in the drive. And there, standing beside my camper, was the Ice Queen of a woman I'd been avoiding for months. The state archaeologist with a medical examiner's license. Gail Bergeron.

Chapter Five

"Fancy meeting you in my neck of the woods," Gail Bergeron quipped. "I was on my way to see Sheriff Blair about an unusual case when I heard your name on the scanner. Annabelle dated my cousin one summer so I knew exactly where this place was. Thought I'd make my pitch before Twilla Sue got her hooks into you. By the way, nice tag-along camper you got here."

The state archaeologist looked right at home at my campsite, what with her gleaming hiking boots, finely creased jeans, silver-studded leather belt, and bright white blouse. A crisp navy-blue-and-white-patterned scarf at her neck completed her chic ensemble. Her short blonde hair was styled like a grown-up pixie, giving her a waif-like appearance, except I knew better. I'd watched her chew men up and spit them out like old gum.

"Hello, Gail." My legs felt heavier as I approached. I'd rather have my fate in Sheriff Wayne Thompson's hands than this woman's. She'd been after me for months to help her with her cold cases. We'd been on opposite sides of a previous case, and I couldn't forget how unpleasant she'd been to me. I didn't want anything to do with her or her moldy old bones.

She caught the eye of the man beside me. "Deputy Duncan, nice to see you again. If you don't mind, I'd like to have a few moments in private with this woman regarding a cold case."

Deputy Duncan's hand closed on my arm again. "I have orders to deliver Ms. Powell to my boss, ma'am. You'll need to take your request up with the sheriff."

My estimation of Deputy Duncan rose several notches. He must've gotten trampled by Gail before. Nice to know she didn't cow everyone.

Gail fumed and I listened as the deputy made arrangements for one of the new officers to ride back on the lake with Deputy Loggins while Duncan took a car.

He marched me over to a squad car and opened the back door. "Get in."

I tried to catch sight of Larissa and Charlotte, but there were too many trees between us. Climbing in the cruiser, I wrinkled my nose at the faint whiff of urine and vomit. The door slammed shut behind me.

Gail approached the car and tried to slip past the deputy. He spoke to her sharply, probably repeating the same line he gave me about doing his job, and she argued loudly with him. He didn't respond, only held up his hand and made a circular motion. Two armed deputies approached and escorted Gail away from our vehicle.

Gail's retreating back gave me a perverse sense of satisfaction. Ha! Divide and conquer trumps political connections in this county. You'll have to wait to sink your talons into me, Ice Queen.

Deputy Duncan climbed into the front seat and started off. I gazed back at the campsite to see Gail hurrying to the black Hummer parked nearby. One cop car remained. For Charlotte and Larissa. I gulped. We drove past Annabelle's cabin. Two more cop cars were parked there, and the door yawned ominously before us. What was it about the vacant cabin that drew their attention?

"This looks serious," I said. "What's going on?"

"You reported Sayer as last seen in this area. We need to question him. He's sheltered in this cabin before."

I dashed off another telepathic message to my daughter. *They're taking me to the local sheriff. They have no reason to hold us, so I'll be back soon. Love you.*

I wished like anything Larissa could do more than receive my messages. I would feel better if I knew her state of mind. I hoped and prayed my mother-in-law didn't get wind of this. I'd foiled her attempt to get custody of Larissa earlier this summer, but I didn't trust her to let it go. She'd use any information she could to prove I was an unfit mother. I pursed my lips in frustration. She wouldn't hear about this from me.

The cop's radio squelched loudly. Immediately following the abrupt noise, the person at the other end rattled off a series of numerical codes. Deputy Duncan clicked a button. "Roger that."

"When this is over, will I get my gun and my personal possessions back?" I asked as we rolled along the grassy driveway and onto the paved road.

"Yes, ma'am, you will have them today, but the timing depends on the sheriff."

"Can you tell me what this is about?"

My question rated no response. I stared glumly out the window as we negotiated a curvy mountain road. We weren't headed down the mountain to town. We were going up the hill. What?

I tapped on the metal grate between the front and back seat. "Hey, town's the other direction. You're going the wrong way."

"Not headed to town."

"Where are we going?"

Duncan took the next curve a little too fast for my comfort. I braced myself against the door to keep from sliding across the vinyl seat. Finally, the man spared me a glance. "What kind of consulting do you do for your sheriff? My boss is over the moon that you're here."

My skin prickled for no good reason. I had a bad feeling about this. "If I'm not under arrest, can you pull over and let me out?"

"Afraid not. The best I can figure, the sheriffs have done a deal."

What had my sheriff, Wayne Thompson, gotten me into? I owed him, for sure, for helping get my in-laws off my back two months ago when they'd tried to pull a custody grab of my daughter, but I had planned to repay him with a favor, not to have him pimp me out. Gloom settled heavily on my shoulders. I eyed the doors. No handles. I wasn't getting out of this car without Deputy Duncan's help. "I don't understand."

"You're the sheriff's ticket to the big tent. Sheriff Blair's sights are set on being the next governor. She's licking her chops. Says you're gonna be her lucky charm. Do you have special insight into criminology? Are you a profiler?"

As a rule, I never mention dreamwalking to strangers. It's better that way. "I'm a mother who happens to consult for my local police department. I don't work crime scenes in other jurisdictions. I'm on vacation."

"Not anymore. According to the chatter in my ear com, your sheriff officially loaned you to us. Said to remind you it's time for payback."

Payback. He would call in the debt when I was on vacation.

Deputy Duncan cleared his throat. His gaze met mine in the rearview mirror. "I couldn't help noticing your unusual hair, ma'am. That white streak looks natural, but it's so different from your darker hair."

Allowing my dreamwalking abilities to be part of my daily life came at a cost. All my psychic relatives started with normal hair. The ones who gave their talents free rein bore the visible sign of power. Because I'd denied my gift until this year, the striped look still surprised me when I gazed at my reflection.

I sighed. “The white forelock came from the universe in January. Some higher power’s idea of making me a beacon.”

“I don’t understand.”

I shoved a few errant strands of hair behind my ear. “Me either.”

Chapter Six

The cruiser bounced down a narrow, grassy path. Underbrush scraped the sides and bottom of the car. Ahead, I saw a cluster of emergency vehicles, lights flashing red, blue, and yellow. Uniformed officers bustled about a tight knot of people.

Sheriff Blair would be in that mix. Dead center, I estimated. She expected me to propel her to fame. Worse, my sheriff back home had called in the favor I owed him and promised my help. There was too much static and despair in the backseat of this car, which kept me from opening my senses and figuring out what the heck was going on, but that was my plan once I stepped foot outside this vehicle.

People scattered like ants as we approached. Deputy Duncan stopped the car behind a black SUV. "Here you go: your next assignment."

Great. A case I didn't want, with people I

didn't know or trust. I didn't like surprises, and this day had been chock full of them. I took a slow breath. Perhaps it wouldn't be bad. Perhaps I could breeze in and solve their case on the spot.

Yeah, right.

I was still upset over being strong-armed here. These people must've been raised by wild animals with no concept of manners. But even as I chewed on my wounded pride, another part of me yearned to know what was on the other side of these vehicles. What was so strange that they had to practically kidnap a Dreamwalker?

My pulse raced, and I felt like I could leap tall buildings. I was becoming an adrenaline junkie, but I couldn't deny that I needed to know what was going on.

I sat up straighter. "What happened here?"

His cop-sharp eyes met mine in the rear-view mirror. "You're supposed to tell us." Deputy Duncan sprang from the car and let me out.

An emotional collage flooded my normal senses as I stood, but the jingle-jangle on my other line held my attention. This was no ordinary crime scene. Something twisted had happened here, and the unknown always freaked people out.

Automatically, I blended my vision, looking to see if a person with a wildly flaming aura had inserted himself into the recovery operation. People appeared to be concerned, scared, upset, and agitated. No one seemed to be in the midst of a sociopathic meltdown.

I changed channels, willing my vision into another spectrum. The light shimmered, and a haze appeared around people. Deputy Duncan glowed a nice blue, but the person in the center of the knot of people radiated a fiery orange fog. As I glanced her way, the redheaded woman stepped clear of hangers-on and strode over to us.

I needed to be one hundred percent around this powerful dynamo, so I shielded my extra senses again. The sheriff was short, though you'd never know it from the authority that rolled off her sturdy shoulders. Her uniform was different in color than the sheriff's at home, but the garments looked like they came from the same catalog. She wore a baby-blue polo shirt with an official emblem over the heart and creased navy slacks. On her feet were hiking boots that had seen their share of muddy creek beds.

So she wasn't afraid to get dirty. My respect for her rose a notch.

I jammed my hands in my pockets, not wanting to shake hands with anyone, not wanting to waste precious energy on anyone I didn't need to read. Everyone had secrets. Not all secrets needed to see the light of day. That was a fact.

"I'm Sheriff Twilla Sue Blair. You're the psychic?" the sheriff asked in a green-apple-tart voice.

"My name's Baxley Powell. I'm a dreamwalker."

"You see visions of dead people?"

"Sometimes." *And sometimes I talk with them, but that isn't the norm.*

She nodded curtly. "You're a psychic. I need your help solving a man's murder."

My jaw clenched. If she expected me to perform a public séance, she'd gotten the wrong message from Wayne back home. Maybe if I pointed out her error, she'd let me off the hook.

"With all due respect, I'm not a traveling sideshow, ma'am," I said. "I'm here on vacation with my family. And for the record, I fail to understand why you couldn't have just asked politely, instead of dragging me away from my family with no explanation."

"Sheriff Thompson told me all about you. I understand your reservations, but I need your expertise." Sheriff Blair's focus flitted to the tree line behind me before she lanced me with a needle-sharp gaze. "There's something extra about this case, something that's in your wheelhouse."

"I doubt that."

"Certain elements here appear ritualistic, but there are no footprints, no obvious means of death. My second-in-command is part Cherokee. He keeps muttering about the Little People. Claims the Nunne'hi did this."

I didn't want to be interested, but I was. My tattoos heated a bit. An entity from the Other Side named Rose had marked me with two inked images of her namesake flower, one for every favor she'd done for me. My debt to her was an hour of my life for each tattoo, which scared the bejeebers out of me. According to Rose, she was an angel working an undercover assignment in the netherworld. I'd witnessed her black wings and her unusual powers firsthand. Since she'd tagged me as hers, I hoped like anything she was telling the truth. Unfortunately, my lie-detecting ability didn't work on Rose, so I had no choice but to do her bidding.

I glanced around, hoping this tattooed mentor and sometime nemesis wouldn't draw me into a dreamwalk right now. Rose had rescued my father and saved my mother's best friend, and now I owed her two hours of my life — a fact she liked to dangle over my head.

Thinking about Rose was just borrowing trouble; instead, I focused on what the female sheriff had said. "Are the Little People and the Nunne'hi the same thing?"

"According to Deputy Mayes, they are interchangeable in Native American folklore." Sheriff Blair's face reddened. "When I heard you were up here, I knew you were exactly what I needed." She paused again. "I apologize for getting you here first and asking you second. You will do it, won't you? I'll pay your standard consulting fee."

Curiosity, outrage, or self-preservation? What response would get me away from here? I spun the roulette wheel of my thoughts and let 'em rip. "I've listened to you, which is more courtesy than you've shown me. I'm not happy about being shanghaied. Deputy Duncan could've explained everything before he stuck me in the back of a cruiser like a prisoner. I don't appreciate being manhandled, and I'm not in the mood to do you any favors. I want my gun and my possessions returned, and I want to be transported back to my camper. Now."

Twilla Sue raised her hands in mock surrender. "Easy. I'll return your gun right this second if that helps. My deputy did exactly what I ordered him to do. I apologize if I've hurt your feelings, but I was desperate."

"My *feelings*?" Air huffed out my nose. "You trampled my civil rights, not my feelings, though I am definitely angry. I should take you to court."

"Please, please. Just hear me out. I needed you to see this place, to feel the unnatural stillness. Something right up your alley happened here. I know it in my bones. No way did this kid just lie down and die."

I didn't want to listen, but in the ensuing silence, I did. Not a single bird chirp. No hums from insects. How was that possible?

She must have taken my silence as acquiescence. "Let me brief you on the particulars and show you the murder victim. If you want to walk away after that, I will respect your wishes."

I glanced around the wide-open space. It should've felt peaceful with so much sky and water, but it didn't. It felt morbid. I wanted to know why. I looked the sheriff dead in the eye. "My Beretta."

Twilla Sue waved Deputy Duncan forward. He handed me my gun, which I stuck in my waistband. "A good faith gesture on my part," the sheriff said. "Normally I would not allow armed civilians or consultants onto my crime scenes. But I need your help. Will you examine the scene?"

The Sheriff's Lucky Charm — that's what Deputy Duncan called me. I was to be instrumental in this woman's gubernatorial campaign. I'd be best served to remember Sheriff Blair had an agenda here.

Hopefully, I could take a look, give her my opinion, and be on my way. In the event I did a dreamwalk, which should only take a few extra minutes, the whole thing would take an hour tops. I'd be back fishing with my family before lunchtime. And earn a healthy donation to Larissa's college fund.

I named an exorbitant hourly rate.

The sheriff nodded. "Done."

"The clock started ticking from the moment your guys picked me up."

"Sure."

She was mighty agreeable all of a sudden. I had one more caveat. "I'll help you as long as we have an understanding about my abilities. I don't control what the dead show me. The visions aren't always related to the investigation. There's usually no Q and A."

"Sounds grossly inefficient, but I'll take anything you can give me. We're stumped."

I relaxed a little more. This was going to work out fine for both of us. "And another thing. Dreamwalks burn a lot of energy. I need time to recharge between episodes. At home, I have a support team and an environment rich in rejuvenation. I have no idea what my rate of recovery will be at Stony Creek Lake. You gotta promise me something. No hospitals and no drugs after a dreamwalk. Even if I appear to be unconscious. That's a natural process for me of my body shutting down to sleep off the exhaustion."

She waved off my remarks. "I got a similar lecture from your handler."

"What?"

"Your handler. Sheriff Thompson."

"He's *not* my *handler.* I consult for him. Big difference."

"He's got big plans for the two of you."

"He needs to have his head examined." Though I was undeniably interested in the case, I had other priorities to consider first. "Where's my kid?"

"Your daughter and friend are with a deputy at your campsite. I'm prepared to foot their entertainment bill while you help us."

"Like what?"

"Whatever they'd like. A boat ride on the reservoir with a picnic lunch. A spa day. A matinee and lunch in Gainesville. I'm flexible."

Sheriff Blair must be in a jam to spring for all that. "I need to speak with them. Right now."

"Call your daughter, let me know what she wants to do, and let's get to work. Daylight's burning."

The sheriff stalked off. I heard rustling behind me in the car, then the deputy handed me a manila envelope with my name on it. I snatched the phone out and called Charlotte. She answered on the first ring.

"We're fine," Charlotte said in a squeaky voice, which let me know someone was there, listening. "How about you?"

"Better now that they're leveling with me. They want me to work a case, Char. I realize it's lousy timing, but when they ran my name through the system, Sheriff Blair thought she'd won the lottery. Worse, she called Wayne, and he promised I'd help her. Anyway, the sheriff has assigned a deputy to spend the day with you and Larissa."

"No deal. If there's a case, I want to be part of it."

I lowered my voice to make sure it didn't carry. "I have no authority here, but I'll give you the same aftermath access you get at home."

"I don't like it, but I understand. What are we supposed to do?"

I ran through all the entertainment options offered, and Charlotte repeated them aloud for Larissa's sake. They quickly settled on a movie and lunch in nearby Gainesville. Charlotte agreed to update my parents on the situation.

Business concluded, I had one more request. "I'd like to speak to Larissa."

"Just a sec."

Larissa came on. "Mom? You okay?"

"Yeah. Sorry about the scare. The police need my help with a case, and they have the manners of wild boars." I turned to see Deputy Duncan trying to hide a smile. "However, once we got the issues sorted out, I agreed to take a look. I apologize for the interruption in our holiday. Can we reschedule paddleboarding?"

"Sure. I'm fine, Mom. Charlotte and I will look after each other."

"I've got my phone back. You need me anytime today, call, okay?"

"Got it."

I wish I had "it." Larissa and Charlotte's outing of lunch and a show sounded great. I hung up, passed along their outing preference to Deputy Duncan, and then picked my way through the cluster of emergency vehicles.

The crime scene tape stopped me like an

invisible force field. Something glimmered at the edge of my field of vision. I turned but wasn't fast enough to catch it. Reflexively, I touched the moldavite pendant I wore. The cherished gift from my husband immediately focused my thoughts.

Dead guy.

Straight ahead.

Chapter Seven

While the last murder case I'd worked had been a bloodbath, this lake frontage crime scene seemed pristine. Not a drop of blood anywhere. The body of the barefooted man laid out like a five-pointed star looked unblemished. No visible gunshot or stabbing holes in his T-shirt or jeans. No sign of a fight. If someone hadn't told me he was dead, I would have assumed this guy was sleeping.

"Ms. Powell," the sheriff called from a clump of officers, "over here."

I ducked under the crime tape and headed toward the sheriff. She'd convened a meeting to the right of the victim. The group included eight deputies, two EMTs, and my not-so-favorite state archeologist, Gail Bergeron. Her high-dollar jeans and white lab coat stood out among the dark uniforms.

Why was Gail here? She'd been quite chummy with Deputy Duncan, so I believed she'd worked with them on an earlier case. Made sense when you considered how relatively close the mountains were to Atlanta, where Gail was based.

I'd met her on a homicide case that also involved old bones. Gail had been arrogant, rude, insufferable, and annoyingly right.

"The first team on scene combed the immediate vicinity for evidence, so this area is completed," the sheriff said. "Pair up and work the search grid until shift change and then we'll reevaluate. Keep your eyes open and your radios on. We don't know who," she winked at me, "or what is out there. Dr. Bergeron and my consultant will add their expertise to our investigation into the death of John Doe. Any questions?" She glanced around and nodded. "Dismissed."

To one side of the corpse was the lake. Long grasses bordered the other three sides, which soon gave way to thick forest on the mountainside. The water flashed and sparkled in the sunlight, mirroring the clear, blue sky. I was drawn to the light show, and it struck me as odd that someone could've been murdered in such a picture-perfect setting.

This should've been a happy, peaceful place. But it felt curiously empty. Drained, even.

"Ms. Powell?"

I was startled by the sheriff's voice. "Yes?"

"I'd like to get started."

"Of course. What would you like me to do?"

"Cut right to the chase. Find the killer." She held up a hand. "I know. You already told me your process isn't linear. However it works, just get started."

I cast a dubious glance at Gail, hovering nearby. "What about your coroner? Doesn't he need to examine the body?"

"Tied up in court temporarily. In his absence, Dr. Bergeron has agreed to examine the body and share her findings." The sheriff moved to touch my arm, and I shied away.

I didn't miss the eyebrow she arched at me. "Your energy," I explained as I slowly walked toward the dead guy, "will dilute my focus on the victim. No one must touch me while I'm doing a dreamwalk. And it would be better if you kept folks away from my general vicinity."

"As you wish. Dr. Bergeron will give her analysis first. That way, if your vision quest takes some time, she won't be held up out here. I've got my recorder on, Dr. B. Anytime you're ready."

I stopped a few feet away, giving Gail

center stage.

"John Doe presents an atypical, healthy appearance with no obvious cause of death," Gail said after she'd circled the corpse. "He's a Caucasian male, about five-ten and one hundred eighty pounds. Tanned skin and closely cropped dark hair." She knelt beside the man's head and opened his eye with her gloved fingers. From there she opened his mouth, then examined his neck, trunk, and limbs.

She stood, snapping the gloves off her hands. "In addition, Mr. Doe has brown eyes with no sign of petechial hemorrhaging. His airways appear clear and open. His neck is unblemished and otherwise unremarkable. He's displayed in an open-armed crucifixion-like pose. His hands and feet show signs of calluses, as if he were accustomed to manual labor and walked barefoot frequently.

"No jewelry, billfold, watch, or other identification is on the body or at the scene. With no obvious cause of death, I suggest you run an extended tox screen to check for poisons. There is no sign of a struggle, no obvious means of death. The body is in full rigor, and decomp is just beginning. I estimate time of death as being less than twenty-four hours. If I had my equipment, I could be more definitive."

The sheriff took a long moment to consider Gail's findings, then a fleeting smile crossed her lips. "You're quite thorough, Dr. B. As usual."

Usual? What the hay? Were these two best friends?

Gail stretched and preened in that arrogant, self-satisfied way she had. "I would like to assist with the autopsy. Two sets of eyes are better than one. If there's an injection site, or a bug bite on his body, I'll find it."

"As long as the coroner is on board. Powell, you're up next."

I waved them aside. "If you ladies would step back, I'd appreciate it. Thank you." I'd been analyzing the scene while Gail ran through her paces. Thanks to my studying up on crime scenes between cases, I'd learned a bit about professional observation.

"Do you want a pair of gloves?" the sheriff asked.

"No thanks. It's hard for me to get a reading with gloves. Like Dr. Bergeron, I see no sign of a physical struggle, no obvious wounds. The body looks placed, as if he died elsewhere and was deposited here. His limb position reminds me of compass ordinals, but that may not be significant."

I glanced around again. There were no objects nearby, no way to tell what the victim or his killer might have touched. The only thing left to do was to try my Spidey senses.

"That's not much to go on, I know, so I'll try a dreamwalk next. Please keep your distance from me during this time."

I lay down beside the body, and my tattoos heated. My supernatural mentor must be in the vicinity. Cool. *Rose, are you here?* Rose didn't answer, but that didn't mean she wasn't interested in what I was doing. "I've never solved a case on the first dreamwalk. Oftentimes, the people don't realize they are dead. They don't know how to be spirits." I paused, catching the sheriff's eye. "I need to touch him. That all right?"

"Sure, but grab the arm instead of the hand. I want to make sure the coroner swabs the hands for DNA."

I reached for John Doe's arm and plunged down a rabbit hole.

Chapter Eight

What is it with spirits and total darkness? Why can't they transition to the netherworld with open eyes and rainbow brightness? Because they don't want to be dead, I reasoned. With closed eyes, they can deny anything is happening to them.

At last, the darkness thinned to a familiar murk. I'd made it through the transition to the Other Side. Distorted sounds tumbled at me like a plastic bag in an errant wind. Standing still made me feel like a target. I trudged forward, waiting for the vision to unfold. A group of bad-boy spirits wandered by with jeers and catcalls. I growled at them, and they moved on.

I summoned the dead guy's face to mind, and the oddest thing started happening. Black and white cartoon images flashed before my eyes, flipbook style. A stick man appeared, followed by a bouncing ball. More detail appeared on the page, and the stick figure was now sporting a skirt and corkscrew curls. A doorway appeared beside her. A much larger figure appeared behind her, mouth turned down in a frown. Tears flowed from the woman. The big figure shouted "Go." The stick woman walked through the doorway and vanished.

The words "THE END" flipped by. Then I heard children's voices, saw their faces. Young boys about Larissa's age.

"It's mine. I found it," Blue Shirt insisted.

"Nuh-uh." Red Shirt tried to wrest the flipbook from the other boy. "You got to keep the last one we found here."

Blue Shirt stashed the book in his pants pocket. "Can't help it if I'm a better finder than you."

Red Shirt kicked the floor, rustling old newspapers that littered the wooden planks. "This place is creepy. What does he do out here?"

Blue Shirt's eyes rounded. He pointed up, to the rafter. A fat spider clung to an old fraying rope. Red Shirt followed his gaze. Both boys yelled, "Ayyyyy!" and ran out of the shack.

But the vision didn't follow them. Instead, the room fluttered and then came into crisp focus again. The perspective was different, higher. Another person had watched the boys from the rafters.

"Who are you?" I asked.

The scene shifted again. The boy from the rafters reappeared near me, but he looked older, teenaged possibly. He wore a grimy white T-shirt and torn jeans. He had close-cropped dark hair and dark eyes like our victim. "Haney," he said in a cotton-soft drawl. "My friends call me Haney."

Finally. I was on the right track. "You make the flipbook?"

"I did."

"What does it mean?"

"What does anything mean? How'd I get here? I haven't seen my dad's fishing shack in years."

A lie. He knew this place well. "Is the cabin on the reservoir?"

"Who are you? Did you drive me here?"

"I'm . . . a traveler. I stopped because of you. This place have a name?"

He shook his head, drifted toward the rafters again. His appearance altered until he once again looked younger, gangly like a boy. "Mama told me not to talk to strangers."

"It's okay," I said. Was he regressing in age with each thought? Was this part of the process of accepting you were dead? "I'm trying to help. What's your mom's last name?"

He muttered something I couldn't quite catch. "Haney, please, tell me your last name."

"None of your beeswax." He picked up an old broom, began working it across the unfinished floor. "I have chores to do, so go away. Daddy will beat me if I'm not done when he gets back."

This was the part I hated, but why let him spend eternity pushing a broom? "Haney, you don't have to do chores ever again. Your dad can't hurt you now. Something made you want to share this life scene with me."

Haney leaned on the scruffy broom, which was nearly as tall as he was. "You don't make any sense." Suddenly he whirled and threw the broom at me. Since neither I nor the broom had actual mass, the broom went right through me.

The boy gasped and recoiled. "Are you dead? Are you a ghost?"

"Not dead, but I'm temporarily a spirit like you."

"I'm no spirit. I have a family, and they will be home for supper soon. Mama's fetching vegetables from the garden. Daddy's fishing. I'm cleaning the house."

"You're dead, Haney. I'm sorry to break

the news to you."

He scanned the room. "I can't be dead." Without warning, he vanished.

I hated it when that happened. At least I'd gotten a name. The cops would have something to start with. Might as well go home, because if past experience was any indication, Haney wouldn't show himself again right away.

A flutter of wings sounded behind me. I whirled, ready to go on the offensive, but it was Rose, my Other World mentor and guide, decked out in her badass biker clothes. Tattoo ink blackened both her arms and neck. Her heavy, Goth-styled makeup and blackened fingernails added to her sinister appearance. Just what the day needed to be perfect. A visit from a powerful entity with a bad attitude.

Chapter Nine

Rose's leather outfit creaked like an old saddle as she moved to my side. "Catch a new case?" she asked. She generally adopted one of two personas when we met up. Today she was in biker chick mode. A leather halter top and miniskirt, along with perilously high-heeled boots, barely covered enough of her tattooed body for decency.

I'd met Rose when my dad got lost on the Other Side. We'd done a deal to get him back. Ever since then, this undercover angel in the demon realm thought she owned me. I didn't want to anger Rose, but I wouldn't roll over and play dead either. I barred my arms across my chest. "I did. What's it to ya?"

"Disrespect doesn't cut it," Rose said, morphing to her fearsome Medusa-headed, larger-than-life size before returning to her biker-babe human size. "You belong to me."

I'd been pushed around enough today by

rude people. Time to redraw equitable boundary lines for this opportunistic spirit. "I belong to no one. We're associates. On an equal footing."

Rose smiled. The sinister curve of her dark lips, the fiery glow in her eyes, the malice lancing out from her in jagged pulses was scarier than anything I'd ever seen. Worried, I glanced around for a boulder or a cave — any place to hide from Rose — but there was nothing solid in the land of the dead, only unrelenting gloom. Merciful heavens. Had I trusted the wrong entity?

My right arm flapped sideways like a chicken wing, then my left. Terrified, I tried to bring them under control, but my animated limbs kept moving of their own accord. What was this? How was this possible? My thoughts stuttered and spun. I couldn't control my spirit-body. Was this the end? Would I ever see my family again?

"Still think we're equal associates?" Rose leaned in close, her sulfur stench nearly knocking me down. "Every being in here is free game in the war of souls. I told you from the start there was a cost to our association. Sure, I charged you a toll for my help, but every time we work together, some of my essence lingers inside you. Remember that, the next time you think about getting uppity with me. I own you, apprentice. You are truly my minion."

My arms fell limply to my side, and I wanted to crawl into a sinkhole and hide for the next millennium. Daddy warned me about the rules of traversing the veil. He'd made it through his entire dreamwalker career without ever making a bargain with anyone over here. I'd been doing this for less than a year, and from all appearances, I'd bartered my soul away without realizing it.

But I'd saved my father. And Gentle Dove. At the time, I thought the end justified the means: an hour of my life in return for each favor. That hadn't changed. Rose may have influence over me, but my thoughts were still my own.

"I can hear you, worm," Rose sneered. "Bow down to your maker."

My knees gave way of their own accord. Rose again. She laughed, a maniacal blast of noise like supertankers scraping together. Instinctively, I covered my ears and closed my eyes, but nothing blocked that metal-on-metal screech. I couldn't stop trembling.

"What do you want?" I managed to stammer out, afraid to look up. Afraid to do anything.

"Total obedience," she said.

Rose smiled again, sinister and malevolent. Then she faded from sight.

I scrambled to my feet. Glancing around the gloom, I hugged myself. Shivers ran down my spine. I had to get out of here. Now.

I tried to get home but nothing happened. My spirit seemed stuck in this realm. The thought stirred my feet into action. I ran down a long corridor of fog until I had a stitch in my side. Everything looked the same, no matter where I went.

Rose. She was messing with me. I shook my head and tried to force my spirit back into my body. No matter what I tried, the passageway home refused to open.

"You win, Rose." I sank to my knees and pleaded for her help. "I can't do this without you."

Chapter Ten

"Baxley? You in there? Can you let go of the dead guy? The coroner's arrived, and they want to move him now."

My good friend Charlotte's voice penetrated my fugue, hovering around the edges of total exhaustion. My fingers were so cold I couldn't work them. As sensation returned, I flexed the pins-and-needles feeling from my left hand, but the right remained locked on Haney's body.

"She's waking up," Charlotte said. "Give her another minute."

The daylight seemed thin, the rim of the sky burnished with rust. I'd made it back to the land of the living, but at what cost? Who was I? What was I?

Something warm brushed against my hand. Charlotte's stable energy added another level of comfort. "Thank you," I managed to say. People hovered nearby as if I were a three-headed monster. A snort blasted out my nose. Maybe I was.

"Mom, I have Elvis," Larissa said. "Do you want to hold him?"

I didn't want to frighten my daughter. I had to do better than this. "I'm okay. You keep him for now." With that, I pushed up to a sit from my prone position. Cops scattered. Did they think I'd zap them with lightning bolts or nightmares? Could they smell Rose's sulfur stench on me? It filled my head. "Thanks, Char. I'm good now." Her hand uncovered mine, and I released the victim. "His name is Haney."

The sheriff knelt down beside me, pen and notepad in her hand. "First or last name."

"Nickname, I think. He said folks call him Haney." I waved her forward and told her the rest in a soft voice. She may have trusted everyone here, but her crew were strangers to me. "Said his family had a place near here. It has open rafters like a barn. Outside it looks like a log cabin. I'm not sure if the shack is still around, but he mentioned a garden. I saw a noose hanging from the rafters. I think something bad happened there. Haney seemed to be a loner. He showed me a scene from his childhood where the other boys his age snuck in his home and were afraid of him."

"You get an address? A landmark?"

"I told you. The first contact with a victim is usually unproductive. Haney didn't even know he was dead. He freaked out once I told him."

"Seems like you should have known better."

I didn't care for her tone. I was cold, hungry, and exhausted. "Look, lady, I did you a favor. This information is relevant to who your victim was, to the events that shaped his life. I can't tell you anything more just yet. Locate the cabin, and I'll be able to contact him again."

"Can't you touch him again tomorrow for another reading?"

"Doesn't work that way. I'll get the same reading from him again. You find anything else while I was out?"

"No car, no boat, no footprints," the sheriff said. "It's as if he was dropped here by an alien spaceship. Deputy Mayes keeps insisting the Little People are responsible, but I don't put any credence in superstition or folklore. I wouldn't believe in you, if not for Sheriff Thompson."

Good old Wayne. What had he been telling his sheriff buddies? We would definitely have a conversation about boundaries when I returned home. With each breath, I felt stronger, more able to get up and walk out of here. I scanned the sky again. Seemed like late afternoon, by the sun's position.

If Charlotte and Larissa were here, I must've been dreamwalking for several hours. They'd gone to lunch and a movie in another town. Dreamwalks weren't usually so long. Fifteen minutes or so, max.

Where had I been?

Why couldn't I remember?

"What time is it?" I asked.

"A little after four." Gail Bergeron knelt in front of me, stethoscope around her neck. "Let me check you again before you stand."

"Good idea," the sheriff said, edging out of the way.

"Where's that stethoscope been?" I asked, remembering that our former coroner, Dr. Sugar, used his exclusively on dead people. I shielded my senses before she touched me. The lateness of the hour startled me. Dreamwalks didn't last this long. Something had gone wrong.

Rose had been messing with me on the Other Side. She wanted total obedience. I couldn't give it to her. I wouldn't, no matter what she did to me.

"Today, it's been on you," Gail said brusquely. "I knew you were coming around when your respirations and heart rate changed. Are you lightheaded or dizzy?"

After a quick self-check, I shook my head. "I feel normal."

Gail monitored my pulse, then my heart and lungs. "Your vitals are good. Ready to stand?"

"Sure." I pushed myself up. Larissa ran forward and hugged me. From the safety of her arms, Elvis, the little Chihuahua, licked my face. Charlotte moved forward to flank us. I wanted to weep at the family support. "I'd like to return to our camper."

The sheriff started to say something, stopped, then waved Deputy Duncan forward. "Take the Powells and Ms. Ambrose home. Stay with them until you're relieved at shift change."

"You think we need a guard?" I asked.

"A man is dead up here under suspicious circumstances, and you're my best chance to figure out what happened. I would do the same for one of my officers."

"Tomorrow, I want you on the scene with Deputy Chief Mayes. He's been called away today on a personal matter. Meanwhile, we'll sift through the property digest and see who owns these parcels up here."

Was living with a name like Twilla Sue Blair sufficient reason to be so annoyingly despotic? I was too tired to argue. I glanced over at Deputy Duncan. "Which way?"

He pointed to a large SUV. At least it was an upgrade from the police cruiser I'd arrived in. I must be moving up the food chain of the sheriff's good will.

We walked over, climbed in, and drove away. The inside of the spacious vehicle was quiet as a tomb, until Charlotte started talking.

Chapter Eleven

"Are you hungry? Did you get lunch?" Charlotte asked, rapid fire. "We had the most marvelous lunch, and the show was fantastic. Tell her, Larissa."

"It was amazing," Larissa said.

We sat in the backseat, with Deputy Duncan chauffeuring us to the campsite. Since Elvis was the only one of our pets here, I assumed Larissa and Charlotte had smuggled him along on their jaunt. I reached for my necklace, but instead of the usual surge of peace, I got nothing. I'd drained it on my dreamwalk.

Not good.

I realized Charlotte had said something else, and I'd missed it. "Sorry. I'm a little scattered from today. Do you mind if we catch up later?"

Charlotte's mouth formed an O. She nodded toward the officer like she got the message. "Absolutely. We'll table this for now."

Larissa reached for my hand. I saw the worry in her bright green eyes, so like her father's. *I'm tired, hon. That's all. I need to sleep it off. Nothing's wrong.*

She gave a slight nod and squeezed my hand. What had I been thinking to take on a case so far from home? My blitz of adrenaline wore off. A yawn overtook me, and my eyes drifted shut again. Charlotte's loud voice in my ear startled me awake. "We're here. Wake up, or you'll spend the night in this guy's car."

Somehow, I clambered to my feet and trudged to my bed in the camper. I fell into it face first.

Pale light bathed the camper. I inhaled the faint citrus aroma of my detergent on the bedding, felt the welcome press of warm pets and Larissa on the firm mattress beside me. The light was thin and pink-tinged. Dawn. I'd slept from dusk to dawn.

My stomach grumbled, letting me know I'd missed dinner. Come to think of it, I didn't remember eating lunch yesterday either. That was some dreamwalk. Way longer than usual, and with a distressing void in my memory. After I'd heard from Haney, something else had happened, and it kept me out of my body for hours.

I turned over onto my back, feeling the comforting energy of gemstones in the bed as the blanket shifted with me. My mom must've added those last night after I crashed.

Wood smoke scented the air. Charlotte and Larissa were still in the camper with me. That left my parents or the deputy outside; most likely my dad was tending the campfire. I lifted the thin curtain and struggled to discern the shapes outside. Officer Duncan's SUV was gone. In its place was a regular police cruiser, complete with another deputy.

A quick questing of my other senses revealed two other people nearby. One at the fire and one in the camper. My parents. Joy replaced the worry in my thoughts.

The dogs edged into my warm spot on the bed as soon as I left it. The cats claimed the pillow. I kept the spare blanket around my shoulders, slipped my feet into sneakers, and exited the camper.

My mother had already dressed for the day, and her thick gray braid hung over her right shoulder. I leaned down and hugged her. "Hey, you're up early."

Mom's entire body radiated love and comfort. "I hoped you'd awaken soon. I made you some of my special broth." She patted the ground beside her. "Join me."

I took the offered bowl in my hands and drank it greedily. "Where's Dad?" I managed between sips.

"Sleeping. He had a restless night."

Mom's voice sounded stilted. I noticed her rounded shoulders and became concerned. "Anything wrong?"

"Nope. Just regular stuff."

A truth and yet not a truth. "Hmm."

Mom handed me my necklace. "I recharged this for you first thing this morning, and I brought along your spare."

My fingers closed over it, and the gemstone hummed happily in my hand. I clasped it around my neck, feeling worlds better by the second. "Thank you. I don't know how you do the things you do, but you certainly are a blessing to me. After the long dreamwalk yesterday, I realized I was lucky you guys came along on the trip."

"Don't fret. We're happy to be here. I can't recall the last time Tab and I visited our friends in the mountains. Annabelle's meadow has such good energy."

"It's nice, especially the scenery, except for wondering if Burl Sayer will blaze through here again. But our guard will take care of it if he does. Anyway, the strange death I'm working to help solve happened a few coves down the lake. I'm hoping that by now Sheriff Blair has more on Haney, which is the name the dead guy gave me in the dreamwalk yesterday."

"Your father spoke with Gail last night. She said Haney's prints were in the system. Randolph "Haney" Haynesworth, son of working class parents, grew up less than an hour from here. He has a history of disappearing, including about two weeks ago, when the group home he lived in reported him missing."

"Does he have a criminal history?" Group home meant Haney had an issue and couldn't live alone. "Is there something wrong with him?"

"I don't know anything more than what the cops told your father," Mom said. "He has some petty theft charges. We're looking at his known associates."

I met her steady gaze. "You thinking to investigate Sheriff Blair's case? She won't like the competition."

"Sorry. I misspoke. The cops are checking Haney out. Not me. I leave all the investigating in the family to you."

"I'm helping with the investigation because I owe Wayne for getting Larissa back from her Powell grandparents. I'd rather be hanging out with y'all, even though I am flattered they want my help. This case isn't open and shut. It will take time to figure out what happened to Haney."

"You'll figure it out. I have confidence in you."

"Thanks, but I'm not doing anything special. I use my talents same as you do when you retune the crystals. I couldn't do my part without your help."

Mom blushed.

The fire crackled and hissed. I set my empty mug down and stretched. "It feels weird, though, not knowing the people here, their background, or the place. I wish I had more context. Being an outsider makes an investigation twice as hard."

"You're no ordinary outsider. You've got a direct pipeline to the victim's thoughts. Every sheriff in this state wants you on their payroll."

I recoiled. "How do they even know about me?"

"Word gets around."

Her simple statement rang true, but I didn't want to believe it. "No, it doesn't. Dad kept a very low profile. People all over the state didn't know about him. He wasn't invited to solve cases everywhere."

"Sorry to disillusion you, dear, but your

father consulted on numerous outside cases."

"I'm not medicating myself to bed every night. My stock in trade is dreams. What kind of dreamwalker is afraid to dream?"

"I wish my friend Gentle Dove had come with us," Mom mused as if I hadn't spoken. "She knows ways to expunge evil spirits from the mind."

"You're saying I can block the crime scenes I've worked?"

"Not *block,* love. Whitewash them and lock those memories in a safe place. You don't need to forget, but you need to partition your thoughts."

"I've never heard of such a thing. Why didn't you or Dad mention this process before?"

My mother shrugged. "Didn't know we needed to."

"Seems like there's always more to dreamwalking than I understand. When will I get caught up?"

"I don't know, dear. But your father and I are proud of you. This year you've helped many people and that hasn't gone unnoticed. Is it so terrible to help cops close their cases?"

"Not terrible. But not good, either. More like going to the dentist for a procedure. It has to be done or worse pain will follow."

"This was good," Mom said, covering a

yawn. "We've been meaning to have this talk with you for weeks now, but the timing wasn't right. Always remember that you're not in this alone."

I'd been so focused on me that I hadn't considered anyone else's needs. My parents wanted and expected to help me. Chances are that Mom kept watch by the fire so my father could sleep. In addition to watching over us, she'd recharged my crystals and managed to cook her special soup. Could I ever repay her for her many acts of kindness?

"I'm good now, Mom. Why don't you get some rest?"

"I will. Thanks." She unfolded gracefully and got to her feet. Her white braid hung over her shoulder, her thin cotton jumper and tie-died jacket seemed inadequate for the mountain air. Had she overdone it?

"She'll be fine," Dad said as I watched Mom climb into the other camper.

I turned to find his steady gaze on me. "What? You can read minds now?"

He inclined his head. "I saw when it hit you, when you turned your needs off and realized Lacey had been up all night."

The logs on the campfire popped and crackled. I was glad to see a ring of rocks around the fire and a bucket of water nearby. My father's handiwork.

"What now?" I asked. "Do you know anything more about the case?"

His eyes lit up with amusement. "Oh, yeah. But first, you need to tell me why you were so zonked last night."

"I don't know what happened. The transition through the veil was flawless. I encountered Haney right away. He freaked out when he learned he was dead."

My father clucked knowingly.

Encouraged, I continued, "I had a brief conversation with a guide on the Other Side. The whole experience should've taken half an hour or less. Instead, I have no memory of the next five hours."

"Interesting. Something wiped your memory, but only a portion of it."

"Did that ever happen to you?"

"Can't say that it did."

"It bothers me."

Dad nodded. "You were exhausted last night when you arrived at the campsite. Not even Elvis was enough to keep you awake. I was plenty worried, but your mom said you'd be all right."

"Mom's amazing. Until recently, I never realized how much she must have helped you."

Smiling broadly, he said, "Couldn't have

made it this far without her."

His praise faded beneath the sudden intrusion of high-beam headlights attached to a jet-black Hummer driving on our grassy lane. Our police guard got out of his car, one hand on his sidearm.

The identity of our visitor must've hit him the same time as I recognized the vehicle because he noticeably relaxed. Gail Bergeron had arrived. *Oh, goody.*

Chapter Thirteen

"Morning," I said, lifting a mug of broth Gail's way. My father took one look at the state archeologist's intense expression and bolted for the lake to watch the sunrise. Our guard ran a lap around the campsite and returned to his vehicle.

"I was in the neighborhood and thought I'd stop by," Gail said, settling on the fireside cushion my father had vacated. She'd dressed in slate gray and styled her hair. She'd even applied lipstick and tossed on a matching mauve scarf.

She'd be in good shape if the fashion police happened by our campfire. In my jeans and faded T-shirt, I was my usual fashion disaster. "Oh?"

"I phoned Mrs. Kinsey once I realized her cabin was a vacation rental. I'm tired of the sameness of hotels."

This vacation kept getting stranger and stranger. "You're staying there?"

She nodded. "I thought we might chat a few minutes this morning about my cold case."

I unclenched my back teeth. "I'm on vacation."

"But you're working Twilla Sue's case. It wouldn't be anything more to work mine as well. This one with the dead child —"

"I hate cases with children. Their faces haunt me."

She brushed aside my reservation. "DNA confirms this victim was a state senator's child. One who was missing for five years. Her remains were recently found. The family initially believed Regina had been abducted for ransom, but the call never came."

The name struck a familiar chord. After his daughter's disappearance, the senator had a breakdown and withdrew from politics. Knox Sandelman became a recluse, refusing all interviews. Charlotte had talked my ear off about the politician when the story first hit the news.

"Senator Sandelman's daughter? What was she, five?"

"Six."

"She was so young. I don't get some people. Hurting a child is so wrong, and killing a child is beyond terrible."

"Agreed, which is why we could never

identify a suspect. But now, with hindsight, it's clear that someone benefited from this child's disappearance. That's motive in my book."

Understanding flashed in my head. "Senator Hudson?" Even a person like me from the sticks recognized his name. He'd campaigned through our county several times. "You're looking at a state senator as a suspect? This could blow up in your face."

"No kidding. We need you to work this case. If we can place where they held Regina or a vehicle type, we might find evidence linking Hudson to the crime."

"Where'd you find her, um, remains?"

"In an abandoned park in an Atlanta suburb. The area was slated for refurbishment last month, but they discovered a lot of bones when they started digging. The park is apparently an old unmarked cemetery, and since I'm the state archeologist, they called me in. While dating the bones, we found that one set wasn't the same age. We ran DNA and got a hit. The thing is, no one thinks this is where she was killed. The park is a dumpsite. I need to find the crime scene."

"Does the father know?"

"Yes, but they've kept the investigation and the discovery quiet to prevent the suspect from destroying evidence. We have a narrow window of time until the press gets wind of this. I have something of the girl's for you to examine."

Dad was right. The parent in me ached for justice for this child. What would it hurt to try one cold case? If it didn't work out, I would know I'd been right to trust my instincts to stick to current investigations. I took a deep breath and met Gail's steady gaze.

"I'll do what I can, but I'm already on loan to Sheriff Blair. Her case takes priority." The sky was pinking up. A new day was coming, ready or not. "Breakfast?"

Gail grinned. "Thought you'd never ask."

Chapter Fourteen

"You're mine for the next hour." Gail Bergeron retrieved a satchel from her Hummer. Would she hand me a stuffed animal or an item of clothing?

My crew had eaten a hearty breakfast, fed the new guard, and dispersed. Larissa, my father, and Charlotte were at the lake with the animals. My mom dozed in her camper. The guard hovered in my vicinity. Whoopee, I was safe.

Even so, it didn't feel right to work on a case in our family area. Being in close proximity to Larissa, I might inadvertently broadcast my thoughts into her head. I'd rather not have any of my thoughts or dream energy spill over into my daughter's head on this case. A little distance would be preferable. "Not here. Let's take a ride in my truck."

"Mine is better. I told Deputy Duncan I'd haul you to the crime scene so he wouldn't have to return for you."

I sighed with regret. "Sounds like my day is being planned out for me again."

"You're in high demand. I'm staying as close to you as I can get."

I dashed off a note to Larissa and Charlotte, stuck another pouch of crystals in my front pocket, and joined Gail in her Hummer.

As she drove down the wooded lane away from the lake, she recounted the familiars of the case. Six-year-old Regina Sandelman went missing on a Friday afternoon five years ago. She'd been playing in her backyard and then she was gone. Her distraught parents had been all over the news, begging for their blonde, blue-eyed daughter to be returned.

"When the kid didn't turn up, the cops believed the parents had done it," Gail said as we bounced along. "They checked the Sandelman household and yard repeatedly. Nothing. Senator Knox Sandelman resigned from the Georgia legislature. His wife gave up her charity work. They closed the city house, moved to the country, and haven't been heard from since."

Regina would've been a year older than Larissa. I would die inside if something happened to my daughter. I wished the cop behind us was trailing my daughter instead of me.

"My, it's suddenly freezing in here," Gail said. "Let me flip on the heat."

I had a suspicion that a certain ghost dog might have joined us. The big black Great Dane had been haunting an abandoned home in my county for years when I ran across him. Oliver had been so grateful to have the virtual chains removed from his neck that he'd attached himself to me.

"No need to turn on the heat on my account," I said breezily. "Probably just a cold pocket. Happens in the mountains. It will pass in a minute." I used my other vision and saw Oliver sitting on the console between us. With a jerk of my head, I indicated I wanted him in the back. The ghost dog jumped over and leaned his head on my shoulder.

"That's much better," Gail said, angling the hot air away from her face. "Now, where was I?"

"The kid's gone, the parents dropped out of life, but the cops. . . ."

"The cops looked at this thing every way but sideways. Mrs. Sandelman led a blameless life. She donated her time, money, and energy to many high-profile charities. The senator made a few enemies in politics —

only natural — but none of them benefited from the void left by Knox's departure. None, that is, except Jared Lee Hudson. He'd been home alone at the time of the abduction. No witnesses, no one to corroborate his alibi."

"Did they question Hudson?"

"They did. Once with no lawyer, and then every time after that with one of Atlanta's most exclusive attorneys. The lawyer shut down the full court press the cops had on Hudson."

I nodded to the pull-off just ahead. "This looks like a good spot."

"Agreed." Gail turned in. Soon trees surrounded three sides of the Hummer. Our police escort hunkered down in our rearview mirror.

"The cops think Hudson did it, but they have no proof."

"Exactly."

"You've got photos of these people?"

Gail snapped open a folder. She withdrew a picture of the parents from the press conference, one of Senator Hudson's election posters, and a school photo of little Regina. I studied them, unable to ascertain guilt or innocence from a photo. Still, knowing what the key players looked like was a start.

I handed the photos over. “How can I help?”

“I need solid proof. Can you get it for me?”

“I can’t promise anything. But I’ll try.” I gazed at the satchel with trepidation. “What’s in there?”

“All that’s left of her. I typed the bones from that park in Atlanta, and everything in the world that used to be Regina Sandelman is in my bag. Don’t tell me you’re squeamish? I know you’ve touched bones before.”

The energy coming off Gail flashed red and ugly. She literally seethed with the need to solve this case. I’d learned a thing or two about my abilities during my short stint as a dreamwalker. “Whatever you want me to use as a focal point, put it on the seat beside me. I should be about fifteen minutes or so, max.”

Gail reached down into the bag and fiddled around a little bit. Finally she came up with a small white bone, which she placed on the console. “From her hand.”

Oliver whined on the seat behind me.

“Steady,” I cautioned.

“I am steady,” Gail said, her tone brusque.

“Wasn’t talking to you.”

"Something else is with us? Is it the child?"

"Not the child. I'll be right back." With that, I grabbed the bone and Oliver. Light bent and whirled. My stomach shot down to my toes and up to my tonsils. Dark rushed in, extinguishing the light, and then the unremitting murk of the Other Side surfaced. All things considered, it was a smooth transition to the realm of spirits.

A scene came into focus nearby. I drifted closer, unsure if this would be a montage of a prior event in this person's life or if I'd be lucky enough for this dreamwalk to be interactive. A young girl played in her yard at a kid-sized table and chairs set. Her sun-kissed hair glistened with purity and light.

She turned to me with a radiant smile. "Did you come for my tea party?"

I squatted down, pleased by the rare treat of interaction with a spirit. Maybe I could close this case with one dreamwalk. The child's oversized black-silk sheath with a beaded collar looked too fancy for the backyard. "My name's Baxley. I came to visit you, Regina. You like to play dress up?"

"Sometimes, though Mommy doesn't like me to take her clothes. But my princess gown is too small and it ripped last time I put it on. I borrowed this one from Mommy because she has so many." She glanced at Oliver, who lay at my feet. "I like your doggie."

I perched on one of her tiny chairs, and we pretended to take tea. Glancing around at the gloom outside the vision, I tried getting to the point. "How'd you get here?"

She shrugged.

"Did someone hurt you?" I asked.

Regina looked down at her pretend tea. She wouldn't meet my gaze.

"They can't hurt you anymore," I said. "Can you tell me what you remember?"

"I was playing tea party," Regina began in a soft voice. "My mom was yelling at my dad. I don't like that. They argue all the time, and I come out here where it's quiet."

Discord in the Sandelman household. Interesting. "What were they arguing about? Was it about you?"

"Daddy's work. He wouldn't do something. Mama wanted him to do it, but he said no. Said he had f-ticks. I tried to help him look for the ticks but he pushed me away, told me to go outside."

F-ticks? I rolled the word around on my tongue for a few minutes before I got it. "Ethics? They were talking about his professional ethics?"

Larissa nodded solemnly. "I don't like

F-ticks. They make my ears hurt."

"So you were outside alone. Then what happened? Did one of them come outside for you?"

She shook her head. Her shape thinned then reformed. I had to hurry.

"Did someone else come for you?"

She shook her head. Her spirit wavered. *Think, Baxley.* "Do you have any owies?"

Regina nodded and turned around. "My head hurts."

I gasped at the indentation in her skull. She'd sustained a blow from the rear. "Did you fall down?" I asked, hoping no one had been awful enough to bash in her skull.

Regina turned around, pain etched in her face, tears in her eyes. "It hurts. Make it stop. Make it better. *Owwieee.*"

"May I hug you? I'll kiss it and make it better."

She nodded, and I opened my arms to her. She nestled in my arms, shuddering. When she calmed, I looked her in the eye. "Who hurt you?"

"A bad man."

"What did he do?"

"He hit me. Then he put me in his red car. He never came back. It was dark."

I stroked her back again. "Do you know the man's name?"

"No, but once Mommy called him Pug. That's a silly name for a grownup."

"He was a friend of your parents?"

"Mommy's friend. Daddy didn't like him."

"Why was he in your yard?"

Regina's lip quivered. "I don't know. He has a black thing on his neck."

"I'm sorry he hurt you, but you're safe now."

"Where are my mommy and daddy? Why won't they find me?"

Oh, I didn't want to tell this child she was dead. I tried to vector my thoughts in Rose's direction. Surely my guardian angel was eavesdropping. "Do you have a grandma or grandpa, Regina?"

"Grandpa Eddie, but he died."

"Can you picture him in your mind?"

The backyard scenery wavered as Regina gestured with her arms. "He's big like Santa Claus, and he gives the best hugs."

Someone came toward us in the swirling mist. A large gentleman who called Regina's name. She squealed happily. "That's him. Grandpa Eddie, you found me!"

The spirit nodded at me and took the child by the hand. The shapes of their bodies thinned into nothing. I knelt down beside Oliver, my trusty ghost dog. "Imagine that, Oliver. Out of all the people over here, her grandpa comes for her."

Oliver wagged his entire body.

A rustle of wings alerted me to another visitor. Rose landed in front of me with a sulfuric blast. "There you are."

"I'm here, but not for long," I said. It paid to be cautious around Rose. "Thanks for helping with the child's relative. I didn't want to have the 'You're dead' conversation with her."

"I owe you one for yesterday."

"Speaking of which, why do I have no memory of the five hours over here?"

"We had a job to do, then I erased it."

"Why?"

"Because you don't need to have *those* nightmares."

More nightmares. I needed to come up to speed on this mental partitioning fast. But wait a minute. . . . She'd used *hours* of my life. "So we're even now? You used the time I owed you and more."

"Didn't count. That time wasn't spent among the living."

"Funny, you didn't mention that rule before."

"Nothing funny about it. The rules are different over here. That's a known fact."

"Still, it doesn't seem fair."

"Sue me."

Not a possibility. *Crap.* She had me coming and going. Time to focus on why I was over here. "You know anything else about the guy who killed Regina?" I asked. "The cops need solid evidence."

"She told you. The red car. A man with a black spot on his neck."

Rose faded, and I headed back to my reality. Light dawned bright around me. I blinked against it. Recognizing the dashboard of Gail's Hummer, I knew I was in the right place. The clock on the dash showed less than ten minutes had elapsed. That was good.

However, the quiet sobbing I heard veered into the uh-oh category.

What'd I step in now?

Chapter Fifteen

A glance to my left showed the weeping noise was coming from Gail. Tears streamed down her cheeks, and her arm seemed bent at an awkward angle. "What on earth?" I asked.

"Thank goodness you're back," Gail managed. "I wasn't sure what to do. I tried to reach over the seat for my briefcase and couldn't manage, so I got out to go in through the rear door, only the seatbelt caught my left arm. I yanked on the arm when it didn't come free. Only the belt had me good. I was just about to call our cop guard over here. I need to see a doctor."

"Yes, you do. Switch places with me, and let's drive to the nearest clinic."

"Can't. I promised the cops I'd take you to them."

"They'll have to wait. Your need is greater than theirs. Hang on while I come around and let you out."

Hurriedly I switched positions with her, noting in passing her shoulder was at a weird angle, not her arm. Looked to me like she'd dislocated it, but I was no doctor. I backed her Hummer out of the wooded spot off our driveway, with our guard easing out of our way, and called the sheriff. "Change in plan. I'm with Dr. Bergeron, and she's injured her shoulder. I'm driving her to the nearest medical facility."

Gail murmured the name of the nearest clinic, and I repeated it for Twilla Sue. "We'll meet you there after we get our warrant," the sheriff said. "I'll have my guy clear the way with lights and sirens."

Once on the highway, the cruiser pulled in front of us and created an open pathway. Nice. This job came with some perks after all.

"Tell me what you learned in the dreamwalk. Please tell me it was worthwhile," Gail said as we rolled down the highway.

I recounted the dreamwalk as it had happened, followed by my recap. "The killer is nicknamed Pug. He has a black something on his neck and drives a red car. According to my contact on the Other Side, the trunk of the red car contains all the evidence you need."

"I'll check the record to see if Senator

Hudson owns a red car. I sure hope so. Did you get anything on the means of death?"

"I didn't see the murder weapon, but whoever killed her struck her from behind and caved in her head. She didn't die immediately from the wound." My hands fisted. "He left her to die alone in the trunk. What a monster."

"I'll find that red car. There wasn't one mentioned in the search we did before," Gail said. "Thank you for the information. I'm surprised you got through to her so quickly. I wish I understood how your process works."

"Let me know when you figure it out. All I know is that I think about the person and I find them. What they show me is another story."

After a moment, Gail asked, "Was it horrible seeing Regina like that?"

I shuddered. "It was. Can't you figure out what struck her from the fracture itself?"

"The object didn't appear to be round like a hammer or baseball bat. It was more linear. Like a two-by-four, only not quite as thick."

That matched with the impression I'd seen. "Anyone that would do that to a child deserves the worst punishment our court system can inflict. The death penalty seems too good for him."

Hands on her weapon-clad hips, Twilla Sue Blair nodded at her striking male companion as she said, "Ms. Powell, this is my chief deputy, Sam Mayes. He'll be with us today. Looks like y'all got Gail's arm sorted out." We were just exiting the medical clinic.

Though she was shorter than me, the crisp authoritarian uniform and her larger-than-life personality made her seem to tower over us.

The dark-haired man in blue beside the sheriff was trim in a solid sort of way and right at my height of five-six. He wore his long hair in a low ponytail down his back. High cheekbones and a blade of a nose attested to his Native American heritage. I switched to my other vision because of the charged atmosphere. He had a dark, emerald-green aura, but it wasn't negative. It drew me in for a closer look.

His energy felt familiar to me, as if I knew him, only I'd never met this man before. He returned my steady gaze with steely determination, as if he'd drawn the short straw by having to work with me. *Hmm.* Cool exterior reserve, but on the spiritual level, I was picking up a warmer reception. For instance, his protective energy melded nicely with mine. I liked him before he'd said a single word. I sure hoped I felt the same way after I got to know him.

"Nothing's broken," I said. "Gail twisted her arm the wrong way and popped the shoulder out of joint. They put it back in, and she's good to go."

"Are you doped up?" Twilla Sue asked Gail. "Do you need a ride back to your rental cabin? I sent Deputy Noble out on patrol, but he could be back here in five minutes."

"I can drive," Gail said, favoring the arm in a sling. "I can get myself back to the lake house, if need be, but I'd rather come with you in case Baxley thinks of anything else from that dreamwalk she did for me."

"Whoa, there," Sheriff Blair said. "You already had your time with our dreamwalker this morning. Ms. Powell is mine for the rest of the day."

"My shoulder is the least of my worries," Gail insisted. "Thanks to Baxley, I now have a new direction to investigate. We might have a murderer in the Georgia legislature. I have to keep this momentum going."

"Stand in line. You've got a very cold case, at best. My corpse is fresh, and I've got the hottest psychic in the country at my disposal. I've got dibs. I aim to solve my homicide today."

"You don't have a means of death yet. The autopsy findings were inconclusive as to cause of death. His heart, lungs, and other tissues were fine. We ordered an extensive tox panel and that will take time. Based on my professional experience, Haney Haynesworth just up and died."

"Dr. B, I respect your expertise, but I don't believe that BS for one minute. People don't just chose to quit living without wasting away or harming themselves." Sheriff Blair motioned me toward her vehicle. "Powell. You and Mayes are with me."

Mayes and I trotted obediently after Twilla Sue Blair and climbed into her SUV, me in the backseat. I touched my moldavite pendant, and it sang under my fingertips. I had enough juice to carry me through another dreamwalk. Good to know.

I didn't miss the quick look the sheriff shot Mayes. "What's the latest on Burl Sayer?" the sheriff asked her second in command.

Mayes shook his head. "He's gone to ground, but we'll get him. I've got 'ins' with the shopkeepers and restaurants up here. If he shows his face, I'll know about it."

We careened down the mountain. "Where are we going?" I asked.

"The vic lived in a group home over on Bear Claw Lane. I heard you can do a reading off inanimate objects. Good thing we called the placement service. They were about to box Haney's possessions and clear out his room, what with the end of the month coming up fast. Nothing's been moved yet. We'll have complete access to his stuff."

Point and click. That's how she saw me. My eyes drowsed shut. Though it was only eleven, it had already been a busy day for me. "Any luck finding his associates?"

"Working on it. Should have one or two of them rounded up by mid-afternoon. You planning on sleeping on the job?"

My eyelids flickered open. "I'm resting. Dreamwalking is active and exhausting."

"Recharge, because I'm expecting useful answers this time."

"What about his parents' place at the lake?" I asked. "What did you find there?"

"Deputy Pruitt is scouting the lake house this afternoon after he finishes a presentation at the elementary school. If it looks like someone has been there recently, especially if it's Haney, we'll go there immediately."

I raised my hand. "Let's wait and see how long Haney keeps me on the Other Side this morning. There's a limit to how much I can safely do in a day, and I already did a dreamwalk for Gail earlier."

The sheriff snorted. "Gail's case is a loser. Everyone knows the kid's mom slept around and the dad ignored her disloyal and dangerous behavior. Her name may be Tawny Sandelman but everyone calls her Tawdry behind her back. And Knox — his aides called him Fort Knox because no matter what she did, he held it together and soldiered on. It's a wonder those two haven't killed each other in their secret hideaway."

"Does Gail know this?" I asked.

"Unless she's been living under a rock. I knew the details, and I don't live anywhere near Atlanta."

If Tawny had been sleeping with Pug, maybe he was sneaking in or out of the house and Regina saw him. I hoped Gail found that red car. I didn't want to deal with politicos, much less mourning parents.

On one side of the road, the mountain jutted out almost to the asphalt. On my side, the shoulder gave way to a sheer drop. I kept a tight grip on the armrest. "Anything else I should know about your victim?"

"Randolph 'Haney' Haynesworth was no choir boy, but he wasn't a hardened criminal either. He fell in between on the crime continuum. Those B and Es, loitering, and trespassing charges could be as far as he was willing to go, or his record could be an indication he was ready to move to the next level of crime. I've seen teens go both ways."

In the dreamwalk, Haney had seemed childlike to me. Whether that meant a young heart, arrested mental development, or a denial of what happened that he'd expressed by hiding in a familiar memory, I didn't know.

"Will his parents join us at the group home?" I asked.

"His mom up and disappeared about ten years ago. Just didn't come home one evening. No note, no nothing. There was no sign of foul play. The cop who worked the case said he figured she just walked off and started over somewhere else. His Dad worked construction until he couldn't anymore. Then he drank himself into an early grave last year."

"Haney was an only child?" I asked.

"Yep."

I'd known kids from single-child families. Some, like Charlotte, turned out okay. Others didn't fare well in social situations. Everything was about *them.* The next question begged to be asked. "What kind of group home is this? Is it for reintegration of felons or more like a way station for the mentally challenged?"

Twilla Sue stared me down. "You know more about Haney than you're letting on?"

"You know what I know."

"He . . . had problems. Some mental issues. Didn't finish high school. Hung out with the wrong crowd. Got in trouble with them, that sort of thing. This group home is a fresh start for young men who got off on the wrong foot."

"You think those wrong-crowd people took advantage of him?"

"Right up until they killed him."

Chapter Sixteen

The modest house at 300 Bear Claw Lane looked like every other cube in this narrow slice of suburbia, only this one was cookie-cutter gray with a black roof. The lawn was scruffy and brown, the front porch littered with an assortment of rickety chairs. A rusty bike rack stood on the edge of the lawn near the gravel driveway.

I followed the sheriff and Mayes up the creaky stairs. A teen answered the sheriff's knock. Said he was Jonas Canyon. He wore dark-framed glasses over his nearly black eyes, a wrinkled, untucked Oxford cloth shirt, and khakis that had been hacked into shorts by an unsteady hand.

Though I kept my senses fully guarded, my palms itched at the sight of the unhappy young man. He gazed at the badges and waved us inside.

The living room was messy and smelled like garbage. Flies buzzed over the dirty dishes left on every solid surface. A few plates littered the floor. There were no lamps, no decorative items, no pictures on the wall.

This was the oddest group home I'd ever seen, and it certainly would fail every minimum public health criterion.

"We weren't expecting anyone today," Jonas said, grabbing up a few of the plates and dropping them in the sink. "We usually have at least twenty-four-hours' notice before inspections."

Sheriff Blair blocked his exit from the kitchen. "Who's in charge here?"

Jonas' smooth façade slipped for a minute, and I saw something that made me wary as he lifted his glasses to rub his eyes. Then he met the sheriff's level gaze. "My mom, but she's resting. We had a difficult night, to tell the truth. Everyone is still in bed."

It was going on eleven o'clock. How odd. The vibe here was weird. I had the sensation of standing in front of a powerful vacuum, and I fought the invisible tug to pitch forward.

"What's your mother's name?" Twilla Sue asked.

"Lizella Tice."

"Tice. And your last name is Canyon."

"She remarried a few years back."

"I need to speak to Lizella and to see Randolph Haynesworth's room," the sheriff said.

Jonas twitched and shifted his weight from one foot to the other. He took off his glasses. "Not a good idea. My mom will be angry with me. No one's allowed upstairs."

"All right," the sheriff said in a quiet voice. "We can come back later."

"No, we can't," Mayes said loudly from over my shoulder. "We have a warrant. We're working a case. Time is of the essence."

Jonas flicked his gaze to Mayes. "No need to rush off. Sit down. Let me fix you something to drink. Coffee. Would you like a cup of coffee?"

"I like coffee," Mayes said agreeably.

Whoa. Something seriously creepy was happening. I didn't do this often, but I drew deep and extended my psychic barriers to include Mayes and Twilla Sue. I linked my arms in theirs. "We're going upstairs to look into the unexplained death of a young man," I said. "We aren't sitting down, and we aren't drinking or eating anything in this house."

The sheriff blinked in confusion. "Of course not. We're here to investigate Haney's death."

Mayes muttered something under his

breath that sounded like "ptomaine palace," so I knew he was back to his senses. *Good.*

Keeping the shielding barrier intact, I faced Jonas Canyon. He shot his best gaze at me, and I reflected it back at him. "Don't mess with me. I've got your number. Anything you send at us will be reflected back three-fold on you."

His face contorted and darkened. "What are you?"

"Doesn't matter, but I know what you are. An energy vampire. You steal people's energy. Stop it right now, you hear me? Quit draining them."

He shook his head. "You're not the boss of me."

"It's wrong to steal energy from people. Is that what's happening in this place? Is that how you killed Haney?"

Jonas raised his hands and stepped back. "Haney's dead? Dude, that's messed up."

He turned away from us, as if he were trying to control his emotions, and the spiritual assault lessened. I hadn't felt any draining power when we first encountered Jonas. Inspiration struck. "Put your glasses back on."

"No."

"Yes."

After I put Jonas' glasses on, I turned to

Sheriff Blair. "We need someone to watch him while we check this place out. I'll stay with him if you like. The people upstairs might need medical attention if he's siphoned off too much of their energy. I suggest calling for backup before anyone goes upstairs."

Blair ordered Jonas to sit in a chair while she called for reinforcements and sent Mayes upstairs. After the call was placed, she pulled me aside and nailed me with two questions. "How did Jonas get me to change my mind before? And how come I feel so tired right now?"

I hoped Mayes would be safe upstairs because I couldn't shield him from here. As long as I stayed close to Sheriff Blair, she was safe from attack. "This guy is an energy vampire. He steals energy from others."

The sheriff's head bobbed as if I'd struck her. "Vampire? The garlic-and-wooden-stakes kind of vampire?"

"There's no bloodletting involved, but energy vampires can be malicious. You need to be strong and to shield yourself, like I'm doing for you."

"I don't believe what I'm hearing, but seeing is believing. That kid hypnotized me a moment ago."

I nodded. "He mesmerized you all right.

If I hadn't been here, you and Mayes would've been his next victims. Don't look into his eyes. He didn't try to hack your energy until his glasses were off earlier. I don't know this for certain, but perhaps his glasses shield him in some way."

"If he can bend people to his will, how will I keep him in custody? Won't he compromise anyone who is nearby?"

"I don't know a lot about energy vampires, but my dad and his friend back home might have answers. You have a handy resource in your Native American deputy. He might know how to cancel out the effect Jonas has on people."

Mayes came back downstairs. "Four bedrooms upstairs, all double-occupied. None of the people stirred when I entered each room. I found a forty-something female and seven males in their early twenties. Given what Jonas nearly did to us, I didn't check for pulses, but I watched long enough to make sure everyone was breathing."

"Unbelievable." Sheriff Blair called for ambulances. She also tapped two additional deputies to come to our location. Then she turned to me. "You're the only one he can't fool. Put my cuffs on him, then secure the glasses to his head. We need more mobility than having us all moving in lockstep. I need you upstairs ASAP so we know what we're dealing with here."

I took her cuffs and leaned down to put them on his hands.

"Not that way," the sheriff said. "Put his arms behind him. He could knock the glasses off if his hands are in front."

"Stand up, Jonas," I said.

He lumbered to his feet. "You people don't get it. Energy is a valuable resource, and I require a lot of it. You're making a big mistake. This is the natural order of things."

I snapped the cuffs on and tightened them. Good thing I'd been training in police techniques during my down time between cases. "Save it for someone who cares."

Mayes found some twine in a kitchen drawer. I tied the temples of the eyeglass frames without raising the lenses from his eyes. "Done."

The sheriff pointed to the man's feet with her gun. "Secure his feet to the chair with the twine while you're at it."

When I finished, Sheriff Blair nodded her approval. "Head upstairs with Mayes and do your thing. If this guy so much as twitches, I'll pepper his sorry hide with bullets."

"No need for that, ma'am," Jonas said with a contrite smile. "I am your humble servant."

"Don't trust him," I said. "We'll be right back." Mayes and I tromped up the stairs, my pulse thrumming in my ears. I'd only encountered two energy vampires in my lifetime, but none had been as focused or as scary as Jonas.

"I thought I'd seen it all," Mayes said. "That leech latched onto me, and I turned to goo in his hands. I feel like I've pulled an all-nighter. Hard to believe. Thanks for saving my hide back there."

"We nearly had ourselves a situation, but we're a good team. I'm glad I could help."

The woman, Lizella Tice, and the young men upstairs were thin — too thin. Mayes was right. None of them responded to our presence. Reluctantly, I touched them all. They were caught in a deep, dreamless sleep. No telling how long they'd been in this condition.

"Are they victims or the bad guys?" Mayes asked as I finished with the last young man.

"I don't know. They seem to be in comas, and their dreams aren't troubled. I have no idea what that means."

"We'll get them to the hospital. Let the professionals evaluate them."

A car cranked outside. Mayes and I hurried to the window in time to see the sheriff driving away. As if he knew we were watching, Jonas Canyon made a crude hand gesture out the passenger window.

"Damn!" Mayes turned and raced down the steps. "He's got Twilla Sue."

Chapter Seventeen

Calls to Twilla Sue's mobile phone went unanswered. Mayes, her second in command, notified Dispatch of her abduction. "Tell Pruitt to track the GPS chip in Twilla Sue's SUV and reroute Loggins and Wardell to intercept the vehicle," he said. "Suspect is armed and dangerous. Repeat. Suspect Jonas Canyon is armed and dangerous. Keep me apprised of the situation."

He ended the call, and I cleared my throat. "We should go after her," I said, following him onto the front porch. "The other cops won't be able to stop Jonas." Though the warm sunshine on my shoulders felt wonderful, I kept a protective barrier around myself and Mayes. I couldn't take a chance another cop would fall victim to foul play with so much at stake.

"We don't have a car, unless there's one around back with the keys in it," Mayes pointed out. He glanced at the shabby house and shook his head. "What happened? How'd Jonas Canyon get to Twilla Sue?"

"I don't know. I'm keeping both of us shielded until we have backup, so stay close. Meanwhile, I'm calling my dad for answers. He has some knowledge of unusual powers. Perhaps he's run across someone like Jonas before."

"Good idea. Put the phone on speaker so I can hear too, if you will."

My mom answered the phone. "Tab said you'd be calling. Hold on while I get him."

Mayes arched an eyebrow at me. I shrugged. "It's a Nesbitt family thing."

"Doesn't matter, as long as it gets us information," Mayes said.

"Baxley?" my father said. "What do you need?"

I held the phone between us. "Hey, Dad. Deputy Mayes is here with me, and you're on speaker phone. We've run across an energy vampire in the case we're working. What can you tell us about them?"

"Don't look in their eyes, for starters," Dad said.

"Figured that one out right after this one attacked. I thought maybe his glasses were shielding his eyes initially, but that wasn't the case."

"Never heard of glasses having a shielding effect. That was a trick it used to get you to lower your guard."

"Kind of figured that out too."

Mayes reached for the phone. "Mr. Nesbitt, how do we stop this thing? He kidnapped the sheriff."

"You're not going to like the answers I have. They veer to the occult."

"I'll try anything at this point."

"Avoidance is your best strategy, followed by and in conjunction with psychic protection."

"Can't avoid this one. He's preying on members of my community. Besides, we need to get Sheriff Blair back ASAP."

I wrested my phone from Mayes' hand. "Specifics, Dad. What can we do? I'm able to shield two cops if they are in close proximity, but other than that, I can't help them."

"In general, cops shouldn't be vulnerable. They're not the weak-willed individuals who are a PV's normal victim."

"PV?" Mayes asked.

"Psychic vampire," I explained. "It's another term for an energy vampire."

"I need to check into this more with my people," Mayes said. "How do we catch this man?"

"Stay close to my daughter for your personal safety. That's the first thing. Most PVs can't harm dreamwalkers."

"Most?"

"I would say all of them, but some PVs invite other entities inside them, things that don't belong on this side of the veil. If this PV is possessed, steel bars won't hold him."

"What are the odds we've got one of those rogue PVs?" Mayes asked.

This vamp was clever and manipulative. Jonas Canyon tricked us into thinking we were safe if he was secured. Now I knew better.

"Gosh. Figures aren't my strong suit," Dad said.

I imagined my dad standing there scratching his grizzled head. I felt the same way about math as he did, and it was all I could do to squelch the inappropriate grin that threatened to come out.

"Maybe one in a thousand or one in a million," Dad said.

"That's a pretty wide swing," Mayes grumbled. "If we've got a rogue PV, what's the deal?"

"You could try exorcism, though getting a demon out of a PV is a problem."

"How about a bullet?" Mayes asked.

"Might temporarily stop the host, but

some entities aren't fazed by bullets."

"Not a promising solution, but we have to stop the immediate trouble in our area. Jonas Canyon looked me dead in the eye and mesmerized me from the get-go. If not for Baxley, I'd be in the same fix as the sheriff. I hope we're in time to save Twilla Sue."

Sirens wailed in the distance. Help was nearly here. I leaned in close to the phone. "About that . . . this guy must've been fully charged if he was able to hypnotize two law enforcement types simultaneously. Do you agree, Dad, that due to the PV's high energy level, he wouldn't completely drain Twilla Sue?"

"Not right away, in any event. We don't know what his rate of burn is, so the sooner you find her, the better."

Heartened, I kept going with my list of questions. "The house has eight people in comas upstairs. They're nothing but skin and bones. What does that mean?"

"Must be his private herd. He's drained them until they're at the brink of death. Few people can come back once they've been drained that far."

"He identified one of the people as his mother. If that's true, I pity her. Is it possible that's what happened to our vic,

Haney Haynesworth? He didn't have a mark on him."

"Entirely possible, unless he was in good health."

A chill shivered down my spine. Haney had looked to be in good health. "What does that have to do with it?"

"He'd regenerate and recover until he couldn't. Each time he bounced back from being partly drained, he'd use up more of his energy reserves. That tends to slim a body down."

"You're saying our vic should've been emaciated if he was killed by total energy theft? He'd look like the people upstairs?"

My father coughed. "That's been my experience with PVs."

So much for my hope to quickly resolve Haney's cause of death. My dad knew way more about this stuff than I did, so I believed him. "We'll get the survivors on their way to the hospital, then hopefully, I can read this crime scene. Mayes suggested we consider also that the Little People might have killed Haney."

"The Nunne'hi?"

The interest in my father's voice vibrated through the line. I spoke louder over the approaching dual sirens. "You know about the fae folk here in the Georgia mountains?"

"I do. They're about knee high to a child, with long black hair, though they can also appear as tall as we are, temporarily. They're rumored to live in caves or caverns, such as in these mountains. Legend says they come out at night to farm and dance."

Interesting and highly specific information. "Where'd you learn about them?"

"Running Bear has shared much with me about his people. He's quite versed in Cherokee lore as well."

My father's friend Running Bear embraced his Native American heritage and still practiced the old ways. Many nights of my childhood had been spent with Running Bear and his wife Gentle Dove at our home. They were my parents' best friends, and I enjoyed being around their peaceful energy.

Beside me, Mayes nodded his head.

I directed my attention back to the phone. "Have you ever seen one?"

"No. And if you see a Nunne'hi, don't follow it. You'll end up in their world with no idea of how much time is passing."

"Understood." The ambulances turned down Bear Claw Lane. I could barely hear myself think. I held the phone close, even though it was on speaker mode.

"You need me to come get you?" Dad asked.

"I'm good for now. Thanks."

I ended the call.

"Your father is a knowledgeable man," Mayes said. "He understands what we're up against. We're trying to catch a psychic vampire for the crimes committed here, but Haney's killer might be fae folk. We have to be careful about releasing the information. No one will believe this."

"Then we'll keep the mysterious part out of your report."

CHAPTER EIGHTEEN

The last pair of the eight comatose people from the house were being loaded into ambulances when Gail Bergeron joined us in the yard. She moved slowly, favoring her injured arm.

I patted the bike rack we perched on. "Wanna sit with us? There's plenty of room."

Gail ignored my offer and fixed her gaze on Mayes. "Any word yet on Sheriff Blair?"

"Her vehicle and cell phone were abandoned in a busy shopping plaza," he said. "A senior citizen from the same plaza reported her vehicle stolen. We're searching for her sedan."

"I've heard the rumors going around the grapevine. I don't believe in this woo-woo stuff, not unless I witness it firsthand." Gail spared me a glance. "You're the real deal, but you're the exception, not the norm." She nodded at the last gurney. "What happened to these people?"

I weighed the possible responses, rejected all but one. "We don't know. They were unresponsive when we found them."

"Curious. I'll follow up with them at the hospital."

Awkward silence followed. Two techs were inside, taking photos and collecting fingerprint evidence.

"Why are you waiting here?" Gail asked.

"Ms. Powell and I will conduct a walk-through as soon as the house is cleared," Mayes said. "Meanwhile, another crew is processing the sheriff's SUV. We're throwing everything we've got at getting the sheriff back."

"So you're stuck here temporarily?" Gail asked.

I didn't like that speculative gleam in her eye. Last time I'd run across Gail on a case, she'd more than earned her nickname of Ice Queen. A natural authority figure, she took the lead on cases and told people what to do. Worse, she didn't take no for an answer.

I met her laser-like gaze. "There's nothing else I can do on your case without additional people to read or new evidence to touch. Plus, I need to direct my energies to this active case. The sheriff's life is in danger."

Two crime scene techs came out with sealed cartons. They took footies, coveralls, gloves, and masks off at the door and bagged them. One of them nodded to Mayes. He stretched and stood, then held a hand out for me. "We're up," he said.

I took his hand to steady myself as I eased off the bike rack. "About time."

Gail darted in front of us and waved her good arm. "Wait. As a medical professional, I should examine that house. To check for contagion."

"If something in there is contagious, Ms. Powell and I are already infected," Mayes said.

Gail blocked Mayes as he tried to step around her. "In that case, I should establish a baseline for your biometrics."

"Not on your life." Mayes steered me around the roadblock. His tone wasn't pleasant. "Twilla Sue's in trouble. Let Ms. Powell do her thing and get a bead on what's going on. Then you can examine the house ad nauseum."

We donned protective gear and entered, while Gail fumed on the porch. "Just as well," I said in a voice only Mayes could hear. "We don't have to worry about her rummaging around while we're in here."

"Where do you want to start?" he asked.

The brooding sense I'd felt before in the house was gone. Now the place seemed empty. "I don't know if one of your guys touched the doorknobs, but I suspect no one who was in a state of great stress touched the plates. That's our best shot. Jonas grabbed this handful of dirty plates and placed them in the sink once we arrived."

"How can I help?" Mayes asked.

I passed him my phone. "Run interference if this takes a while. Jonas is still alive, so his spirit can't trap me on the Other Side. But I never know what I'll come across while in a meditative trance or a dreamwalk. Call my father if you become concerned for any reason."

He nodded, his eyes cop-sharp as he scanned the room. "What social worker approved this place? No way in hell should this dump be a group home."

I stood in front of the stack of plates. Since I knew I'd be dreamwalking, I hadn't put on my right glove. Physical barriers like gloves weakened my tactile reception. I waggled my fingers and steeled my nerve. "Going in."

Mayes said something, but I barely heard

him as I slipped into a meditative trance. Light fractured into kaleidoscopic panels whirling and turning and making me dizzy. At the same time, rage vectored up my arm, turning my stomach, making me want to puke. In a flash of light, I saw a clearing where nothing grew. The image whirled and stopped at a strangely shaped tree. The earth was disturbed there. Blackbirds cawed and flew at my face.

I willed myself back to the group home and found Mayes supporting me, his hands holding my hips in a snug grip. "What?" I asked, gazing at the refrigerator and the sink. Hadn't I been in front of the sink when this started?

"You're okay," he said. "I've got you."

Being held felt nice. More than nice. But this was wrong on several counts. My marriage. His being a stranger. I stepped away from him. "Did something happen?"

"You dropped the plates immediately. Your eyes twitched, then you started walking. Tried to walk right through the refrigerator. That's when I grabbed you, so you wouldn't hurt yourself."

Odd. I'd never moved during a dreamwalk before. "Thanks, I think."

"I'd offer you something to drink or a seat, but you don't want to do either in this strange house."

Something else was different about this vision. Something that had *not* happened. For the first time, I'd felt truly alone on the dreamwalk. "You're right."

"Was it worthwhile?" Mayes asked. "Did you learn anything to help us find Twilla Sue?"

Instead of touching my necklace, as I often did to center myself after a vision or a dreamwalk, I touched the tattoo on the back of my hand. Cold as ice. Usually Rose's tattoos heated when I crossed the curtain. Not this time. Hard to say I missed Rose, but her absence puzzled me.

"The vision was filled with changing images, light, and rage," I said. "I saw a weird tree with disturbed earth nearby. Not a leaf on this skeleton tree, just black bark. The limbs twisted in every direction."

"How does this help us find the sheriff?"

"I don't know. I'd like to talk with you later about the images, about the places I saw. I'm unfamiliar with the area so I don't know if they are landmarks or remote areas we might never identify."

"We will." He seemed to draw into himself for a moment. "Meanwhile, during your dreamwalk, we found the stolen car, but no Twilla Sue. I've ordered scent-tracking dogs to the location."

"We'll find her," I said with more conviction than I felt. I had no idea what we were dealing with in Jonas Canyon. Was he more than an energy vampire? That was enough, truly, but how did he bend people to his will so easily? "Did they find any computers or phones in the house?"

"Nope. Nothing modern like that. Not even a TV. These folks didn't read or play games either. Other than the dirty dishes, this place has none of the usual clutter of life. No books, no photos, no games, no mementos. You up for more touch tests?"

We walked around the house, me touching doorknobs and bedposts and lamps. Nothing in the way of a zing. There were only a few items of clothing in each closet. Nothing jumped out at me when I touched them. The refrigerator was empty. Absolutely empty.

"Did the lab guys take all the food?" I asked as I closed the fridge door.

"I can check the evidence log."

"Not necessary. I think your initial assessment is correct. This place feels like a rest stop, only the people weren't in any shape to travel."

"You moving away from the psychic-vampire-enslaving-them theory?"

"Jonas was an energy vamp, that's for sure. But something else is bothering me. How'd he get the people to come inside this place? Why would they stay after he drained their energy partially? And how is our victim associated with Jonas other than this address? I see nothing to indicate Haney ever lived here. It's like these people are living ghosts."

Mayes' radio squawked. We listened to the update from the deputy with the scent-tracking dogs. No news on the sheriff's whereabouts. The dogs had lost her trail by the highway. Worse, two of the comatose people evacuated from the victim's house had died on the way to the hospital.

Sweat trickled down my spine. These darn protective coveralls didn't breathe. "I'm not getting anything else in here. Let's wait for our ride outside, where it's cooler."

We trudged to the front porch. "That's weird," Mayes said.

I wrestled with a coverall sleeve. "What?"

He pointed. "There's an ice cream truck parked in the driveway."

Chapter Nineteen

Ice cream? Could there be any better treat after roasting in these coveralls? I peeled the protective gear off and raced out to the truck. My mouth watered at the prospect of something cold and comforting. I ordered a chocolate and toffee-covered bar of ice cream. Gail stood talking to the driver, an older white male in a crisp aqua uniform shirt and hat. The name embroidered on the shirt was Joe.

"Do you usually stop here?" Gail asked, voice recorder in hand.

"Not hardly," Joe said. "This place always looks deserted. Never saw a face in the window. Never saw anyone on the porch or in the yard. Never saw a single bike in that rack out front. That's saying something, because I've had this route for over a year now."

"What about cars? Ever notice any vehicles here?"

Joe shook his head. "Nary a one. I can't believe people lived there. Seems like I should've known."

Mayes flashed Haney's picture on his cell phone at the ice cream vendor. "Ever seen this guy?"

"Sure. That's Haney." Joe beamed. "He lives across town. I usually see him out walking. He goes for orange sherbet every time." Joe studied the picture closer. "Why's he sleeping? Did something happen to him?"

I wondered if Mayes would say Haney was dead. Technically, Haney's family hadn't been notified, but just as technically, he didn't appear to have any family.

"Haney died," Mayes said in a matter-of-fact voice. "His body was found yesterday. We're trying to locate folks who knew him."

"Haney. God love 'im," Joe said, "Haney wasn't quite all there, you know? A few quarts shy of a full tank, but he loved Atlanta Braves baseball. He knew stats for all the players. That guy could talk your ear off about baseball."

"Where did he live?" Mayes asked, edging in front of Gail.

"I don't know. I assumed he was homeless because I never saw him at a house. He was always out walking on the road. He'd flag me down and get a treat. Never had dollar bills. Paid me in coins."

"Did he ever talk about family, friends, or work?"

"Noooo. He'd talk baseball, even in the winter. I saw him last week, and he was all fired up about the playoffs."

"We need you to show us where you saw Haney. All the places."

"Can't do that. I have my route. My customers expect me at certain times of the day."

"Call your boss. We'll square it with him."

"I don't want to do that. The boss thinks I goof off as it is. He's looking for a reason to fire me because his nephew got laid off from the car place."

"Call your boss. Or me, you, and your boss will have an extended meeting in Sheriff Blair's office in fifteen minutes."

Joe shook his head real fast. "If we don't take long, I can make up the time later on the route."

"I'll have another of those chocolate-toffee things," I added.

Gail and Wayne looked at me as if I'd lost my mind. "I need to stay hydrated," I protested. "No telling what will happen next. Life's short. Eat dessert first."

"Good point. I'll take another one in that

case," Mayes said, reaching for his wallet. "And I'll ride with you. We'll note the GPS coordinates of every location where you saw Haney. Gail, you and Baxley follow us in the Hummer."

The ice cream bars weren't cheap, but they were worth every cent. I felt worlds better after my belly was full. Which made me wonder if a sugar boost would help after every dreamwalk. Except then I'd be taking in too many calories.

We followed the van up and down streets, even waited while two different families stopped Joe, and Mayes served ice cream to them.

"I did some checking on my case while you were inside the house on Bear Claw Lane," Gail said. She maintained a steady six-car-length distance between us and the ice cream truck.

"Oh?"

"Neither the Sandelmans nor Jared Lee Hudson owns red vehicles, now or five years ago."

"Someone they knew owned one," I said. "Maybe an aunt or grandparent or family friend. The red car is important. Regina died in the trunk."

"Five years is a long time. Why would anyone keep the car if it linked them to her murder?"

"That's why I think the car belongs to someone else. It isn't the murderer's to dispose of."

Gail appeared to consider that line of reasoning. "Perhaps. I'll have my people keep digging."

"What about the man named Pug?"

"We did a records search. Pug isn't a known alias for anyone in the case. And on the basis of suspect photos from person-of-interest interviews, no male had a black spot on his neck. The lead's a dead end."

Why was she so quick to dismiss the leads Regina had given us? "The mark could be on the back of his neck."

"Could be, but odds are Pug wasn't one of the original suspects. These leads aren't helpful."

"Think again." I couldn't believe she didn't see the obvious connection. Talk about being too close to the investigation. "You have someone on your list who knows the murderer's identity. Someone who knew him well enough to call him by a nickname."

Reality dawned. Gail swerved off the road and recovered. "You're right. Tawny Sandelman. She knows who Pug is."

"Be careful how you ask her. If she felt loyalty to Pug, a call from her would likely have him destroying any remaining evidence. You'd need to have a search warrant in hand."

"Without solid evidence implicating him, a warrant's out of the question, but I can certainly get the cops to haul this Pug in and question him. I can put those wheels in motion today."

I studied her profile. Gail didn't seem as haughty as usual. She seemed . . . human. Vulnerable even. "Don't you want to be there to see Tawny's reaction?"

"Justice for Regina is all I want. If Tawny brought this on her family by her bad behavior, I want nothing to do with her. Besides, Twilla Sue and I go way back. She's a personal friend. I need to stay right here and do what I can to help her."

Her last words didn't ring true. I thought about the big picture. Tawny was yesterday's political powerhouse. Twilla Sue was tomorrow's powerbroker. Gail had her own best interests at heart. No surprise there.

The ice cream truck stopped in the street. Mayes dashed out the passenger door and hurried to Gail's Hummer. "Hospital. Right now. Twilla Sue's been found."

He didn't scare me. "They don't have a choice. The sheriff got hurt on our watch. That doesn't sit well with me. I need you to make sure we're not disturbed."

Mayes took his time answering. "You don't ask for much, do you?"

"I'm not asking."

"Yes, ma'am."

To his credit, Mayes didn't rattle my cage, didn't tease me about being bossy. Dare I try a dreamwalk with Twilla Sue before everyone showed up? I wanted to help her, but trying to reach her in deep sleep would exhaust me. Best to recharge her reserves first so that I wouldn't have to go down so deep to find her.

His gaze narrowed, and I suspected he was giving me a once-over. Probably checking out my aura. No worries there. My aura glowed with health and vitality. A few seconds later, he nodded, as if I'd passed an important test.

I'd only met Mayes today. He wasn't a personal friend like Running Bear. Just because he was Native American didn't mean he embraced the same beliefs. "Twilla Sue's brief captivity was very draining and took a heavy toll. Have you seen this before?"

He studied me again, as if he were also

weighing his words. "I know what you are."

Hmm. That sounded accusatory. "I want to help her."

Deputy Mayes said nothing, but his gaze increased in intensity.

Verbal sparring wasn't my forte. "Do you trust me or not?"

"I don't know you."

"But you checked me out with your second sight just now. I felt it."

"Tell me something about me, something you couldn't know ordinarily."

Uh-oh. My respect for him tanked. "I don't do party tricks."

He glared at me. "I could have you barred from this room."

"But you won't. Because you know I can help."

"I know your reputation. I know you've helped others. But. . . ."

His trailing voice alarmed me. "What?"

"You have a ghost attached to you."

A laugh welled up inside. I nearly snorted it out. "You're hesitating about me because of Oliver? He's a friendly spirit."

"Call him."

"No party tricks, remember?"

"This is important, Walks With Ghosts."

My turn to study him. He must be softening toward me because he'd given me an

Indian name. What would it hurt? *Oliver? This man wants to see you.*

Energy wavered in the room, then Oliver materialized with a deep bark. I knew Deputy Mayes saw the ghostly Great Dane because his eyes widened. He knelt and called the dog's spirit. Oliver crossed to the deputy and licked his hand.

The deputy said some words I didn't understand, then Oliver returned to me. I gave him a pat and sent him on his way.

"Thank you," Deputy Mayes said. "I had to be certain. Many are called. Few are chosen."

Cryptic words. Great. "Uh, sure."

"What's your plan?"

"To restore her energy."

His eyes glinted. "How?"

He wasn't giving me anything, and I'd already shown him my ghost dog. Suddenly, I felt like I had overstepped. I'd best be careful what I said. Mayes was a stranger and a cop. "The usual way."

"You need a special ceremony for that. And a facilitator."

"Not a problem."

"I'd like to participate. I offer my energy for her healing."

His request stunned me. "Thanks, but I'm sure we can handle it."

"I insist." His eyes narrowed, and the air vibrated with intent. "This is my boss. You're not playing fast and loose with her life."

"Her energy is dissipating as we speak. If we don't intervene, she won't make it until morning. The PV took her too low, just like he took the guys in house. Four of them died today, and the rest are at death's door."

"You misunderstand, Walks With Ghosts. You have my permission to do the healing ceremony, but only if I'm included."

Great. Just what this three-ring circus needed. Another Indian chief.

Chapter Twenty-One

My parents arrived, and Mayes began sneaking people into the hospital cubicle. Twilla Sue's room was at the end of the hall, so I hoped we wouldn't attract unwanted attention. My mom helped me drape my crystal shirt over Twilla Sue. When my dad came in and learned of Deputy Mayes' intent to participate, he sent word by the deputy stationed outside for Charlotte and Larissa to wait in the car.

I didn't catch the soft words my father and Deputy Mayes exchanged, but they seemed satisfied with each other. My father turned to me. "The sheriff's man has more experience than I have with this. He will lead the healing ceremony."

Protests rose and died in my dry throat. If my father was yielding, Deputy Mayes must be a powerful shaman. "As you wish. She doesn't have long, so we should get started."

Mayes took note of the supplies my father

had brought and grunted. He turned and opened a satchel I hadn't noticed before. With brisk efficiency, he added a tunic over his uniform. We gathered around Twilla Sue's bed. Mayes stood at her head, my father at her feet, and my mom and I beside each of her hands.

The vibe coming off Mayes was not harmonious. "You sure you can do this?" I asked.

"I can. First, only believers are allowed to participate. The flow of energy must be true."

"Mayes is right," my father added. "The channel must be opened correctly. Negative energy will block the transfer. Everyone must put aside suspicion and negativity."

I nodded my understanding. I'd benefited from these ceremonies, but I'd never been a donor. I hoped it was easy.

"We have four ordinals," Mayes said. "That is sufficient."

Deputy Mayes placed both hands on Twilla Sue's head and instructed us to lay hands on her as well. He began chanting. His voice had a hypnotic quality and soon, I found myself in a meditative trance. I recognized the peaceful state of mind from the healing ceremonies my parents and their Native American friends had performed on me after my dreamwalks.

"Walks With Ghosts, Sparrow, Lives In The Woods, and Raven stand beside this fallen warrior, Twilla Sue Blair," Mayes intoned. "We freely offer our energy to her spirit so that, if she chooses, she may live."

I marveled silently at my parents' Native American names. They were so apt. My mother's nurturing blue energy flowed through me, as did my father's protective yellow energy. Mayes' energy buffeted me next, powerful and emerald green. I chafed at the odd sensation of his fierce and dominant authority, instinctively resisting the level of submission he demanded.

Blocking him was like trying to roll a wooden wheel with a flat side. Each revolution jarred my entire being. I struggled against the energy field disturbance, wanting and needing everything to return to status quo. I had responsibilities. A child. I couldn't afford to be so vulnerable.

"Let go," my mother urged quietly. "To help your police friend, you must surrender all."

Having never been on this side of the healing circle, I hadn't known that I would totally lose my identity. The prospect of being adrift and not knowing who I was terrified me. If this transfer went awry, I'd spend eternity shackled to Mayes and my parents.

"Daughter," my father prompted, "trust in the circle. Lose yourself and gain the world."

"I'm afraid," I admitted.

"I am with you," my father said. "You are safe."

A great chasm opened up beneath me. The glass bridge I stood on thinned and narrowed. The light, airy quality of the trance darkened and pulsed erratically. Intuitively, I realized the fault was mine. I had jeopardized the link by refusing to surrender. My parents' faces swirled through the gathering gloom. I couldn't allow them to be harmed. They'd survived this process many times. I could at least cooperate.

"I am ready," I announced. "I surrender to the link."

The dark power Mayes exerted flowed inside me, overwriting my will. Instinct drove me to retreat into the safety of a dreamwalk, but Mayes yanked me to the surface of the trance. His harsh words bristled. "You cannot help her there, Dreamwalker. Trust in me. Stop wasting valuable time and energy."

"We are strangers," I added lamely.

"We are kindred spirits. Trust. You must trust, or a great warrior will suffer."

Twilla Sue. This was about Twilla Sue. Not about me. I would give my life for anyone in my family. Never had I imagined healing the sheriff would demand this level of sacrifice from me.

Trust, my father had said. It was easy to trust when you knew the answer. Not so easy when the winds of death howled in your ear.

Chapter Twenty-Two

The dark energy subsided, and my parents' energy surfaced. It seemed as if they were reaching for me, and I reached for them, going all in. The sense of self fell away, and I saw without eyes, without senses. I just was.

Only I was more than myself. I was my mom, my dad, and Mayes. My enhanced senses wanted to soar, but Mayes' insistent urging gave focus to my liberated spirit. I still retained my physicality and normal senses, but the extrasensory part of me had formed an intangible bond with my help-mates.

Twilla Sue lay before us on the hospital bed, struggling to survive. We stood around her, touching her head, feet, and hands. I wanted her to live. We all wanted her to live. Energy rose and flowed through the extra-sensory circuit we'd created, seeking a way out.

She did not so much as stir as she became bathed in the energy field. Through the spirit-link, we sought her empty well. I nearly jumped for joy when Mayes located a barren spot in her psyche. Slowly, ever so slowly, he massaged healing energy into that area.

Anticipation soared and crashed as she did not respond. I wished I knew her better. With effort, I found my voice. "We're not reaching her. We need another plan."

"What about singing? She likes music," Mayes said. "Old time spirituals."

I'd recently overcome my fear of singing in public, so I launched into a rendition of "Wade in the Water," making it soft and tender. At the same time, I stoked her arm and hand. My parents followed suit. Twilla Sue stirred, and our combined energy wrapped her in love.

Mayes added his voice to mine, and the enhanced energy brightened the room. I likened the sensation to the rosy glow of dawn. Twilla Sue's labored breathing eased. We were on the right track. Finally.

"Slow and steady," Mayes cautioned, as if he knew I was thinking to fire hose our energy gift into her.

I was a newcomer to this process, and the last thing I wanted was to harm our recipient or any of us. Mayes patiently held our focus and directed the flow. Soon, Twilla Sue's color brightened. Her hand twitched in mine.

My relief was instantaneous. It was working. *We* were working. I'd never had this heady feeling of healing someone. I'd never savored the sweetness or the moral rightness I felt from helping the sheriff. It was amazing.

"Just a little more juice and she'll be back to normal." I pushed a little extra energy forward, and the sheriff absorbed it. Giddy with power, I fought an absurd desire to laugh like a maniac. I could vault mountains. I could skim over the ocean waves. I could dance with the stars.

"Disengage," Mayes ordered, "now."

My parents obeyed at once. I saw Mayes had physically released the sheriff and stepped away as well. With regret, I mentally pulled back from Twilla Sue.

"We've done our part. Now we wait," Mayes said. "I'm releasing the mind-link."

The room brightened as I came fully into myself. I shivered against the unexpected chill in the sterile cubicle. Questions stuck in my throat, but I was too tired to utter a word. My knees felt all squishy and rubbery, so I sank into the nearest chair.

"Masterfully done." My father came around the bed and shook the deputy's hand. "You were the right man for the job."

"She's turned the corner now," my mom added, snuggling up to my dad. "Now she must finish the healing process."

"I wanted to keep going," I said, hugging myself for warmth, "but I'm so tired now, I need a nap. Thank you for monitoring all of us. Your delicate touch and your timing were awesome."

Mayes bowed his head. "Thank you for sharing your energy with my boss. She's a fighter. I have every confidence she will revive and be whole once more." He lifted his head and fixed me with a glare. "You are reckless and undisciplined."

"Guilty. But I have good intentions."

"When you are rested, we will speak again."

I didn't like his bossy attitude, so I brushed it off. "Sure."

Mayes handed me a blanket, which I immediately wrapped around my shivering body. At first it didn't make a difference, then slowly, surely, warmth seeped into my bones. I yawned, too tired to do one more thing. I had questions for everyone, especially Twilla Sue, but it was too late for me to gather information. I'd exceeded my energy limits, and Mayes had the good sense to pull me back from the abyss.

My eyes drifted shut.

Chapter Twenty-Three

I awoke to the muted sounds of quiet conversation. The light was weak, and I blinked until my vision adjusted. Definitely thin light, possibly late afternoon. I must've slept the day away. Shapes resolved until I realized I was in my bed in the camper. A mouthwatering scent tempted me. My mom's restorative broth.

Blessed be.

Memories poured into my consciousness. We'd given Twilla Sue a kick-start on her recovery energy, which in turn drained each of us. I must have passed out afterward. Had my parents experienced the same effect? If so, how'd my mom manage to revive so quickly to make her soup?

My stirring must have alerted the dogs outside. They came to the door and waited expectantly. I made a quick pit stop and then joined everyone at the campfire ring. Larissa ran over and hugged me like I'd been gone a week. Charlotte smiled in greeting, as did my parents.

"There she is," my mom said with a lilt in her voice. She got busy ladling broth into a bowl. "How're you feeling?"

Larissa and I sat cross-legged beside my mom. Elvis climbed into my lap, and the other dogs lay beside us. I cuddled the little Chihuahua close before I put him down. "Better. But a little embarrassed. How come you and Dad are up and about while I conked out?"

Charlotte cleared her throat. "I heard you commandeered the link and disproportionately shared your energy, whatever that means."

"Neither of us felt any ill effects from the mind-link," my dad said. "You shared too much of yourself, and you were poised to keep going."

"I had no idea," I said, accepting the steaming mug of soup from my mom. Warmth and peace emanated from the savory broth. I sipped slowly as the familiar and delicious aroma filled me. "Please accept my apology. I meant no harm. The energy channel opened to me, and my instinct to help took over. I should've taken my cue from you pros. It felt so good to finally reach the sheriff that I lost track of my sense of self. I tried to be expedient, if that makes any sense."

"Expediency has its place," my father said. "But experience should always be honored. We were lucky to have a man of Mayes' talent to oversee the transfer."

I nodded, my face flushing uncomfortably. "I made a mistake. It won't happen again."

Mom smoothed my hair behind my ear. "You are so powerful. We're amazed at what you can do."

"I keep making mistakes, but I learned another lesson today." I stared at the fire. "What I know is much less than what I don't know. Everything I do here and on the Other Side has a ripple effect. In my ignorance today, I put the people I love in jeopardy, and I'm so sorry. I seem to have two gears, full speed ahead or dead stop. I can't do this alone. Both of you amplify my abilities. If not for you, I'd be lying in that hospital with Twilla Sue getting pumped full of meds after collapsing on the job."

"You seem okay now," Charlotte pointed out.

"I *am* okay. A bit tired and a little muzzy-headed like the day before a cold sets in. I feel bad because this was supposed to be a week away from the pressures of home and work. It was supposed to be restful. We've hardly had a chance to spend an entire afternoon together, and I'm in the midst of two, maybe three cases."

"Three cases?" Larissa asked.

I drank the last bit of my soup and set the mug aside. "You know about the young man they found at the lake. And the state archeologist brought me a cold case that's a few years old involving a missing girl."

Larissa nodded. "That's two cases. What's number three?"

"The inhabitants of the Bear Claw Lane house. Whether they are related to the local case, I don't know. But I'm concerned for your safety, and if we didn't have so many folks here to keep an eye out for danger, I'd insist you go home right now."

"I don't want to go home," Larissa said. "I want to stay here with you."

The entire group gazed at me in expectation. I wanted to be the hero, the fun mom, but I was mired in responsibility. "We'll play it by ear. You need to have a buddy all the time."

Larissa nodded eagerly. "I will."

After a lull in the conversation, Dad asked, "Have any dreams during that four-hour nap?"

"I got nothing. When I'm down that low, I don't dream. Sorry. But, what about Twilla

Sue? Any news?"

"Her vitals improved," Dad said. "The doctors say she's close to waking up. The deputies guarding her will call once she's alert."

"What about the others we found in that house?"

Dad cut his eyes to Larissa and back. "It doesn't look good for the young men. The woman, though . . . she seems to be stabilizing. Perhaps she will recover. That's what we're hoping, at least."

"And Mayes?"

"He took some time off this afternoon as well, but he's back in the office. I heard from him just before you awakened."

I nodded. As usual, the world had gone on without me, but I had the strong sense I was missing something. A switch clicked in my head. "What about Gail Bergeron?"

"Gail spent the day observing autopsies at the morgue. She said she'd swing by in the morning to update you on her case."

I gazed at my family and best friend. "I know I don't say this often enough, but thank you, everyone. I couldn't help people without you and couldn't cope with everything else without your love."

Larissa wrapped her arms around my neck. "Love you back, Mom."

We spent the evening relaxing together, and it wasn't until everyone was bedded down for the night that I thought to do a perimeter energy check. The only people present were those in our travel party and the deputy who watched the camp, which was a relief.

All should've felt calm and serene, but the peace of the meadow had been replaced with a silent, edgy watchfulness. Something had changed the energy of this place. Whether it was living or dead, I wouldn't let it harm my family. Not while I had breath in my body.

Chapter Twenty-Four

True to her word, Gail Bergeron showed up promptly at nine the next morning. I wasn't fooled by her feminine, mossy-green pant-suit. This woman was as relentless as a riptide and as aggressive as a shark.

Deputies Mayes and Duncan followed Gail's Hummer into our campsite. My parents and Larissa were fishing on the lake, so Charlotte and I greeted our guests with hellos. Our words fell on deaf ears.

Mayes intercepted Gail. "You can't have her today."

"Your emergency is contained," Gail argued. "My need for Ms. Powell is urgent. Things are breaking in my case because of her. This family needs closure."

"In cases like yours, the family blames themselves, so finding the killer won't bring them closure. They need counseling," Mayes pointed out. "I've got a killer on the loose and an unconscious sheriff. I need Ms.

Powell to contact Twilla Sue this morning. We must locate and arrest her abductor before he hurts someone else. There hasn't been a rash of child abductions and murders in Atlanta since your victim went missing five years ago. Ms. Powell comes with me and works on my case."

"I could call the governor." Gail's face darkened. "I could have you removed from this case."

Mayes shrugged, his granite-hewn features revealing nothing. "Go ahead. Public safety trumps cold justice every time. Even if your pal orders me to step aside, whoever takes my place will have the same priorities. Someone went after a cop. We don't take that lightly."

I was getting a headache from their raised voices. An idea glimmered briefly.

Gail pinched the top of her nose. "This isn't fair. I have an obligation to that family."

"A self-imposed obligation," Mayes said. "You mean well, I get that, but —"

"Hey folks, I have an idea," I interjected, moving to stand between them. "Gail and I can consult in her car on the way to the hospital. I'm back to a hundred percent, so I'll have no problem with my energy level today."

"That's an excellent idea." Gail beamed her approval. "A compromise. Mayes still gets you at the hospital right away, and I'll have a new direction to follow."

Mayes scowled at me. "I have a problem with your divided attention. I need you at the top of your game when you work with Twilla Sue."

"The ladies are in agreement, Mayes." Duncan's gravelly voice rumbled through the meadow. "What say you to us riding together and allowing the ladies to travel with Dr. Bergeron?"

Mayes glared at him. "You approve of this?"

Duncan bobbed his head. "Boss always defers to Dr. B. Let's play nice by sharing our consultant. Then we'll have Ms. Powell's help for the rest of the day."

I took Mayes' continued silence as tacit approval. "Great. I'll grab my book bag, and we can go. Charlotte, you're welcome to tag along."

Charlotte had been talking about hunky Deputy Duncan since dawn. She grinned. "Wouldn't miss it. I need my purse as well."

We hurried up the camper's steps and collected our stuff. I debated packing my crystal shirt in my book bag, just in case, then rejected the idea. Much better to have it waiting at home for me.

"This is so fun," Charlotte confided as she touched up her makeup. "Not only am I part of an investigation, I've had six calls from Kip so far asking me where things are at the office. He needs me. Life is good."

I dashed off a quick note to my family. I could send a telepathic message to Larissa and my father, but I didn't want to horn in on their fishing. I stashed the gun under my pillow. "Betcha your boss is feeling the pinch with you gone. No way is Bernard doing all the extras you routinely take care of every day."

"Right-o." Charlotte beamed, the light glinting on her glasses. "Don't get me wrong. I don't want Bernard to be fired. My goal is to be considered his equal."

"If Kip doesn't realize what a gem he has in you, that's his loss."

"I like the way you think."

A horn blasted outside. I winced, not looking forward to the coming skirmish with Gail. "Our chariot awaits."

Outside, Gail stood beside her Hummer. The guys were watching from inside Mayes' cruiser.

"You there, Candace," Gail said, "I want you to drive."

"My name's Charlotte, but I'm happy to

take the wheel. Where to?"

"The hospital, but there's no rush. Ms. Powell and I will be in the backseat working on my case. Your job is to allow us to have discovery time, understand?"

"Got it."

We climbed in, with Gail sitting in the captain's chair behind Charlotte. A tote bag rested at her feet. "Can you do this on the move?" she asked.

I buckled my seatbelt, glad of the personal space protection offered by this style of seating. "I've awakened in different places when someone moved my body during a dreamwalk. It's disorienting, like being out of phase with yourself, but it is possible. My preference is to dreamwalk and awaken in the same place," I admitted, though my explanation sounded weak. "What's your news? Did they make an arrest?"

"A pair of Atlanta detectives will visit the Sandelmans this morning. If Tawny knows who Pug is, they'll get it out of her. But I started thinking about what you said yesterday, and it jarred a memory. I've seen that dress before."

I waited while she grabbed a photo from her bag.

"I had a few things shipped overnight here from the evidence locker," Gail said. "Is this the gown you saw?"

She turned the photo over, and there was the tea-party gown Regina had worn in the vision. On her mom, the fabric stretched tight across her buxom figure.

I met Gail's intense gaze. "That's the dress. Why?"

"Because it was found in the far corner of the yard. Senator Knox blew up because he thought Tawny had stripped outside for one of her lovers. She denied it, of course. And he started in on her infidelities. According to the detectives, it was an awful scene. Bottom line, the dress was collected in evidence."

"I'll look at it, but there's a chance the same scene I already witnessed will be attached to the fabric."

"And another chance we may learn something different."

"Was it tested for DNA?"

"Not at the time, but it could be tested now, especially if the killer's DNA is on it. Will you examine it now?"

"A touch test is different from a dreamwalk. Touch tests pick up emotion. What happened before with Regina was a gift. I'm almost never allowed interaction with murdered spirits."

"Whatever. Let's try it."

Charlotte eased down the lane by the creek. As Gail dug into her tote bag, a dirty fog enveloped the car. "Y'all see that?" I asked.

"I don't see anything," Charlotte said, her syllables dragging out in slow motion.

An awful sense of foreboding flooded my body as the mist thickened. This was not the way to the hospital.

Chapter Twenty-Five

Utter darkness descended as the entire vehicle passed through the veil of life. Ludicrous as that sounded, the disorienting sensation was the same as when I went into a dreamwalk. I gripped the sides of my seat and braced myself for what would come next. Sure enough, the Hummer began spinning, rolling end over end, and yawing from side to side. Something had us. They'd taken the entire car from our campground.

The last time I'd carried someone along accidentally on a dreamwalk, I'd nearly died. Now I was responsible for two people, myself, and an expensive vehicle. I focused on stabilizing our freefall and eventually oriented us so we were upright and level, though still plunging downward in the dark. The seatbelt held me firmly in place.

Suddenly, the wheels touched down, and I pinched myself to see if I was in spirit or human form. Oddly, I was flesh and blood.

How was that possible?

I gazed around. "Charlotte? Gail? Are you all right?"

No answer. Of course not. That would've been too easy. I unbuckled my seatbelt and climbed over the center console to switch the car lights on. I touched every knob, moved every lever. Nothing happened. Not even a click. No juice at all. But the fog was lifting. I could make out my hand in front of my face. That was good news.

I unbuckled Gail's belt and patted her face. "Wake up!"

She stirred uneasily but I hadn't awakened her. I climbed to the front and tried the same with Charlotte. No response. Whatever had us, I felt sure I was the reason for the abduction. This was not right, and I had to fix it.

Reaching deep for courage, I opened my door and exited the vehicle. "Hello? Anybody out here?"

This place didn't resemble my dreamwalker world on the Other Side. For one thing, the ground felt solid and cold beneath my feet, and the air smelled damp and earthy. Were we in a cave? If so, how'd we get here?

I ventured a few steps away from the car. "Hello?"

At a soft moan, I inched behind the Hummer and stumbled across another vehicle. What was this? Feeling my way down the side of the car, I opened the passenger door and traced a man's craggy features with my fingertips. My gut clenched. Deputies Mayes and Duncan in the police cruiser had also been transported to this creepy place. *Great,* now my responsibilities included two more people and a police cruiser.

Like Charlotte and Gail, Duncan was unconscious. Mayes, however, was twitching and stirring.

"Too soon," Mayes mumbled. "I told you I'd bring her."

"Who are you talking to?" I asked, reaching over and tapping his chest. His energy level spiked, and I knew he'd fully awakened.

He turned to face me in the cloying mist. "The Little People. They've brought us to their land."

Only recently had I heard about the Little People. Twilla Sue had mentioned them in a comment about Mayes and the murder. Was Mayes working for someone else? Was he on my side? I wasn't sure if I could trust him. "It's a dark place," I replied in a neutral tone.

"That's part of their charm. The tunnel is

the only darkness here. Outside the passageway, there is light, and life, and merriment."

I shrugged, and truth be told, felt a wave of relief. "Doesn't sound half-bad."

"It's meant to confound you. If you venture out of this cave, you'll lose track of normal time."

His words alarmed me. I couldn't afford to waste time. My vacation kept getting cut. "What should we do?"

"We summon them."

"Is that wise?"

"They're our only way out. The vehicles won't work here. Theoretically, we could walk back through the portal, but we'd have to abandon the vehicles."

My vision seemed to be crisping up. I could see Mayes more clearly in the murk. "No way is Gail going to leave her new Hummer."

"Twilla Sue would be pissed if I left a cruiser here as well."

I tried to wrap my head around that. "Will the others awaken?"

"In time." He took a slow breath, as if debating what to say next. "You and I are used to alternate realities, so we came to our senses immediately. The others won't awaken as quickly."

Was he concerned about trusting me? How bizarre. "How do you know about this place?"

"It is the lore of my people. When the gatekeeper comes, I'll speak for us. You will follow my lead. No jumping in and playing hero. Our lives and our friends' lives are at stake."

I hated being chastised, but I understood. He was the expert here. I was treading in uncharted waters. If he could make these Little People let us go, more power to him. Back in the real world, I had things to do, people to see.

A faint thumping sound grew louder. I pivoted and cocked my head to hear better. "What's that?"

"The drums. Ignore them."

I strained toward the sound. "The beat is catchy. We should check it out."

"Block the sound. Now. If you get lured by the drums, we're doomed."

"I don't want to block it. I want to see it for myself."

I turned, vaguely aware of Mayes exiting the cruiser. My feet moved of their own accord. As I cleared the Hummer, a bright light dawned ahead. I yearned to be in that perfect light. I desperately wanted to feel its warmth on my skin.

Mayes blocked me. His hands covered my ears. I tried to shake him off, but he kept his hands in place. After a moment, I glanced up. His face was darkened by shadows, his expression fierce.

The physical contact brought him close to my face. "Baxley, block the drums," he said. "You have the power. Don't be lured by false pretenses. Hold fast to your reality."

I shook my head like a dog shaking off river water, but Mayes stuck to me like a sandspur. Defeated, I resorted to the truth. "My reality? Are you kidding? My reality is meeting strange creatures on the Other Side. My reality is stopping killers from striking again. This place feels like the holiday I've been seeking, a place where I can kick back and forget my responsibilities."

"If you follow this path, you will miss seeing your daughter grow up. You will not share the companionship of your parents' golden years. Is that the future you want?"

The thought of missing so much of life stopped me cold. "No. I love Larissa." Blocking the drums was my only hope of getting out of here. But how?

"Focus on your loved one," Mayes said. "Visualize her face and keep it in the forefront of your thoughts while we are here."

My thoughts must have spilled into his head inadvertently. Nevertheless, I did as he said. When I had the image of Larissa firmly in my thoughts, I nodded, and he slowly lowered his hands. I gave him a cautious thumbs-up.

"Do *not* lower your guard," he cautioned. "They're very curious about you, Walks With Ghosts."

My thoughts drifted to Oliver, the ghost dog who'd attached himself to me. Was he here? In that instant, the drums boomed loud and clear in my head. I clapped my hands over my ears and summoned my daughter's face until the din receded.

When I had a firm grip on my thoughts, I lowered my hands and locked eyes with Mayes. "They're persistent."

He nodded. "Hold that thought. They come."

Chapter Twenty-Six

I wracked my brain for the meager information I'd gleaned about the Little People. They were thought to be the subject of tales the Scots had brought over from their homeland. They'd been likened to elves, dwarfs, and fairies. Experiencing their abilities firsthand, I believed they were more than that.

They'd somehow transported two vehicles and five people through the veil of life to their land of milk and honey. Did they have superpowers? Would they trap me here with them? I couldn't allow that. I had to get us all safely home, and for that reason, I'd follow Mayes' lead.

Instead of coming from the brightness of outside the cave, a host of glowing warriors walked from the depths of the tunnel to greet us. Three tall men clad in ceremonial Indian buckskins, their hair bound in long black braids, separated from the others and continued toward us. Each wore a round medallion with a cross bisecting the circle. They greeted Mayes like a long-lost brother.

My thoughts pinged like crazy. What were these people? They certainly weren't little. Where was I? Had I lost my mind? This was no spirit realm, but it wasn't my Earth either.

The most implacable of the three, the one Mayes addressed as Trahearn, stepped around Mayes to approach me. I was enveloped in the glow of his light. "We have long awaited your arrival, Spiritwalker."

"My name's Baxley, and I'm a dreamwalker. I have no Native American heritage."

Trahearn pointed to my white forelock. "You wear the sign of power as prophesied."

His buddies, who introduced themselves as Meuric and Arwel, joined him, nodding their approval. Meuric reached for my hair, and I instinctively retreated toward Gail's Hummer. I didn't like being hijacked, kidnapped, or whatever this was. One thing I was sure of: these fierce warriors wouldn't respect weakness. I shot a glance at the Cherokee who knew them. "Mayes?"

"He meant no harm. They are in awe of your power."

"Me? I'm as human as anyone." Now that I'd started talking, I couldn't seem to stop.

"Why aren't they little?"

"We have many guises, Dreamwalker." Trahearn waved his companions to the other side of me. "This is how we appear to the Cherokee. Mayes has walked among us many times, so we sought to put him at ease. Forgive us for staring, but to us, you're the stuff of myths and legends."

I couldn't help it. I snorted my disbelief. "What are you?"

"We are like you but not like you." Trahearn made another motion with his hand, bowed, and took a few steps backward. Simultaneously, the men behind me crowded closer. I inched into the open space beside Mayes.

"You are strong," Trahearn continued, "and according to Mayes, courageous."

The men behind me were breathing on my neck. I shot them a glare and moved forward. "I believe the term he used was 'reckless.' Why have you brought us here? What do you want?"

"We seek to bring our friend Haney's killer to justice." Trahearn's dark eyes gleamed with emotion.

Every nerve in my body strained to run out of this cave, but where would I go? These people had me surrounded, and I didn't know the way back to my world. His words finally registered. My feet stopped. "You know something about Haney's death?"

He backpedaled into the cave. The cluster of others melted to the side, forming a corridor for us. "We know who killed Haney. We saw it come to pass."

His cavalier attitude about witnessing a brutal crime angered me. I followed him. "Why didn't you stop the killer?"

"Why would we intervene? Human affairs are not our concern."

But now they wanted his killer brought to justice? My hands fisted at his callous remark, but Mayes touched my arm until I glanced at him. "Let's keep calm heads here," Mayes said before he refocused on the spokesman. "We need your information. Tell us what you know."

Trahearn smiled indulgently. "You used to have more patience, Raven. Your spirit is weakened by the white man's ways. Honor your heritage. Listen with more than your ears."

Mayes stiffened. "You're wasting our time."

"We have information you seek," Trahearn insisted. "We wish to make a trade."

Was it my eyes, or was the cave becoming brighter? Or was Trahearn's glow dimmer? I really didn't like feeling so helpless. We'd been guided away from our vehicles, separated from Charlotte, Gail, and Deputy Duncan. This was not good.

"No deals," Mayes said. "We'll catch Haney's killer through solid detective work. Send us above ground."

"You would deny us? We are linked, your people and mine. When the Nunne'hi leave the mountain, your people will cease to exist here. Do you want that on your soul?"

Mayes shrugged. "The old ways are dying out. My people leave the mountain every day and don't come back."

Trahearn bent forward, nearly touching me. I jumped back. "A thief from your world stole from us. The wrong must be avenged."

I'd had enough of being pushed around, and it seemed I was trapped inside a mountain. There had to be a way out. If Mayes wasn't willing to look, I'd do it myself. But first I'd try reason again. "We want to go home. Tell us the terms of your deal so that we may discuss it with the sheriff."

Trahearn gave me a long, considering look. "You are also impatient, Dreamwalker, but your directness is commendable. Your time in this region is limited, so you wish to conclude the matter swiftly."

So much for reason. We were getting the runaround. I turned to Mayes. "Can you get us out?"

He didn't answer at first. His gaze slipped over to Trahearn's then met mine again. "Depends."

"On what?"

He nodded to the crowd of about thirty tall men surrounding us. "On whether they allow us to leave."

"No one is leaving," Trahearn said, walking away.

The knot of glowing people swept Mayes and me along in Trahearn's direction. Now I knew how it felt to be a cow in a herd. It was either move or be trampled. I glanced over my shoulder, but there wasn't even a hint of the vehicles or people we'd come with.

"Let's rethink this," I began slowly. "We want to go home. You have information for sale. We should be able to come to terms."

Trahearn entered a large cavern and strode toward the center. "First, you must see what unfolded. Sit." He gestured to the area around the cold fire pit. A flick of his wrist drew flames from the stones. A young boy's face appeared amid the flames.

The face was familiar, but I couldn't place it. I sat cross-legged beside Mayes and hoped this wouldn't take long.

"Haney was our friend," Trahearn insisted. "He walked with us many times throughout his short life. We accepted him among us because of his kind and gentle spirit. He could've stayed here forever, but he said this wasn't his place. He made a friend in your world, but that friend betrayed Haney and stole from us."

Mayes' brow furrowed. "Who was his friend?"

"Haney called him Jonesy. We allowed Jonesy entrance to our land because we trusted Haney. But Jonesy had an ulterior motive. He discovered our wells of power and stole from us. Then he enslaved Haney and made him do terrible things. Jonesy is evil."

"What does Jonesy look like?" I hoped they would describe Jonas so we could leave.

Trahearn shook his head. "He is a master of disguise. He deceived us by visiting here in the guise of Haney . . . and of others."

An image of another boy's face appeared in the flames. Scraggly dark hair framed a thin face and a strong nose. The dark eyes burned with hate.

I recognized the child. From Haney's dreamscape. The first boy was Haney, when he was a kid. I understood now. Jonesy had befriended Haney all those years ago, earned his trust, and then used him to become powerful.

"I don't recognize him," Mayes said. "I've never seen that boy in our county."

"He wears another appearance now. We know he's still in the area because our power will only work near this mountain. That is why he cannot move out of range."

Keeping my thoughts about Jonesy and Haney to myself, I asked about the stolen item. "What is this power you refer to?"

Trahearn blanched. He glanced to a tall, white-haired man who'd come into the cavern from the opposite side. Whatever he saw must have encouraged him. "A memory churner. We use it to recall events in our long lives, but in the wrong hands, the power can be harmful."

"As in making people forget who they are and where they are because their memories are so vivid?" I asked, putting more of the case together in my head.

"The churner can have that effect," Trahearn admitted. "But that was not its intent. We have no need to trap humans in their memories."

"In that case, we already know who Jonesy is and where he lived. There's no supernatural device in his house, or I would've sensed it." I didn't know if that was true or not, but I was on a roll. "The killer is in the wind with your superpower, but even so, we don't have evidence to hold him accountable for the murder."

"Proof is a construct. Jonesy is a thief and a murderer."

"He kidnapped my boss and used the device on her," Mayes said. "When we catch him, we can charge him with that crime."

"We want our memory churner back," Trahearn said.

"How?" I asked. "We don't know what it looks like or where it is."

"Your guide can retrieve it. Summon her."

My guide. Who was he talking about? An awful feeling filled my gut. *Dear God.* He wanted Rose.

Chapter Twenty-Seven

"Not a good idea," I stammered. "The one of whom you speak exacts payment for every favor she grants. She's a wild card."

My tattoos heated. The one on my back felt like it was burning into a shoulder blade. I chewed my lip to keep from crying out in pain. The tattoo on my hand out and out throbbed. I did not want to summon Rose. She already owned two hours of my life on Earth to use whenever she saw fit. I couldn't afford to be any deeper in her debt.

"We are used to such demands," Trahearn said. "Summon her."

Dreamwalking here would be a bad idea, especially when I had no idea where *here* was. "No. If I decide to help you, I contact her on my terms, from my world."

Muttering filled the cavern, rising and pulsing like a living, breathing creature. They weren't happy with me? Well, I wasn't happy with them either.

Mayes whispered in my ear, "Give them what they want."

"Then I'll lose any leverage I have to get us out of here," I whispered back. "They kidnapped five of us, if you recall."

"I'm aware of that, but I know these people. They do not tolerate defiance or insubordination."

"I can't risk a dreamwalk from wherever we are. It's too risky."

Mayes had the good grace to look troubled. About time he realized these strange folks didn't rule the world. So what if they could bend reality somehow? They weren't as fearsome as Rose.

Trahearn brought his arms up. "Silence!"

The cave quieted, though the mood of the place remained unsettled, and that discomfort wasn't coming entirely from the humans in the room. I'd held my ground, but at what cost? Would I be trapped forever in their world?

"We have decided to grant your request," Trahearn said. "Mayes knows the place. We will meet there at dusk today."

I gulped. Had I just called their bluff? Was I a super negotiator or what?

"However, we have learned our lesson with humans, and as an incentive for you to follow through, your friends will remain with us in our world."

My newfound confidence tanked. I scrambled to my feet, with Mayes following suit. "My word is good," I said. "I'll meet you and make the connection you seek. You don't need to hold my friends hostage."

The flames tripled in size, and in their midst, I saw Charlotte clinging to Deputy Duncan in what looked like a park. Gail stood nearby, chatting with a woman with long, dark hair. They were unharmed.

I gulped as the image faded from view. Charlotte, Deputy Duncan, and Gail would be held hostage somewhere in an illusion trap while we waited for dusk in the real world. "Why delay? Why don't we go right back to my world and summon my guide?"

Mayes touched my arm. "Dusk is the gloaming time," he said. "It is when the portal between worlds is easiest to access."

His stony expression confused me. "You're okay with this?"

"No harm will come to our friends and associates. They are safe with the Nunne'hi."

"They're hostages. We can't leave them behind."

Mayes' face turned red. "Those are the terms we were offered. The Little People will honor their word. Our people will be returned to us after we have fulfilled our part of the bargain."

"I'm not so trusting."

Mayes' cheek twitched. "I know."

"Enough quibbling," Trahearn said. "Do you accept the terms, Baxley Powell?"

"How about if I stay here until dusk, and everyone else goes free?"

Trahearn shook his head. "No change in terms. Besides, you are needed in your world."

My heart jumped right into my throat. "My family? Are they okay?"

"Do you accept the terms?"

I pictured my family injured or dead by the roadside. I had to get back to them, even if it meant throwing the rest of our travel party under the bus. "Yes, I agree."

The room grayed to black. Freefall started again. I hated this stomach-in-your-throat part of whole body transport. I affixed Larissa's face on my mental chalkboard and stopped spinning. My thoughts narrowed to a pinpoint then expanded out in a bright kaleidoscope. I hoped my brain wasn't exploding.

Chapter Twenty-Eight

The sun blazed high overhead. Birds chirped in the nearby forest. All indications pointed to a normal day, but nothing had been normal about this morning.

My trembling legs could not support my weight. I sank to the ground, hugging my middle as my abs tensed. Nausea overtook me, and I dry-heaved until the urge passed.

Natural sounds slowly overcame the thrumming of my pulse in my ears. Wind sighed in the pines and oaks, water lapped the nearby lakeshore, but nothing caught my attention like the cold knot of dread in my core as I processed what I'd been through.

I'd failed, and that failure ate at me. Poor Charlotte. Poor Gail and Duncan, too.

Granted, the circumstances were extreme, but I'd left my best friend behind. Would I ever see her again? The thought of such a terrible loss brought on a new wave of nausea. Sweat beaded in my scalp, dribbled down my spine. I clung to the ground for dear life.

The sound of retching nearby startled me. I shrunk into myself, not wanting anyone to see me in such a weakened condition. Then I realized the noise had come from Deputy Chief Mayes. He must be having the same visceral side effects from being transported body and soul.

Oddly, his distress cheered me. *What do you know? Misery does love company.* I began to take stock. I was alive and back in the world I knew and loved. My fingers and toes worked. My thoughts were my own. So far, so good.

I scrambled to my feet and glanced around. A police cruiser sat on the grassy lane that passed for a driveway on Annabelle's property. Our camper was visible through the trees. I knew exactly where I was, but the sun's position high in the sky told me I'd lost the morning.

As if on cue, my phone shrilled. My father. I answered the call.

"You all right?" he asked.

"Getting there."

"I see." Silence pinged. "Can you talk about it?"

"Not sure anyone would believe the tale,

but I need something from you."

"Oh?"

"Please make sure Larissa isn't worried about me. Tell her I'm okay."

"Rough dreamwalk?"

"You have no idea."

"Should we meet you at the campsite?"

"No." I grimaced at my sharp tone. "Sorry. That didn't come out right. I'm okay. Deputy Mayes and I are working the murder case. I'll be tied up through sundown."

"And Charlotte? She with you?"

I gulped. I didn't want to lie to my father, but how could I explain what happened? "Charlotte's spending the day with Deputy Duncan."

Soft murmuring filled the line before my dad spoke again. "Your mother says to change your crystals." More murmuring. "She says to carry your gun."

A sob choked out of me. My mother's intuition was spot on.

Thank goodness.

Bushes rattled. Mayes walked toward me, his normally tanned face as pale as the thin clouds rimming the eastern sky. "Thanks," I said. "Gotta go."

Mayes stopped near me, right eyebrow arched.

I hardly knew which question he had in

mind. I went for the most expedient answer. "You'll feel better in a few minutes. Before we head to the hospital, I need to return to my camper to change my shirt. Then, we need to talk."

He nodded and went over to sit in the cruiser. Hurrying to the camper, I washed my face, luxuriating in the cold water. It felt like heaven. I swapped out my sweat-dampened tee for another of the same vintage. I hastily dumped my pocketful of crystals on the table and grabbed a fresh set. The Beretta I tucked in my waistband.

On my way out the door, I caught sight of the coolers. No way could I tolerate food right now, but a ginger ale would be great. I found two cans and jogged back to Mayes.

The cruiser door was open. I slid into the passenger seat, leaving my door open to create a cross-breeze. Mayes accepted the soda with a weak smile. "Thanks."

"So," I began after we'd both had several sips of ginger ale, "you do this often?"

"This. . . ." His voice hitched and trailed off. "It's never been like this before. I'm weak as a kitten."

"I'm none too steady myself. Where were we? Are our friends truly safe?"

He stared blankly ahead as he took another swig of ginger ale. "The Little People are said to dwell in the mountain, but as best as I can figure out, the mountain is more like a gateway to their realm."

I'd figured as much, but I needed more information. "Are they living, dead, or something else?"

"Definitely something else."

"Why do they need our help? They seem powerful enough."

Mayes shrugged. "We can't tell anyone what happened."

"Figured that much out already when my dad asked about Charlotte. I explained she was spending the day with your deputy. Can you cover for him and for Gail at work?"

"As long as this doesn't go south on us. You can hold up your end, right?"

"Right." I was certain Rose would answer my call. Unless she didn't.

"What?" Mayes asked.

I let out the breath I'd been holding. "You're very good at reading people."

"Have to be in this job. You thought of something just now. What was it?"

"My *guide* isn't a dog that comes on command. I've only seen her in my dreamwalks. What if she can't or won't make an appearance in the land of the living?"

"Thought of that already. You and I walk between worlds. We can relay the messages back and forth if she can't materialize."

"Seems reasonable. Good. Next question. What do we do between now and dusk?"

He stared at me in a way that had me shrinking inside. "We solve the case."

Chapter Twenty-Nine

Mayes drove to the hospital like the car was on fire. It seemed surreal to be doing ordinary tasks when my best friend was being held hostage by supernatural beings.

Two thoughts eased my fears. First, my time in Little People land had seemed like a mere thirty minutes, while in truth it had been the entire morning. That gave me hope Charlotte wouldn't be watching the clock. Second, I knew she was attracted to Deputy Duncan. Charlotte could very well be having the time of her life. Being stranded with a hunk in a park would not be a hardship for her.

At the hospital, monitors beeped from each room we passed, and our rubber-soled shoes squeaked on the shiny floor. We nodded at the guard outside the sheriff's room, and then we stood at Twilla Sue's bedside. Despite yesterday's energy transfer, the sheriff had not awakened.

Mayes spoke to the guard and closed the door. He gave me a nod. "You're on."

"Are you tagging along on this dream-walk?"

"Not this time. I need to conserve my strength for later today. I can do what you do, but not as easily and not as frequently. What you have is a true gift."

I scowled at him. "Sometimes it seems like a curse. I can't tell you how many times I've wished to be normal."

He shrugged. "You are what you are." With a tip of the head to his boss, he said. "Get her to come back to the surface with you, or at the very least, get me a lead we can use."

"Would you like me to also secure world peace and end poverty?"

He crossed his arms and growled at me.

Men. They had no sense of humor. I edged closer to Twilla Sue. She looked so serene, it seemed wrong to disturb her slumber. *Her unnatural slumber,* I reminded myself.

Girding myself for an ordeal, I wrapped my fingers around her hand. At once, I heard the sweet sound of humming. A lullaby.

A rosy scene unfolded before me in the dream plane. A child's nursery glowed with the soft blush of early dawn. Adorable monkeys decorated the wall and lamp. Two stuffed monkeys guarded the white crib.

I turned toward the soft singing in the corner of the room where a woman rocked an infant. Twilla Sue. I didn't know she had a daughter.

"Shh," she said in a stage whisper, "don't wake the baby."

I reminded myself this was a dream. There was no actual baby that I could disturb. Even so, it wouldn't hurt to play along. I softened my voice. "Twilla Sue, I need you to come with me. This place, it isn't real. It's all in your mind."

She continued to rock the baby and pat its back. Her eyes drifted shut. "I'm here with my darling Miranda. Such a sweet baby. I love her so much."

"Do no harm" was more than an oath taken by those in the medical profession. I also operated under the same philosophy. If Twilla Sue was content in her delusion, could I bring her out of it without upsetting her? I gave it a shot. "The baby's asleep. You can put her down in the crib now. She'll sleep through the night."

The woman snapped to attention. Her eyes bugged out. "I can't put her down. I just can't. She's my precious baby girl."

I matched her sharp tone, needing to jolt her into reality. "This is a dream, Twilla Sue. You're in the hospital. A man hurt you, and we need your help to catch Jonas Canyon. This nursery, even the baby . . . they aren't real."

"Of course they're real. This is Miranda's nursery. I painted these pink walls myself. My mother found the monkey designs for us online. This room is absolutely perfect for a little princess like my daughter."

The nursery was Twilla Sue's refuge, a hideaway where she wasn't the sheriff. Without knowing why she sought refuge in that memory, I had no means of talking her around to waking up. I needed another way in.

I cleared my throat and spoke in a no-nonsense tone, the kind Twilla Sue used routinely. "You're the sheriff, Twilla Sue. A dangerous man named Jonas is hunting people on your turf. He steals their energy and leaves them for dead. You know things about this man we don't know. Things that would help us catch him."

Twilla Sue swatted my words away with a flip of her wrist. "Bah. Police business. Not my concern. I'm on maternity leave right now."

Nothing was working. All I had left was

tough love. I walked over and tapped her on the shoulder. "Snap out of it, woman. Duty calls."

Her jaw trembled, then hardened. "No. I don't have to do what you say. Get out!"

The dream faded, and my consciousness returned to the bright hospital room. I released Twilla Sue's hand and glanced at Mayes. "I'm so sorry. I failed you."

"You couldn't reach her?"

"I spoke with her — that was the easy part. She's reliving an aspect of motherhood, that of rocking a newborn to sleep. There's a pink nursery and monkeys. The infant has on pink jammies. You know anything about that?"

"A little. It happened before I joined the force. Twilla Sue's daughter died a few weeks after her birth. Sudden Infant Death Syndrome, they said." He paused, taking a long look at his sleeping boss. "After the baby's funeral, she poured herself into police work. But all the ground she gained in her career drove her husband away. She's been divorced for years."

The pieces started to fit together. "That explains why I couldn't get her to leave. The mother I saw holding her baby would've traded her entire career to have one more hour with her daughter. That memory is everything to her."

Mayes muttered something under his breath. His next glance at his boss wasn't a kind one. "What about Jonas?"

I shook my head. "I got nothing useful from Twilla Sue. The nursery construct is her only reality right now. She told me she was off duty."

The shrill of Mayes' phone startled us both. Mayes took the call and shepherded us both out the door. With a quick instruction to the guard, he dragged me down the hall.

"What's going on?" I asked.

"Got another victim."

Chapter Thirty

Mayes stopped the cruiser at another lakeside spot, only this one was ringed by his Cherokee brethren. They stood in knots of twos and threes — stoic, dark-haired icons against the blue-green backdrop of forest and lake.

"We just got the call," I said, staring at the crowd. "How'd they get here so quickly — smoke signals?"

Mayes logged his position with HQ and turned off the car. "Wrong cloud. Try social media. The tribe has gone high tech, and there's an app for everything, including bad news."

"Do you know who it is?"

He paused and rubbed his eyes. "White Feather, known outside the tribe as Dana Finley."

I followed him around the car, studying the sadness on his face, registering the slight hitch in his voice. "You sound resigned, like

"Yes. He thinks he's a regular Sherlock Holmes."

"This print could belong to anyone."

His gruff tone sounded much like my sheriff's back home. No way was I letting him ignore this clue. I met his steely gaze. "Except it doesn't. This is proof the killer walked this way. I'm guessing a road is farther along this path."

He nodded. "Hawk's Nest Trail. It's unpaved."

"Get yourself a scent dog up here. It'll track the killer from the body up this path and to the road. I'd wager money on it. You might even get some tire tracks."

Mayes knelt down to study the print. "This is deep and a size-eleven-or-so sneaker. The man who made it must be two-fifty, easy, maybe more. Not Jonas Canyon. I estimate his weight was barely one-fifty."

"It could be Jonas. If he was carrying White Feather."

Mayes stared at the ground some more. "That works." He rose, made a call, then turned to me. "Don't wander off again. I need you to stay in my field of vision."

A team of deputies approached. Mayes directed them to secure the scene and cast the footprint. While they worked, I trailed Mayes to the road, wishing I could do more.

I wanted to help, and yet I needed to conserve energy. A quandary I didn't want or need.

Mayes stopped and pointed to a shrub. A broken branch dangled by the path, about thigh high. Even I could see the whiteness of newly splintered wood. Only, if not for Mayes, I wouldn't have seen it at all.

"Touch it," he said.

Another dreamwalk? I shoved my hands in my pockets. Fingered the crystals there. "I shouldn't. The others . . . I need everything I've got for later today."

"I need you right now. Help me catch White Feather's killer, and every member of my tribe will donate energy to the cause this evening."

The idea horrified me. "I'm no psychic vampire. I don't steal energy from others."

"Don't be hardheaded. Energy is energy, and I'll make sure you have enough. One of my deputies is trapped, as well as your friend and a prominent state official. If you hold back, we all lose." He glared at me. "Do your job."

My *job.* I gritted my teeth. I didn't like him calling what I did a *job.* Dreamwalking was something I did on my terms, and even though a simple touch-read like this branch wouldn't drain much energy, I disliked being ordered about.

Biting back resentment, I grabbed the branch. Immediately, I jolted into the head of the person who broke the branch. He was breathing hard, but the strange thrill coursing through his veins was unlike anything I'd experienced. The path we'd traversed came into view, then the lake. He moved White Feather from his shoulder and gently laid her down at water's edge. The sun's first rays bathed the sky in brilliant glory.

Her eyelids slowly raised to reveal dull brown eyes. The spark of life was faint, but Jonas' face reflected in her dilated pupils. She managed a strangled whisper. It sounded like "Please."

"Patience," Jonas said. Then he walked around her body, sprinkling powder from his pocket along his path. A circle. He made a circle.

He knelt over her, straddling her belly. Tenderly, he interlaced his fingers through hers.

The tepid warmth of her flesh jolted me. I struggled not to interrupt the vision because I knew there was nothing I could do for White Feather. This scene I was viewing had already happened. It was history. I bit my lip and watched as it played out.

Jonas bent forward until his lips hovered

over hers. He applied firm pressure to her hands until her eyes fluttered again. "It's time."

His hands buzzed. That was the only word I could think of to describe the sensation. He gazed into her eyes and watched the light go out. Even then, he didn't release her hands. After a few moments, he kissed her lightly on the lips. "For your gift," he said.

He closed her eyelids and posed her arms in a tee shape. Then he took a branch and brushed the ground to erase his tracks all the way back to the path. Energy writhed like a pulsing serpent within him, White Feather's energy. Jonas exulted in the feeling, jumping for joy as he headed up the path . . . toward someone.

A woman waited for him in a car.

The vision faded.

"Tell me," Mayes said. "What did you see?"

Chapter Thirty-One

"You could've experienced the vision with me," I said, relieved to feel only my thoughts rattling inside my head. The downside of visions is that the vision stays vivid in my consciousness temporarily, as if it were a memory.

Mayes glanced around the wooded path. "Someone had to keep guard. You saw something. I watched your face change. That sick bastard loves doing this, doesn't he?"

I filled him in, then I added my observations. "Jonas killed her in a ritual. He watched her die as he siphoned every drop of her energy into himself. Other than that, he did not harm her. He seemed reverent to some extent, taking care to reassure her."

"This guy is a stone-cold killer."

Something twisted in my gut. "I'm not so sure. White Feather didn't protest. She wanted the transfer to happen."

"I don't believe you."

I cleared my throat gently. "From what you told me, she was a bit of a lost soul. Could her death actually be a suicide? Can a person forfeit their entire life energy?"

"I've never heard of such a thing."

"But is it possible?"

"I don't think so. There are too many safeguards in place in the body, too many systems that go on automatic pilot even during a severe illness."

"What if the person was near death? Jonas' other victims were in comas. Only one survived. The rest were too far gone by the time they reached the hospital."

"A weakened person is close to the veil of life. During illnesses, many of my tribe have reported seeing loved ones and more before they returned to the living."

"Hmm." An idea bubbled into my head, so outrageous I dismissed it immediately.

"What?" Mayes asked.

"Is there anything you don't see?" I jammed my hands back into my pockets, allowed the smooth gemstones to roll across my fingertips. "I had an idea, that's all. It has no basis in fact, no reason to be *The Answer.*"

"From what you said, Jonas Canyon was racing to meet another woman. She could be his next victim. I want to hear your idea."

"What if Jonas offers his services as a pain-free way to kill yourself? What if all those people in his house wanted to die? What if it was a living energy bank?"

"No way."

"How many suicide calls does your emergency services field each month?"

"More than I'd like to admit, but the callers never go through with it. Their attempts are cries for help, cries for attention from the world and loved ones."

"You're right. It does sound preposterous. But if I'm right, we could find out where Jonas meets these prospects and corner him there." I shot Mayes an innocent look. "If only we had a victim to interview."

Mayes snapped his fingers. "The woman from the hospital, Lizella Tice. She was moved over to rehab yesterday."

"Didn't someone already interview her?"

"Duncan and Reyes. They spoke with her. She doesn't remember anything except awakening in the hospital. Jonas originally claimed she was his mom, but she looks much older than that. He must have lied about her identity to confuse us."

"Maybe her memories have returned," I suggested. The more I thought about it, the more likely it was that this woman could aid our investigation. "We need to talk to her. She may know more about what happened in that house than she realizes."

"We'll head there next. Retracing our steps is a valid investigation strategy."

He fell silent, and the woods did too. It felt as if a heavy weight were bearing down on me. I gazed to the western sky and saw a bank of dark clouds approaching. A storm. *Perfect.* We'd get drenched at dusk when we rescued Charlotte and the others.

Strange emotions rolled off Mayes. How did he manage to integrate his various roles? He'd risen through the ranks of the police to become the chief deputy, and from all indications he held a position of respect and leadership among the Cherokee.

Any way I looked at it, he was a force to be reckoned with. And he'd made sure to keep me close. Was that for my benefit or his?

"About White Feather . . ." he began.

I backed away from him, palms raised defensively. "I can't do a dreamwalk in front of all those people."

"Say what you mean. You can, but you won't."

Heat rose from my shirt collar. "You're right. I won't. I have this thing about being seen as a one-trick pony. What I do is private and the fewer living people who know about it, the better."

"Will you ride to the morgue with her?"

"No. Get her to the morgue, and I'll try it there. From past experience, I know it's too soon to get much from her. The newly dead need time to adjust to their changed status. Once she figures out where she is, she will either be happy about it and move on, or she'll stew in anger until someone like me hears her case."

He pinned me with a look. "Are there others like you?"

His intensity made me uneasy, so I glanced away on the pretense of studying the changing sky. In the distance, a woodpecker tapped out a fast beat. The forest must be returning to normal now that the disturbing element had moved on.

I was stalling. I knew it, and Mayes knew it. Dreamwalking was more than a hobby or a vocation: it was everything. Ever since my father passed the reins to me and I'd become the Dreamwalker, I felt whole in a way I never had before.

The clouds held no answers. I glanced at Mayes and shrugged. "What are the odds I'm unique? The title I inherited from my father is County Dreamwalker, only I've never met another full-fledged Dreamwalker. Some of my father's friends can cross the veil, but they are limited in their abilities."

His eyes gleamed. "I would like to meet your father's friends."

"Come to the coast for that. It is a rarity for any of us to leave home like this."

"I accept your invitation." He glanced at the sun before he gave me his full regard. "Your star shines bright among your people and among women, Baxley Powell."

I was nearly blinded by his praise. His face seemed to shed years, and his eyes glowed with approval. The heat that followed surprised me even more. Masculine appreciation. Aye-yi-yi. I wasn't ready to deal with a suitor. Although I was officially a widow, my husband wasn't among the dead. I'd searched for him repeatedly and come up with nothing. Which meant I wasn't really a widow.

Not a subject I wanted to get into with a man I barely knew.

"Uh, shouldn't we get back?" I asked.

He gestured with a hand. "After you."

Chapter Thirty-Two

The low-slung rehab center looked as if it had been built to withstand the mother of all hurricanes. The stucco exterior was the reddish-yellow tint of Georgia clay. With rounded evergreens flanking the bland architecture, the building should have seemed pleasant. Instead, it pulsed with something not quite right.

The harried woman behind the thick glass window told us the center was closed to visitors due to a flu outbreak. Deputy Mayes flashed his badge. "Official police business," he said. "We're here to see Ms. Lizella Tice."

"Let me check my list." We waited while she perused a paper list. "You're in luck. As of this morning, Ms. Tice is in the healthy cohort. She's in Wing B, Room Twelve." The woman handed us hospital masks through the security slot and made us sanitize our hands. "I hope you've both had flu shots. Staff and residents are coming down with flu symptoms in droves."

"How long has this been going on?" I tucked my clean hands in my pockets. Touching a door or anything solid wasn't part of my visitation plan. My extra senses were shielded, but a casual touch of an inanimate object could still jar me, if the person who'd touched it previously had been in the grip of a strong emotion. No telling what emotions were layered on these doorknobs and furnishings. Best to avoid them altogether.

"A few days. Normally we wouldn't miss an aide or two out sick, but a third of our staff are feeling ill effects. The rest are working double shifts to get us through the crisis. Watch out for the box of fire extinguishers in the hall. Our safety officer was supposed to exchange these expired canisters for new ones, but he called in sick today."

The door buzzed open, and the first thing I noticed inside the facility was that the shiny corridors were deserted. This place resembled a ghost town. A box of fire extinguishers sat just inside the doorway. I had no trouble avoiding them, but the sadness in this place had me missing a step.

I shuddered, picturing living out my final days so removed from my normal routine. Institutions were great stopgaps, but I hoped my future didn't require one. People with paranormal sensitivities needed natural and holistic environments.

"You okay?" Mayes asked as we branched off into the B Wing, passing a deserted nurses' station.

"I'm not a medical center kind of gal. They give me the willies."

"We worked hard to get a place like this here." His voice rang with pride. "The next nearest rehab facility is an hour away."

"Nothing against this place in particular. I prefer to be outdoors." I shot him a curious look. "Do you have hypersensitivity to pain meds?"

"Never had any."

My feet quit moving. "Never?"

He stopped a few paces away. "I've always had a healthy constitution."

I pondered that for a moment. "I guess tribal confidence would wane if the medicine man was sick."

"Ah, you're mistaken. I'm no medicine man. He is a healer."

"So, you're a shaman?"

He shook his head. "Shamans are from other cultures. In some Native American tribes, the medicine man and the holy man are the same person. Outsiders called them shamans, a mystic tradition that hails from

Siberia, but we never call our spiritual leaders by that name." He took a long breath. "I'm not a holy man either. Merely a tribal member."

"Who can do amazing things like facilitate the sheriff's energy transfer."

He put a cautionary finger to his mask. "My extra abilities are known only to a select few."

"Why?"

He chose not to answer.

"Are you ashamed?" I asked.

"Never." His eyes glittered with emotion. "It's better this way. You, on the other hand, are too reckless for your own good. You nearly sent us all adrift yesterday."

A deft change of subject, and it hit the bull's-eye of my guilt button. "I'm sorry. I already apologized to my parents, and I meant to say something to you earlier. That was my first time as a donor in the circle."

"It showed."

His censure rattled me. "It won't happen again. I learned my lesson."

"Good. No harm was done. The outcome could have been tragically different."

My turn to go mute. We'd dodged a bullet, thanks to his skill, experience, and patience. "You don't know my history, but I'm also new to dreamwalking and police consulting. I'm a quick study though, and I don't make the same mistake twice."

"We have to stay focused here. Let's talk to Ms. Tice and get out of this place. I can't chance you coming down with the flu."

A masked healthcare worker came out of a room near us and staggered into the wall. Her face glowed with perspiration, and her aura seemed off. Thinner, less visible. I backed away. Every instinct told me to run, not walk, out of this building.

Mayes stepped between me and the young woman in lavender scrubs. "She's ill. Keep your distance." He hustled me into Room Twelve across the hall.

The curtain was drawn, but a low-wattage fluorescent fixture above the bed provided illumination. The humidity seemed higher, making it harder to breathe through the mask I wore.

The brunette on the bed looked less emaciated than the last time I'd seen her, but her features remained drawn, her face skeletally thin. Her wan skin had the sickly sheen of a fever sweat. Even with the naked eye, her energy levels appeared to be fluctuating.

"We shouldn't be in here," I said, latching onto Mayes' arm. "She's sick."

The woman stirred. Her brown eyes

flashed open, a wild look in them. "Help me. I need help."

Mayes stepped forward, but I grabbed him. "We'll call a nurse," I said, pulling him out of the room. To his credit, he left without protest.

The infected nurse lay slumped against the wall. I wanted to help her, but I had no medical training. "Hurry," I urged Mayes, keeping hold of his arm.

He seemed to be receiving an inaudible message. "We should help them," he said. "We should stay here and contain the situation."

"Fresh air. That's what we need." I stopped before the door. "Open it."

He did, and we sailed outside into the weak sunlight. I kept us moving until we made it through the parking lot to the street. With each step, I felt stronger and more clear-headed.

I ripped the mask from my face. Mayes did the same. "What happened?" he said.

"I'll tell you what happened. Once we started down that last wing, I knew something was off, and I'm not talking about illness or contagion. The vibe felt like Jonas Canyon's house on Bear Claw Lane. I had the sense of bodies in cold storage, slowly ebbing away."

Drawing back, Mayes studied the leaden clouds in the pewter sky. "You think Jonas was in there?"

"Don't know of anyone else who can suck the life out of people, but definitely an energy vampire has been in there. May be there still."

Mayes reached for his phone. "We should see about moving our survivor. It wouldn't do for her to fall under Jonas' spell twice. I should have my deputies search the place for Jonas."

That went so well last time. To my credit, I didn't voice that negative thought. "What was it about you and the survivor woman? You wanted to touch her, even after we saw she was sick."

"I wanted to help her." His radio squelched, the sudden noise startling and attention-getting. Mayes tapped the button. "Mayes. What you got?"

"Deputy Pruitt, sir. Hall County came through with their cadaver dog. We searched the grounds of that house on Bear Claw Lane. Got nothing. Then we came out to the old tree in the backside of Meese Park and hit the mother lode. You won't believe this."

I perked up at the sound of a female voice on the radio. Other than Twilla Sue, all the other deputies I'd met to date had been male. Nice to know she'd hired a woman.

"Try me."

"The dog indicated a body. We dug and found human remains. Then the dog lit up again. And again. So far it looks like at least four bodies here, maybe more."

"I'll be right there."

"Copy that. And . . . Mayes?"

"Yeah?"

"We can't reach the state archaeologist lady, Dr. Bergeron. You know anything about her whereabouts?"

Mayes' eyes met mine. "She got called out of town. An urgent matter. She'll return this evening."

I nodded my approval of his truthful answer. It didn't ring false, even to my truth-sensitive ears. *Well done, Mayes.*

"What do we do?" Pruitt asked. "Protocol is to have the coroner pronounce victims dead before we move them. With our coroner out of town, we used the coroner from the next county over for the body earlier today when we couldn't locate Dr. B. The borrowed coroner's tied up in autopsy. We don't want Grayley Beckett, and Foster Winkle from Rabun County is still on his honeymoon. What should we do? Call in the staties?"

I elbowed Mayes. “I know a coroner . . . my dad.”

Chapter Thirty-Three

"Maybe he can fill in temporarily until relief arrives." Mayes turned to me in the parking lot after he relayed the information to Deputy Pruitt. "One thing's for certain. We were stretched to capacity with two murders. Dealing with a mass grave site will exhaust our resources, even if the same guy is responsible. I'll have to call in the GBI."

I didn't want additional exposure of my abilities, especially to the Georgia Bureau of Investigation, but even I could do the math. A small police force was no match for the horror happening here. We'd had Jonas in custody, and yet he'd put the sheriff out of commission and escaped.

"Do what you have to," I conceded. "Just don't let the big guns keep us from our appointment with the Little People at dusk or let the GBI sink their teeth into me. We have to get our people back."

"Trust me, I want them back as much as

you do. Call your father while I begin notifying the outside authorities. Tell your dad we'll meet him at the site. I'll text him the GPS coordinates of Meese Park."

"Uh, my dad's not that high tech. He'll need the roads-and-turns kind of directions."

Mayes looked up from his phone. "What? Oh. Okay. Give me a sec."

While he was busy on his calls, I contacted my father and brought him up to speed. He agreed to drive back early from Luanne's farm. Even better, Luanne knew where Meese Park was.

"Lacey and Larissa will drop me off at the site," Dad said. "If I can catch a ride home with you and Mayes, that'd be great."

"Sure." Too late I remembered about the dusk meeting with the Little People. Oh well, we'd cross that bridge when we came to it.

"Any word on Charlotte and her hot date?" my father asked.

"Charlotte? Yes, Charlotte." I grimaced. "Haven't heard a peep out of her. She's probably having the time of her life."

I squeezed my eyes shut at the realization I'd skirted the truth with my dad. It felt wrong for him to be left out of the knowledge loop. But I couldn't burden him with this, not when he had a mass gravesite in his immediate future. "How's Larissa doing?"

"Happy as a June bug. She did a bit of everything at the farm today, even drove the tractor."

"I feel bad that I didn't get to take her paddleboarding yet."

"Don't fret. We still have time to do that, and she hasn't mentioned it again."

I nodded, then realized he couldn't see me. "Thanks for that, Dad. See you soon."

Talking with my father helped ease the chill in my bones. This day kept going downhill. So many things had happened that it was hard to take it all in.

How could Jonas be stopped? How many would die or be sidelined because of him? How many lives had he already taken? The vision I'd had from the broken branch on the trail replayed in my head. Jonas believed he was helping these people, that they wanted him to take their energy. A "gift," he'd called it when he'd taken life from White Feather.

My head ached when I tried to understand how that could be. Life was sacred. Throwing it away was wrong. Dead wrong. Appalled at my brain's poor choice of words, I choked back a laugh.

"You all right?" Mayes said, opening his car door.

Like a trained seal, I trotted around to the passenger side and got in. "No. I'm not all right. Everywhere we go, people are dying and being drained of their energy. I'm worried sick about Charlotte, and my thoughts are crashing into each other."

He cranked the car and eased away from the rehab center. "Normally, I'd offer an overwhelmed colleague a visit to my sweat lodge to restore clarity, but we don't have time to recharge naturally. I'll make a quick stop on the way to Meese Park. The dead can wait ten more minutes."

It felt good to leave that place behind, though I worried about the welfare of the people trapped inside. "Where are we going?"

"Convenience store."

"Oh?"

"This is the Sam Mayes' official cure for surviving a terrible day."

"What is it? Some kind of Cherokee herbal infusion?"

"Nope. Supersized candy bar and an energy drink. Works every time."

CHAPTER THIRTY-FOUR

As promised, the combination of sugar and caffeine recharged my body in a hurry. Though the jolt would probably be short-lived, it should hold me for another few hours. That was all I needed, and once we had Charlotte back, I planned to conk out.

A glance at the clock on the dash showed me it was nearly four o'clock. This time of year, dusk arrived about seven to eight, depending on the cloud cover. With today's low, thick clouds, dusk would arrive early. I hoped Mayes planned accordingly. The Little People meet-up was one appointment I couldn't afford to miss.

We turned into a wooded area, passing under the carved sign bearing the park's name. The road looped around Meese Park, and at each bend was a nice waterfall or creek-side vista. Finally, the strange tree of my earlier vision came into view. Beneath its barren, spreading arms, cop cars galore hunkered down with their lights awhirl. Two ambulances from fire companies were parked nearby.

Deputies had cordoned off the scene, and only a dog and its handler walked beyond the tape. I saw the woman reach down and plant another marker after the dog circled and lay down on the ground. Another body. How many did that make — five, six? The potential graves seemed to march in a linear progression along the side of the mountain.

Whatever this was, someone had conducted the burials in an orderly fashion. Too many people around for me to do a full-press dreamwalk, but my tattoos tingled. Though I was supposed to focus on the graves, my gaze kept returning to that odd tree. The need to touch it arose in my blood the same way I occasionally craved chocolate. Somehow, someway, I would dip under the crime scene tape and learn what the tree needed to tell me.

The shrouded mountains in the distance gave no hint of what lay ahead. Instead, I had the strong sense of the fleetingness of life. The mountains endured, though they were aging as well. Weren't we all?

"Sitrep, Loggins," Mayes said to the approaching African-American deputy.

Deputy Loggins vibrated with puppy-fresh

excitement. "This could be huge. The body count is up to five at this point, but the cadaver dog is still working the area."

"What can you tell me about the bodies?" Mayes said. "Any way to identify them?"

"None of the bodies we've found appear to be fresh. So far, all we've found are skeletal remains."

"My buddy at GBI is bringing in a forensic team. We'll work the DNA and dental X-ray evidence as well as run the basics of each individual through the NCIC Missing Persons database."

"Dr. Bergeron will be upset she missed this," Loggins pointed out.

I'd been following the ping-pong exchange of conversation, but from the lull in the timing, I could tell Mayes was thinking about his response. Loggins was right though. A few months back, Gail Bergeron delighted in the early settlers I'd accidentally exhumed on a tree installation. This cache of unidentified remains would make her year.

"She'll return this evening," Mayes added, with a quick glance to the sky and the shadows stretching across the parking lot. "This site will take a while to process."

Loggins nodded at me. "What about her? You going to deploy Twilla Sue's secret weapon on the remains?"

"Tomorrow. I don't want to get in the way of the recovery team."

Loggins scratched his head and surveyed the area. "Never thought I'd be saying this, but I'm glad you called in extra help. Once people hear about this, they'll be up here gawking."

"Any artifacts found with the remains?"

"Not yet, but if the graves date back into history, this could be anything. Conquistadores. Your people. Gold rush dreamers. White settlers. Even black folk."

Mayes eyed the straight line of markers the dog and his handler were creating. "Contact the historical society and churches to see if there's any record of this area ever being used as a cemetery."

"Dang. You think that's what we have here?"

"We won't know unless we ask the right questions."

"Will do."

"Loggins, you've got point on this site. The perimeter is your responsibility, even after the GBI gets here. Pruitt is to log everything and make sure we follow procedure."

"Yes, sir."

A smile tugged at Mayes' lips as he noted the parting officer's courtesy, but he hung onto his stern visage and turned to me. "You got anything?"

I shrugged. "Can't dreamwalk so many victims right now, though I am mighty curious about that tree. I've been drawn to it ever since I dreamed of it at Jonas' house."

He nodded knowingly. "The Tree of Secrets. It bears a huge weight for mankind."

"How's that?" I understood his diction clearly enough, but I didn't get the meaning.

"Locals have been coming up here for years and telling their secrets to this tree. The Semage family couldn't keep people off their property. The tree became an attractive nuisance, so they donated the land to the county. Since it became a county park, we've had no complaints or trespassing calls out to this area. People come and go as they like."

Sounded like the tree served as a confessional. "You sure this isn't the Semages' private family graveyard? The interments seem rather orderly. Not like the work of a disturbed mind."

"That'd be a heck of a note, wouldn't it? But it isn't likely. They have several plots of relatives over in the Methodist cemetery."

I slanted him a sideways glance. An odd bit of trivia for Mayes to know, but this was a small town. Taking into consideration my own knowledge about my hometown and Sinclair County, I could put his remarks in perspective.

Mayes must have seen my unspoken question. "I went out with Sabine, the daughter of the family, long ago. Before I knew better."

My thoughts turned one-eighty. "You think the Semage family had something to do with these graves?"

"Anything is possible. We'll question them tomorrow."

I sighed. "Sounds like tomorrow will be busy too. I don't like to whine and complain, but I came up here to spend time with my daughter before school starts next week. We've got more dead people than we know what to do with, and our killer is practically uncatchable. Unless the GBI has a hotline to crime central, we're screwed."

"Priorities. We get our friends back from the Nunne'hi today. We find Jonas Canyon and contain him. We help White Feather and Haney in the afterlife. We work the back-burner case. Simple steps. That's how we navigate."

Even though he'd broken the investigation down into easy tasks, it still seemed overwhelming. I wanted justice for Haney and

White Feather, but at what cost to myself?

"School starts Monday. We're already on Thursday afternoon, and I have to leave time to drive home. You think we can wrap this up in two more days?"

"The timeline is a challenge, but we'll do what we must."

He could double-talk when he wanted. Gauging from the slant of the sun's rays, we'd be leaving this place soon. If that tree had a message for me, I needed to hear it now.

"Where are you going?" Mayes asked as I strode away.

I ignored him. I had a tree to talk to.

Chapter Thirty-Five

Behind me I heard a collective gasp. The local cops knew the tree's reputation. None of them had strayed under its branches. Now I stood beside the Tree of Secrets, marveling at its wide girth and stark, empty branches. I stroked my moldavite pendant. This simple gem had become a touchstone for me since Roland's disappearance, because it helped settle my thoughts and ease my mind.

Mayes hadn't followed me over, so he must not be too worried about the fullness of my dreamwalker tank. He was talking to another deputy. I tuned him out and dialed in to the faint whispers I heard.

I touched the tree, and conversations flowed around me. Of betrayals. Of trysts. Of unbearable sorrow. I sifted through it all, growing despondent. I'd been so sure the tree had something for me. Something about the case. I channeled the sound of

Haney's voice and kept drifting in the current of whispers until at last I caught the right eddy.

Suddenly, I flashed into a dream sequence with Jonas and Haney standing on this very spot.

"You will do as I say," Jonas said, his beady eyes boring into Haney's.

"Nuh-uh," Haney said, his gaze steady on the distant mountains. "You hurt people. I don't like that."

"Only the people who want to transition. I swear it on my mother's grave."

"Not me. I don't want to transition, Jonesy. I like it here. I've got a place and a job. I've got unfinished business."

"We shook hands on it. You said you'd be my helper if I showed you how to get your mother back. I held up my end of the deal, showed you the hidden doorway to walk her out."

Haney shook his head, stepped back from Jonas. "Before. That was before. You hurt me. I slept for three days after we shook hands and nearly lost my job. I don't want to do that no more. And my mom — she doesn't want to go anywhere."

"Even more reason for you to help me find the ones who need me. You'll have more time to convince her to come home. So that you can be together. I can help you with that. Besides, you have a real talent for finding people who need me."

Haney brightened, his features aglow with happiness. "I do?"

"Yeah. You're really good at it. You're my number one guy."

"I've never been anyone's number one guy."

"I rely on you. We're like family."

Haney sobered. "My mom taught me that family doesn't hurt each other."

"She's right." Jonas moved in front of Haney and placed his hand on his shoulder. "Family looks after family."

"I'll do it," Haney said, "for my family."

The vision faded as quickly as it began. I shoved my hand into the pocket of crystals, not out of need, but to protect myself from an incidental touch. The vignette with Jonas and Haney explained a lot. Jonas used Haney to find lost souls. Haney himself was lost, only he hadn't known it. I admired him for trying to help his mom, wherever she was.

From what I remembered, she'd disappeared when Haney was a child. Then he'd grown up alongside his dad, a shambling drunk who'd paid no attention to his boy. Seemed to me Haney had darn near raised himself.

But I understood that feeling of being odd man out in a society where it seemed everyone else was normal. Of wanting to fit in. Of wanting to be loved. Jonas had tapped into Haney's basic need, flattering him and promising him devotion Jonas had no intention of delivering.

He'd played on Haney's emotions and reeled him in like a trout on a line. Poor Haney. He'd lost his life and his chance to be with his mom.

I viewed the knot of police cars. Seemed like they'd doubled in quantity while I was reading the tree. Was the GBI already here?

Mayes was speaking to a group of law enforcement officers. The uniforms were different within the group, so neighboring counties must have loaned a couple of guys to the cause. Back home, my sheriff did the same from time to time.

The shadows were lengthening. I headed toward the group, ducking under the crime-scene tape and stopping at Mayes' vehicle. I felt a familiar tap on my shoulder. Whirling, I faced my father and hugged him. "Glad you're here," I said.

Dad sported white coveralls and booties, so he'd already dressed for his job as coroner. "Lacey dropped me off. Larissa insisted you needed Elvis, so I put him in Mayes' cruiser." He pointed to the ambulance crew and a hearse. "I've got a sweet set-up over there. Having all this gear at my fingertips will spoil me for cases back home."

"If you need supplies, tell Wayne. He'll make sure you get it at home."

"That he will."

"How is everyone? Should I call Larissa?" I asked.

"She's fine. She knew you were dream-walking when we arrived, and she said she was proud of you for helping others."

After the day I'd had, to hear such wisdom from a ten-year-old brought tears to my eyes. I blinked and sniffed to cover my emotional state. "That's good."

"How many are out there?" Dad asked.

"Five was the last count, I believe."

"This is something, all right. Such a pretty place, but terrible things must have happened here."

"I don't know what happened here, or if this is related to my other case. I don't have the full picture yet of my killer. The first victim and the second died suddenly and in a similar manner. There's an energy vampire involved. Those are the facts. These other elements — Twilla Sue refusing to wake up, the Little People's anger at a theft, the flu epidemic at the rehab center, and this mass grave — seem to be independent of the murders. And yet, I can't help thinking it's all related. It's maddening not to know the connections."

"You'll figure it out," my father said. "You always do."

"There's figuring, and there's proving it. That's why Wayne and I are a good team back home. I'm not as confident about this crew. Mayes is nice and friendly and a spirit-walker, but is he up to the task? I don't know."

"He has good energy," my father said, as if that explained everything.

A shadow crossed over us as Mayes approached. "I sense the same about you. Yours is a strong family."

The men studied each other. Finally my father nodded slightly. "Nesbitts don't shy away from our responsibilities, and Baxley, she's picking up where I left off."

Tick tock. Charlotte's life was on the line. "Dad, we've arranged for Deputy Pruitt to drive you to the campsite when you're done." I caught Mayes' gaze. "We need to hurry to make our next appointment."

"That we do."

"Worrying never solved any problems. Our next appointment will happen whether we fret over it or think about something else. I prefer the later strategy." He paused, then glanced over at me. "Tell me about the Tree of Secrets. You were over there for a while. Did you see something?"

Distraction sounded like a great idea. "Haney and Jonas stood under that tree for a talk. I saw the replay of it. Jonas had a hold over Haney. Something to do with springing Haney's mom. She's alive, Mayes, but wherever she is, she doesn't want to leave. Not even to be with her son. I just don't get that. Is there a mental institution or something similar around here?"

He made a dismissive gesture with his hand. "Nothing like that in our county."

"A prison?"

"We have the county jail, but that's it. If Haney's mom was in our system, I'd know about it."

"What's left? A cult? A gang? You got any of those?"

"If she's alive, we'll find her. If she's dead, you and I have a chance of finding her."

"Dead. Dear heaven. If we don't get this right, Charlotte might never again see the light of day. Her body and her soul will be trapped in the mountain or wherever the

Little People exist." I pressed a fist against my mouth to hold in a sob. Elvis whimpered in my arms.

"Breathe, Baxley," Mayes said in a soothing tone. "I don't plan on anyone dying on my watch. We'll get through this."

My skin felt all prickly and too tight. Not even Elvis' good vibes counteracted the ice in my bones. "I can't help it. Charlotte is my best friend. The thought of failing her terrifies me."

"We won't fail her."

His certainty floored me. "How can you be so sure?"

"My dreams."

"You dream of stuff that hasn't happened yet?" I studied his craggy profile. What were his secrets? It bothered me that I really wanted to know them. "How's that possible?"

He shrugged and shot me another unrepentant grin. "It just is."

I digested his words as we barreled down the lonely road. Everything seemed overgrown and neglected on this stretch. I hadn't seen a car since we turned this way. Narrow shadows of trees striped the road and strobed our vehicle.

"This may be just another case to you, but the result matters to me," I said as I stroked little Elvis. "I can't approach this dreamwalk with a 'business as usual' mindset because that isn't how I see it."

He slowed the car and glared at me over the top of his sunglasses. "I've got a stake in this too. Deputy Duncan and Dr. Gail Bergeron are valuable team members, and Dunc is a personal friend. But positive thinking is more than just a wish and a prayer. Positive thinking can change an outcome. We will have a positive outcome. Worry is negative and will burden you. We need to be strong."

"I'm trying."

He shook his head. "Try harder."

For some reason, his patronizing tone cracked me up. I laughed until I was spent.

"Better now?" he asked.

"Yes." I was better. This situation was beyond our control, but I'd do my part. I had dominion over my thoughts and actions.

With the daylight thinning, Mayes veered off the road onto the grassy shoulder and then we bounced along a narrow trail through the deep woods. Absently, I massaged the itchy rose tattoo on my hand. "How's this going to work? Will they find us?"

He snorted. "They will most definitely

find us. We have something they want badly."

"What's that?"

"You."

Chapter Thirty-Seven

"If they wanted me, why didn't they keep me and let the others go?" The vehicle's sides seemed to close in on me. I forced in a few deep breaths.

Mayes punched the accelerator on the straightaway. "They do things in their own time, in their own way."

I clutched the armrest after a jarring bump. "Have you visited them before?"

"Several times."

I noted a soft buzzing in my thoughts. "How odd."

He stopped the vehicle, turned it off, and studied me. "Not that odd. The Nunne'hi are part of my heritage as a Native American. Like you, I can move between worlds. I listened to the stories and sought the Little People out."

"Why?"

"Answers."

"To what?"

He sighed. "This is important?"

"Yes."

Mayes glanced away from me, cocking his head to catch the muted sounds beyond the car. "To why I was different. They walked between worlds. I walked between worlds."

"But they didn't have answers, did they?"

"No."

"Hmm."

"This makes sense to you?"

"For a man who can see some measure of the future, you can be blind at times."

He shook his head. "Not following you."

"Your exploration and soul-searching led us to this moment. The Little People know you. They allowed you in their world. You have insider information. It could come in handy during the negotiations."

He scrunched up his eyes. "Negotiations? I thought this was a straightforward swap."

My heart raced again at his penetrating scrutiny. *Straightforward* wasn't a word I'd use to describe Rose. "I have insider information as well. Nothing is ever easy with my contact."

"What's your plan?"

"The plan is to come out of this with our friends — alive. Beyond that I have no expectations."

"Aiming low." His mouth tugged down at

the corners. "I thought more of you."

"Just being realistic." I nodded outside. The humming noise in my head thrummed louder. Not quite melodic, but a summons nonetheless. "We should go."

He placed a hand on my arm. "One quick point. This place. The things you will see here. They are secret and must remain so."

His dark energy swirled around me, and I shoved it away with all my might. I glanced down at his hand and returned his stony, gunslinger stare. "Trust me. I don't go blabbing about my dreamwalks to anyone. I'd get locked up in the loony bin."

He went all quiet, and the silence in the car pinged in my ears like a hyperactive ticking clock. With each passing second, we were losing light. Urgency seized me. I pulled out of his grip, opened the door, and instructed Elvis to stay in the car.

Mayes followed, but he didn't show me the way. The only path I saw was the grassy lane ahead of us. Before I walked two steps, I pulled up short. Four young men dressed in buckskins, feathers, paint, and not much else joined us.

"Oh!" I pressed my hand against my chest. "Sorry for the yelp. You startled me."

Mayes spoke softly to the men in Cherokee and then turned to me. "We're ready."

My heels dug in, and I gestured to our audience. "Whoa. What's this?"

"These warriors are here to help."

I shook my head. The angry-bee sound in my ears intensified. "We can't risk losing anyone else. Have them wait here."

"These warriors are White Feather's friends. They understand the risk and the danger."

"So be it. After you."

His eyes narrowed. "You shall lead us."

"I've never been here before. I don't know the way."

Mayes said nothing. Worse, he gave no indication of which direction to take. This seemed to be a test. Well then, challenge accepted. In the dim light, I turned in a slow circle, searching for a trail to follow. As I did so, the bees in my head buzzed louder in one direction than another. That had to mean something, and since I had nothing else to go on, I headed in that direction, straight toward a tall oak.

Not hearing anyone behind me, I glanced over my shoulder and saw my posse following me. Reaching the tree, I skirted it and lost the signal. The noise seemed to emanate from the tree trunk. I found the side where the buzzing noise was the loudest and touched the trunk. The tree's center faded, revealing a passageway.

I retreated. "We're doing this on our side of the world. If we go this way, we'll be on their turf again."

Mayes waved me forward. "This is not the land of the Nunne'hi. It's neutral territory. A place where spirit worlds connect."

"A way station?"

"Do not delay," Mayes said. "The light wanes."

I forced a swallow past the lump in my throat. Charlotte. I would walk through a tree for Charlotte. "I'm going."

Chapter Thirty-Eight

Light faded with every step I took into the winding passage. I flicked on a flashlight. My brain tried to make sense of this reality, but it was pointless. Mayes would tell me not to worry. I couldn't force my taut nerves to relax entirely, but I wouldn't let them freeze me into inaction either. Charlotte would be leaving with me, and that was all there was to it.

The way ahead of us brightened. Soon, I stood in a cave-like den with a crackling fire pit in the center. It resembled the cavern from this morning, in Little People land. Panic hit me square between the eyes. Had Mayes tricked me? Dear God, there was no time to reboot and start over.

"Calm yourself." Mayes stopped beside me, the others ringed behind us.

"Easy for you to say. This is scary as all get out for me. You expect me to dreamwalk from a cavern inside a tree."

"You wish to change the appearance of the meeting location? All you have to do is think of a place, and it will appear. But doing so will burn energy. I selected this setting because we have both experienced it before."

I forced in a breath. Okay. He'd designed this space to feel familiar. Both to us and the Little People. It wasn't a trap. It was good strategy.

The rose tattoo on my hand itched like crazy, but thankfully, the buzzing sound had faded from my thoughts. "I'm okay with it. Surprises aren't my strength."

"You're doing well with the surprises of today, Dreamwalker." He lowered his already low voice and leaned close. "Any warrior would be honored to have you at his side."

"Married," I hissed.

He nodded and pulled back. "Good."

Another test. But it had worked. He'd deflected my anxiety. For better or for worse, I was ready to do this.

The wall on the opposite side of the cavern brightened. Three tall men stepped into the open area in full Native-American regalia. I recognized Trahearn, Meuric, and Arwel from this morning. Another half-dozen men crowded behind them. The entourage stopped on their side of the fire pit.

Trahearn nodded in greeting. "Begin."

No point in talking them out of the parlay. This was the only way to get Charlotte and the others back. "I will contact my guide."

I opened my senses to the room, feeling the swirl of Mayes' dark energy, pushing through it for Rose. But before I could transition to the Other Side, I felt the flutter of wings, smelled the acrid, sulfuric scent of brimstone. "No need to dreamwalk. She's on her way here."

A great wind filled the space, followed by flashes of lightning and peals of thunder. The earth shook, and I crouched to keep from falling. Mayes and his brethren did the same. When I glanced across the fire pit, the Nunne'hi lay prostrate on the ground.

With such theatrics, I was afraid to look at Rose full on. I'd seen her in many guises, from a tattooed woman, to a brimstone-scented demon, to her archangel-like wings, to her full-on scare-the-crap-out-of-you monster persona. I guessed she'd opt for super scary to make sure we knew who was in charge.

"Why have you summoned me?" Rose's voice roared lion-strong through the cavern.

I cringed, knowing she was pissed, knowing she was vindictive. I scrambled to my feet and found her standing beside me. Quickly, I backpedaled to stay behind her. I'd guessed correctly. Her three heads writhed with Medusa snakes. Her six eyes glowed demon red. Her burnished crimson body armor reminded me of the color of spilt blood. Her breastplate perfectly reflected the flickering flames of the fire. In one hand, Rose held a scythe with a wicked-looking curved blade, and on her feet she wore midnight-black boots, their outer edges laced with sharp spikes.

Her angel wings were nowhere to be seen. I gulped. With Rose, it was always a good news/bad news deal. However, I'd fulfilled my end of the bargain. Rose had come to the meeting.

One glance at her and any thinking being should know to hide and hope this fierce creature didn't fry them on the spot. I felt that way, even though I knew Rose was showing off. She wasn't all badass. She operated under a code, though I'd yet to figure out the nuances.

Mayes joined me, both of us standing slightly back and to the right of Rose. I felt the dismissive look Mayes gave me. His disdain hurt, but I couldn't undo my connection to Rose. My choices in the past affected my present and my future.

The Little People knelt in a knot on the far side of the cavern. Their image wavered and shrank. Only Trahearn rose to his feet and stood proud and tall. "Ancient One. Our people have a grievance. Something precious was stolen from us, and we demand its return. By the treaty of life, we beg your mercy and ask for swift justice."

Rose breathed fire, searing the hair on my arms. *Mercy.* Would I survive?

"The treaty specifies a blood price to be paid for my help," Rose said.

"We're prepared to pay the price."

Silence billowed in thick waves around us. Finally, Rose responded in an imperial tone. "Proceed."

As Trahearn recounted the tale of the theft, my tattoos heated, my entire birthday suit warmed unpleasantly, and my eyes watered so much from the sulfur stench I could barely see. I hoped that no matter what Rose decided, the Little People would release Charlotte, Gail, and the deputy.

"Bring the thief to me." The ground trembled when Rose spoke. I locked my knees to remain upright and watched to see if the walls would fall down and crush us. To my relief, the walls held.

"He is in the land of the living," Trahearn said. "Beyond our jurisdiction. The man beside the Dreamwalker is an officer of human law."

Rose slanted her fearsome gaze our way. "Explain."

"Jonas Canyon eluded capture," Mayes said from my side.

How could he speak so matter-of-factly? My legs barely held me, and I wanted to throw up.

"In addition to his energy-robbing ability and the stolen memory lock, he mesmerizes those in his presence and escapes," Mayes continued. "The Dreamwalker alone is immune to his wiles."

Rose cut her six demon-red eyes to me, and I quaked. Even knowing we were allies, I couldn't take the intense scrutiny. I scrunched my eyes and covered my head with my hands. I'd never been this terrified in all my life. *I want to wake up now. I want this to go away, like a bad dream in the dead of night. If I count to three, will I wake up in my bed back home?*

The world wobbled once more, and a powerful force lifted me into the air. I didn't like this. I didn't want to be here. Even so, I needed to see what would happen next. Rose's scythe pointed at me, and I found myself upright and poised over the fire. Through my sneakers, I felt the soles of my feet toasted past the point of discomfort. With effort, I curled my knees into my chest and held them there.

I was going to die. Right here. Right now.

Rose flicked her wrist, and I began to rotate like a chicken on a rotisserie spit. The lump in my throat gave way, but I was too scared to move a muscle. Fire crackled beneath me. Heat suffused my body.

"I am displeased with the lot of you," Rose stated, each angry word as toxic as caustic lye. Self-preservation had me ducking my head between my knees. Whatever Rose was about to do, I wanted no part of it. The thought of a blood price scared me to death. Would she outright kill someone in this room? Would it be me?

Was Rose really my ally?

Would she value the sanctity of my life?

As I swiveled, I peeked through slitted eyes. Everyone in the room prostrated themselves in Rose's presence. She now levitated beside the fire pit, her armor glowing so bright my eyes hurt to view it.

"Your actions bring undue attention to my apprentice." She pointed her scythe at the Little People. "You failed to keep your treasure safe." She leveled it at Mayes. "You are helpless in the face of evil. Woe, woe, woe be unto you, human and fae alike."

Despite being scared out of my gourd, I was struck by the humor in Rose's word choice. Who needed three times the woe? Woe was woe. It sucked, big time. I felt pretty woeful myself.

"We throw ourselves on your mercy," Trahearn begged. "Right this wrong."

"Arise," Rose said. "I have a judgment."

In that moment, I found myself standing at her side again, in between the two camps of people, the Native Americans on my right, the Little People on the left. Power swirled around us, lifting my hair and blowing it every which way. I hoped to high heaven I wouldn't be sporting a Medusa-like snake hairdo from now on. Living with a thick white forelock in an otherwise dark head of hair was enough of a fashion no-no.

Rose leveled the scythe at the Little People. "You will release the hostages."

I liked that proclamation.

She directed her stick at Mayes. "You will find the thief with the help of my apprentice. She will bring him to me, and he will be cast into the pit."

Before I could protest, the ground shook and the cavern filled with dense vapor. I fell to my knees, coughing. When the air cleared, Rose was gone.

Chapter Thirty-Nine

In the orangey glow of spent firelight, a strong hand appeared in front of my face. "If she's your friend, I'd hate to see your enemies."

Grabbing Mayes' lifeline, I arose. I patted myself to make sure I still had all my arms and legs. Scorch marks flared up my jeans. Truthfully, I was afraid to wiggle my toes, lest they'd been damaged. I wiggled them anyway and nearly passed out with relief when they worked.

So far, so good. But from the coldness in Mayes' eyes, I knew something else must be different. "My hair. Is it . . . normal?"

"You're concerned about your hair?"

"I'm scared to touch it." I shuddered. "But I have to know. Do I have snakes for hair now?"

His fingers caressed the side of my head. "No snakes, though the ends are singed."

I couldn't suppress a shiver. Human touch

felt wonderful. What I wouldn't give for a hug right now. . . . But this was the wrong place, the wrong man. "Thank God."

"God had nothing to do with any of this. We need to have a serious talk about the friends you keep."

"Who said Rose was my friend?"

"Pardon me. Your master."

"She's my *associate.* We've partnered together for various cases."

He gestured emphatically with his hands. "Face facts. You've sold your soul to the devil."

His anger upset me. "I have not. You have no right to judge me, or Rose for that matter."

"That creature was no 'Rose.' More like the archangel of death."

He was closer to the truth than he knew, but I couldn't talk about Rose's undercover assignment. All I had was bluster. "Shows what you know."

Mayes looked ready to argue until sunrise, but a commotion across the cavern caught our attention. Gail, Charlotte, and Deputy Duncan stumbled into the area, escorted by a group of females.

"What is this place?" Gail asked. "Why is it so dark in here? The air is foul. We shouldn't be here. I demand to know what's going on."

Charlotte and her cop walked toward us with joined fingers. My heart brimmed with relief. She was all right. I ran and hugged her. "Charlotte!"

"There you are," my best friend in the whole world said, her freckled face glowing with happiness. She wrapped her free arm around me and drew me close. "You smell like smoke, and something's different about your hair. Anyway, we've had the most amazing time exploring the park."

Duncan and Mayes exchanged nods in the minimalist way men greeted each other. "Everything all right?" Mayes asked.

"We're fine," Duncan said.

"Are you okay?" I asked Charlotte, stepping away from Mayes and taking in her every feature. Not a mark on her, and she seemed like the best friend I knew and loved. I was declaring victory.

On the opposite side of the cavern, the Little People scurried away, and the wall sealed behind them.

"We're fine," Charlotte said. "We went for a walk in that beautiful park. Then those friendly women asked us to follow them. . . . Where'd they go?" She craned her neck to look around the cavern in the waning firelight. "Anyway, they directed us here.

What a bizarre place this is."

"Let's get out of here," I said. "The light is fading. That's never a good sign."

"Where are we?" Charlotte asked. "I feel lightheaded."

Now that she mentioned it, I felt lightheaded too. And a little nauseous. Not unexpected, after being spun in tight circles. Good thing I hadn't eaten much today.

Our gambit had worked. We had our people back. Charlotte was alive. I'd do it again to save her. I tried to draw a full breath, but the effort exhausted me.

"You'll be fine. The effect will pass soon," Mayes said. "Duncan, take the women out that door. I'll bring up the rear."

"I demand answers." Gail planted her feet, her blue eyes blazing with indignation. "Where were you people? I've been searching for you for most of the past hour."

"I have the answers you seek, but time is of the essence. We must leave this place," Mayes said. "Please follow Deputy Duncan."

We hurried down the flashlight-illuminated passageway, and with each step my limbs felt heavier, as if gravity were reasserting itself. I hadn't felt weightless before, but now I could barely lift my tired feet. My head bobbled as the weight of it became more than I could manage. Mayes noticed my difficulty and waved one of his warriors forward to help support me.

"Sorry," I managed. "I've got nothing left."

I plunged into a dark oblivion of dreams, alternately floating and falling and too tired to do anything about it. In the distance, a light appeared. "Mom, is that you?"

When my mother had pulled me back from the brink before, she'd called my name. I heard no sound, no voices at all in the void. I felt no urge to go toward the light, so I drifted. My body chilled, and the cold felt wonderful after the scorching heat of the fire.

Past visions floated through my consciousness, each more terrible than the last, until I viewed the cavern scene from outside my body. How had I survived the heat of that fire without my blood boiling? That experience had been real. The heat had been real.

I must have died. Nothing else made any sense. I'd passed away, and it was my turn in limbo. *Larissa!* I couldn't die. I had a daughter to raise. But I couldn't get back to her. All I could do was drift. Alone.

Wait. I didn't have to be alone. I knew a ghost dog. I called his name. And kept calling it. When the jet-black Great Dane appeared, I was so relieved, I threw my arms around his body. Oliver licked my face and hands.

Haney and White Feather appeared, their fingers joined as Charlotte and Duncan's had been. They approached as if they saw me, then stopped to kiss each other. I held onto Oliver for dear life.

"Hello? I'm here," I said. They didn't notice me. My thoughts whirled at the implication. Somehow, this was a dreamwalk, and this vision was a prerecorded memory. A dreamwalk. Maybe I wasn't dead after all. I listened.

"I'm sorry," Haney said when they came up for air. "I didn't mean to drag you into my problems."

"You didn't. I'd do anything for you," White Feather said, caressing his face.

"Jonesy, he's a bad man. I thought he would help me, but each time we met, he hurt me. Now, your Nunne'hi are mad at me, I still don't have my mom, and I'm certain Jonesy plans to kill me."

"I'll go to him," White Feather said. "I'll make him see reason."

"No. Stay away from him. Far away. I want you to be safe. Promise me you won't go to the house on Bear Claw Lane."

"You are my heart, my life. You understand me."

"We met for all the wrong reasons. He expects me to bring you to him, but I can't. The only way I can save you is to never see you again."

"I'll find a way to save your mom. All you have to do is show me the passage."

"You're the best thing that's ever happened to me," Haney said. "Never doubt that. I can't show you the way. I'd rather die than have you enslaved by Jonesy or enamored by the Nunne'hi."

He looked to the horizon, his voice roughening. "Now that I've done dirty work for Jonesy and for the Nunne'hi, I'm beginning to believe Mom can't leave their land. Being there changes a person. Each time I come back, my breathing is all messed up."

"I've seen where the warriors go for purification. I could find the place."

"Don't. Please. Let there be one good thing I've done in this life, and that's to save you."

The vision flickered like a power outage. It returned, grainy and transparent, flickered again. I could see them talking, but I could no longer hear them. Oliver nudged me to my feet. I didn't want to stand, didn't want to go anywhere. I liked it right here.

Light flashed, blinding me. I blinked and covered my eyes. Oliver barked, nosing me from behind. The sensation pained me. Sensation. I was feeling something. I was indeed alive. The light appeared again. This time I reached for it with both hands.

Chapter Forty

Voices murmured. Familiar voices. My mom and dad. A deeper voice. Mayes. Pinpoints of light coalesced overhead. Stars. Water lapped against the shore nearby. I smelled the faint thread of campfire. The steady pressure on my palms and soles of my feet. Determined hands caressed my head. For a long moment, I savored the gentle touches. I stretched and hummed like a contented cat.

Longing thrummed through my blood in a way I'd become unfamiliar with. Need feathered throughout my body, whispering of sultry passion. Yes, I was most definitely alive.

"I'm here," I said.

The pressure on my hands tightened and eased. "Yes, you are."

In the faint light, I turned to see my fingers intertwined with a man's. Mayes. He sat astride me, in the same way I'd dreamwalked Jonas taking White Feather's last breath. It seemed to me we were united in thought, mind, and deed.

Then reality hit me in the face like a bucket of ice water. I'd been out cold. Mayes was on top of me, and I was getting intimate messages from every place we intersected. My longing and his longing were tangled up in a Gordian knot. Worse, as I became more aware of the sensual effect, I sensed he was doing this to me.

I bucked. "Get off me."

"Easy, Dreamwalker, or you'll undo all the good we just did," Mayes said, disentangling himself and moving to my side. The others who were at my feet and head also withdrew. Below me a tarp rustled. I was on the ground. In the woods. Starlight filled the night sky. A fire crackled nearby.

Best of all, I was safe and alive.

I pushed up to a sit, amazed at how quickly my head cleared. Doubly amazed by how peppy I felt. More amazed by how close I felt to Mayes, even though we were no longer touching. It was as if he were caressing my thoughts.

Was he in my head?

Outrage flared at the violation of my personal space. I quickly activated all my extrasensory shields as I crabbed away from him. "You were doing it to me. Like in my vision. Exactly as Jonas stole the energy from his marks."

He shot me a look of chagrin. "It's also how you give energy."

That thought clunked in my head and thudded to a clattering full stop. "Are you like him?"

Mayes bowed his head, as though he were ashamed of what he was. Then his energy blazed as bright as his dark eyes. "Everyone has this ability. It's innate in the human race. Those who walk between worlds are strong energy conduits. Because of our similarities, the channel between us is easy for me to access."

I rubbed my temples, appalled at the personal violation. Were my feelings my own? Were they his? Questions exploded in my head like popcorn in hot oil. Worse, my curiosity reared its ugly head. When the energy transfer went the other way, Jonas' victims suffered lasting harm. Some died.

To my eye, Mayes seemed hale and hearty. Sexy, even. "Are you . . . tired?"

His eyes sparkled as if they'd caught the intimate drift of my thoughts. Was he listening in my mind even now? Heat stole up my collar, steaming my neck and face. I felt a masculine nudge at the edge of my thoughts. Was it Mayes? I reinforced my virtual shielding. Enough was enough.

His hopeful expression faded. "Not as much as you might think, since four of my brothers also shared energy with you through me. Your *pal* used your own energy to suspend you over the fire. She drained you on purpose."

My temper spiked, and just as quickly I realized my anger toward him served no purpose. He'd helped me, at a significant cost to himself. I'd survived another encounter with Rose, and as far as I knew, she hadn't put her claws in me for another hour of my life.

Mayes was the good guy, though he clearly wanted to be *my* guy. I'd deal with that later, when we didn't have an audience.

I shrugged. "That's Rose. She exacts a price for each favor she gives."

"You were unconscious. She took you too far down."

The razor edge to his voice relayed his anger. Why wouldn't he let it go? "I'm sorry." Seemed like I'd just apologized to him for something else. "No, I'm not sorry. My friend was in trouble. I got her back."

"You got everyone back. You did good."

The masculine appreciation in his voice zapped my body in all the wrong places. I

Chapter Forty-One

"Tonight?" I asked, downing the rest of my broth.

"Tonight we compare notes," Mayes said. "I've got people working around the clock. Might as well point them at any fresh leads while we sleep."

"Uh, okay," I said softly. "I may have something."

Though his face was shadowed, his teeth flashed briefly in a smile. "Thought you might."

"I had a dreamwalk during my . . . outage. Haney and White Feather knew each other. They liked each other."

Mayes said nothing. I didn't know if that was a cop strategy or if I'd floored him. I hurried to fill the awkward silence. "Haney recruited White Feather for Jonas. From what he said, I gathered his job was to find lost souls for the psychic vampire. In return, Jonas was supposed to help Haney get his mom back from the Little People. Anyway, Haney told White Feather to stay away from Jonas. He tried to save her."

"Jonas got her anyway."

"Yeah, but I think she went to him after Haney died."

"After he was murdered," Mayes corrected.

I waved away his protest. "I know cops need evidence, so this is clearly speculation. I believe Haney became a liability when he refused Jonas. That's what got him killed."

"And White Feather?" His voice sounded brittle.

"She didn't want to live after Haney was gone. A clear case of Romeo and Juliet. She knew about the house on Bear Claw Lane. As troubling as it sounds — and I don't know this for certain — I believe she asked Jonas to take her life. So she could be with Haney again."

Mayes said nothing. His four warriors started keening in a low sound, a universal moan of pain that cut right through my heart. My parents came over and hugged me again, and I needed their support to stand. The grief at the lake blanketed me. It echoed in my veins like a living, melancholy thing.

I didn't understand why this was happening at first, and I fought the emotion. Then I realized that, due to the energy transfer, I was connected on a spiritual level with each of these braves. To honor their feelings, I mourned the loss of their tribeswoman. My vision blurred, and tears spilled down my cheeks. My father's arms tightened around me, and as I basked in the love of my family, I had an idea.

I fed a bit of that steadying, paternal love through the spiritual connection, softly, gently. Soon the sounds of mourning waned, and the lakeshore became tranquil again. Night animals made shuffling sounds in the nearby woods.

I gave my father a return hug and waved him toward the fire. "I'm better. Thanks, Dad. We have a little more police business to cover and then I can go home. If y'all want to head on back to the campers, I won't be long."

"We'll wait for you, Baxley," Dad said.

After Mayes and I had a semblance of privacy again, I resumed the conversation. "That's pretty much it from my dreamwalk. What have the police turned up?"

Mayes cleared his throat, tried to speak, but took another long moment first. "Five people were buried in the park. Adult, skeletonized remains. No soft tissue present. They've been dead awhile. Two were beneath heavy root cover. They could've been there a hundred years or more."

"Any chance of identifying them?"

"The GBI is taking the lead on that site, and Gail is on her way to join their effort. I've got point on the recent killings, though we are sharing information and coordinating efforts."

"We need to find Jonas before he hurts someone else. What about the rehab center?"

"Public health officials are on the scene. They are very interested in that epicenter of disease. There were no new cases as of nine p.m. It seems the *infection* has been contained."

"Because Jonas isn't there to drain anyone. But all those people at the center have limited or no mobility. They are easy prey to a predator like Jonas. Public health won't be able to stop Jonas either."

"You can stop him. I'm outraged that this predator set up shop in my town. He hurt my boss and killed my tribe mate. He's killed twice that we know of, more if we count the seven who died in the hospital after they'd been in his house of horrors."

Mayes' anger at Jonas colored the air. If I wanted to get through this debriefing quickly, I should change the subject. "Any word on Twilla Sue?"

"Stable but unresponsive."

"What about Lizella Tice from the nursing home? Did she survive the flu outbreak?"

"Last I heard, she was alive."

"I wonder why Jonas went there for her. He's capable of subduing a healthy individual and draining them dry. Why would he target a weakened person he'd already drained?"

"Hadn't thought of it that way. Could be personal. Could be she asked him to kill her and he's got some perverted code of honor. Could be he's a complete sociopath."

"We should talk to her again."

"We will. Tomorrow. Our dragnet caught Burl Sayer, the mountain man who brandished a firearm at your family. We'll talk with him first thing."

I remembered the mountain man, though our unpleasant encounter seemed like weeks ago. "A man like him won't do well in captivity."

"He should've thought about that before he went around breaking the law."

"Now that we know Jonas is the killer, why hold Sayer?"

"We want to question him on other matters."

"What other matters?"

"Police matters."

I recognized that curt tone of dismissal. "Have you got someone keeping watch over the sheriff?"

He nodded. "For all the good that will do. Jonas can blow right through anyone we put there. Except for you, and I need you for more than sitting guard. You and I will catch this killer tomorrow and put an end to this."

"Whatever you say."

"Our current thinking is that the recent killings and the mass grave site are unrelated. Our job is to catch Jonas Canyon. To see that he pays for his crimes."

A niggling doubt crept through me. Did he expect to incarcerate Jonas? "We agreed to deliver him to Rose. You won't be able to bring him to human justice."

His shadowed face remained inscrutable. I recognized another conversational dead end. All I could hope was that we agreed about honoring our pledge to Rose. I did not want her mad at me.

I sighed. "Last person on my list is your Deputy Duncan. Does he understand what happened to him?"

"Not exactly. But I offered him the option

to guard your campsite tonight, and he jumped at the chance."

"Charlotte is, well . . . she's Charlotte. I love her like a sister. For all her bluster, she's only dated a few men. I don't want to see her hurt. I'm worried she might be infatuated with your deputy."

"Dunc knows how to handle himself. I wouldn't have posted him in your camp if I thought he'd take advantage of the situation . . . or of your friend."

"Could they still be affected by their exposure to the Little People?"

"Absolutely."

"Is the attraction real?"

"Time will tell." He drew in a slow, weary breath, reached for my hand, and gave it a reassuring squeeze. "I wish Duncan had said no so that I would be there in your camp tonight, but this way I can go home and get some needed rest. We'll meet at daybreak tomorrow."

I groaned at the early hour. "I'm on vacation."

"So you keep saying."

Chapter Forty-Two

I awakened slowly, cocooned by three dogs, two cats, and my daughter. As my eyes adjusted to the faint light, I heard soft voices from the campfire outside. My parents? I hoped not — they really needed an uninterrupted night's sleep. Lifting my head, I noted Charlotte's empty bed at the other end of the camper. Then I heard her soft laughter outside.

Ah. Charlotte was enjoying the dawn hours with her deputy. As best I could tell from in here, they were sitting next to each other. *Good for you, Char. Go for it.*

Larissa edged closer. "I'm awake," she said.

My lungs filled with the sweet scent of youth and innocence as I returned her hug. "I'm sorry I've been so busy with the case. We came up here to spend time together, and I've been everywhere but here with you."

"We are together, and this is where we're supposed to be."

"Oh?"

"I had a feeling about coming here. And I was right. These people need your help."

A feeling? Was she developing precognitive skills like my mother? "Hmm."

"I'm proud of you, Mom."

Her admiration caught me by surprise. "Thank you, but no way am I mother of the year. I get so caught up in these cases, I barely know my name. I've wanted to go paddleboarding with you every day since we arrived."

"We'll get there. Listen to how happy Charlotte is."

More soft laughter wafted into our camper. "I hear them. She's having the time of her life." I gave Larissa another hug. "How'd I get so lucky to be your mom?"

"I don't think luck had anything to do with it."

Her serious tone startled me. "Oh?"

"I'm pretty certain I could only be your kid."

"And your father's kid."

"That, too."

"I miss him."

"I used to think we'd get him back. I hoped for the miracle of him walking in our front door."

Oh, dear. Larissa was ten. She'd already remarked that my best friend deserved a happy romance and declared herself to be content with my all-consuming work. Now she wanted to talk about death? Unease trickled through my veins. Had my dreamwalker vocation robbed her of a childhood?

"I hope I haven't transferred my expectations to you," I began slowly. "I would dearly love the three of us be a family again, but as time passes and we don't hear from your father in this land or the next, I am losing hope. The man I love and married, that man would move heaven and earth to return to us." I paused to get my emotions in check.

"If he's still alive," I went on, "and I say *if,* because the more dreamwalker experiences I have, the more I learn about things I never knew existed. Anyway, if he's alive and can't come home, there must be a reason. He might be trapped in some in-between place. That's where Charlotte and her deputy were yesterday, stuck in an in-between realm. Until that happened, I didn't know such places existed."

"But Charlotte came back from there okay, so Dad might be okay too?"

"It's possible. Anything's possible. I promise you this. I won't stop looking for him."

Larissa didn't say anything for a long moment. "What if someone else asked you out?"

"What? Who? Why would you even ask me that?"

"I notice things."

That was an understatement. My baby's abilities were beginning to make themselves known. Based on a vision she had earlier this summer, I'd assumed her talents would manifest as clairvoyance, but today she'd admitted to a flash of precognition. Multi-talents were rare. She would need all of us to help her understand and manage those extrasensory abilities.

I rubbed her back. "I'm not looking for a boyfriend. No need to worry about that."

She hugged me back. "Good. I want to keep you for myself."

Finally, she sounded like a ten-year-old. I tickled her, and she tickled me back. Gosh, it felt great to laugh. When we were tickled out, I rubbed my nose against hers. "I'm glad you had the idea to come to the mountains."

We lay there entwined, until Larissa levered herself up on an elbow. "I want to see the sunrise. At the lake."

I needed coffee, but this might be the only

private window of time with my daughter. "Sure. Let's get dressed. Maybe we can slip out without alerting the others."

But everyone else was already awake and outside, waiting for us. So much for alone time. After the chorus of good mornings, we padded down the trail to the lake. Using my extra senses, I checked to make sure our group was alone, and we were. No one was within miles of our location.

We hiked a little past the finger of water where I'd tried fishing the other day, stopping at a large rock that faced east. Larissa climbed the rock first, and I followed. Charlotte and Deputy Duncan stood at the rock's base, staring over the misty water. My parents scrambled up like billy goats.

"Careful," I said, knowing how easy it was to twist an ankle or fall.

"We've got this," my dad said, "though I appreciate your concern."

Larissa climbed in my lap to make room for them. My parents sat to my right, Dad with his arm around Mom. Charlotte and her friend wandered farther down the lakeshore to be alone. Hard to miss their joined hands.

I grinned. "This is cozy."

The vibe on the rock was great. I felt connected to the earth and to nature in a way

I'd been too busy to acknowledge recently. The mist on the water intensified, and I found my eyes drawn to it instead of the waking sky.

The rose tattoos on my hand and back flared, and I sucked in a quick breath. I glanced at my parents and my daughter, who seemed enthralled by the mist. What were they seeing? I switched to my extra senses and heard the faint drumming.

My blood iced.

The Little People.

Were they after my entire family?

What was going on?

Two faces appeared in the fog. I recognized them immediately. Haney and White Feather. They beckoned me to follow them onto the water. I shook my head.

Even as I did so, I was aware of my parents rising beside me on the rock. Larissa was squirming a bit in my lap. No way was I giving them up to the Little People. I extended an extrasensory bubble around the four of us. The sound of the drumming faded. My father blinked and sat back down.

Everyone followed my gaze to the water. Had they seen the vision too? I sent a telepathic message to Dad and Larissa. *The Little People are calling us. I blocked the signal temporarily. If you hear those soft drums again, and I'm not around, you must cover your ears.*

My father nodded. Larissa burrowed farther into my arms. I held her close and shot a private message to Dad. *Do you see anything in the mist?*

He shook his head.

My mom said in a monotone voice, "I've got to go."

Alarmed, I touched her arm. A pulse of energy shocked me. The flyaways that never quite stayed in Mom's braid lifted as if electrified.

To my horror, both my daughter and father repeated Mom's words, and they stood on the rock. I clambered after them, strengthening the protection bubble around us. Out on the water, Haney and White Feather were gesturing madly, but the mist was thinning.

Something was happening to us on this rock, but the spirit-infested mist over the water didn't inspire confidence. We weren't four feet above the water in front of us and the ground behind us. Better to jump on land where we could see our footing.

"Off the rock, now," I urged, pointing to the footholds we'd used to ascend.

They listened and slid down the back of the rock. "Group hug," I said, drawing my family into a tight clump. I clung tightly to the people I loved. The sun gleamed above the distant treetops. As the rays met the water, the mist disappeared.

My father laughed. "Good morning to you, dear daughter."

I released them and slowly lowered the bubble of energy around us. The drums were gone, and so were the faces in the mist. I craned my neck and spotted Charlotte and Duncan necking behind the big tree.

"We're safe," I said. "That's what's important."

"Of course we're safe," Mom said, smoothing her loose hairs back behind her ear. "Why wouldn't we be?"

"You don't remember?" I asked.

All three of them looked at me as if I'd lost my mind. I gestured with my hands. "Does any of this ring a bell? Drums? Faces in the mist?"

"Are you all right?" my father asked, concern in his eyes.

"I'm fine. I nearly lost all of you. My two victims appeared in the mist and urged us to walk on the water to them. Meanwhile, you two went into a trance of sorts, speaking in a robotic tone that you had to go. Mom's hair stood on end."

"I don't remember any such thing," my

mother said. "How unusual."

"There are strange forces at work here, forces that are reaching out from beyond the grave. Do me a favor and head to your friend's farm for the day. Take Larissa and Charlotte with you."

Before they could answer, a car horn sounded three times. It repeated three more times in longer increments. Then three final quick blasts.

SOS.

CHAPTER FORTY-THREE

Deputy Mayes had his weapon drawn beside a black SUV when we burst through the path into the campsite. I pulled up short, stepping in front of my family. Deputy Duncan sped past me, bumping my shoulder in his mad dash.

Charlotte followed her friend. Truthfully, I'd never seen her move so fast.

"Report," Mayes spat out. His dark eyes swept us, but he kept glancing around the perimeter. Something had spooked him.

"All quiet here," Duncan said. "Not so much as an owl call in the night."

Mayes nodded, checking the perimeter again. He lowered his service weapon.

I edged toward Mayes. "What happened? Why the SOS signal?"

He shook his head, rubbed his eyes. "The mist. This place. When I arrived, everyone was gone. From the embers in the fire pit, I knew you hadn't been at the campsite in a while. The vehicles were accounted for. I hoped you'd gone for a walk, but what were the odds of everyone going at the same time?"

"Turned out, pretty good, since we all went to see the sunrise at the lake," I said.

"The sun's been up for thirty minutes at least. Maybe an hour." Mayes checked his watch. "Definitely an hour."

"We haven't been gone that long," I said. "But something weird happened at the lake. I saw faces in the mist. And the rock somehow made everything worse."

"What rock?"

"The boulder by the water's edge."

"There are no boulders on this property."

"I don't understand. Are you saying we had some sort of group hallucination about a rock?"

"Show me."

"Can it wait until after breakfast?"

"No. Show me the rock."

"We'll start breakfast," Mom said. "Larissa can help me crack the eggs."

"I need coffee," I said simply.

Mayes reached inside his vehicle and withdrew a carryout cup of Joe. "Thought you might."

I took it and gulped greedily. The brew had cooled enough that it didn't take the skin off my throat. "Thanks. Feeling better already."

Mayes nodded at his deputy. "Stay here with the Powells."

"I'm staying too," Charlotte said.

"Did you see the rock?" I asked.

"What wasn't to see? It was big, gray, and right next to the water."

"Come with us," I said. "Just to make sure I have the place right. I need another set of eyes."

"All right, but just so you know, this is more exercise that I usually have in a month. I'm on vacation. And you have to share your coffee with me."

"This is turning out to be a different sort of vacation for me, too," I said, handing her the cup.

I led the way, with Charlotte right behind me and Mayes bringing up the rear. We got to the fishing part of the lake, turned, and angled up the shore. The sky above was crystal clear, the water glinting in the bright sunlight. No trace of the mist remained. The rock was right where we left it. "There it is." I pointed it out in case Mayes couldn't see the big lump beside the path.

"I didn't know this was here," he said.

"Kind of hard to miss."

"Tell me again what happened."

I ran through the scenario, including the part where I thought the Little People were calling us. Mayes listened impassively, then he walked around to study the rock from all angles.

"This is a rock all right, but it may be more than that."

"Oh?"

"There's another rock — same color, but a different shape — across the lake. Our people avoid it."

"Why's that?"

"For the very reason you mentioned. The drums of the Little People. The rock snares you until they come for you. It is a people trap."

"And, because you fall under the influence of the drums, you don't notice time passing."

"Yes. That's why you were unaware how long y'all had been out here."

"Charlotte and Deputy Powell weren't on the rock."

"They didn't need to be. With their mutual fascination society going on, they were in their own world."

Charlotte looked appalled. I snorted with laughter, then covered up my face, embarrassed by the rude noise.

"Am I right?" he persisted.

"Yes, they are definitely still enamored of each other," I said.

Charlotte's face turned red. "Since when is it a crime to make out?"

"Since my deputy was supposed to be guarding your entire party," Mayes said. "You're keeping him from doing his job."

Charlotte and I looked at each other and burst out laughing. Mayes stiffened. "I fail to see the joke."

I tried to rein it in, but it wasn't easy. "Charlotte is delighted to be cast in the role of Scarlet Lady."

"You might say this is my first starring role," Charlotte added. "Your deputy is a great kisser."

Mayes rubbed his eyes. "You are aware that supernatural beings kidnapped the two of you yesterday, and anything — I mean anything — you're feeling may not be real."

"It's real to me," Charlotte said. "And so what if it is temporary? I've never been in love or even in infatuation before. I would give up my career in a heartbeat to be with the good deputy."

I grabbed her arm. "Charlotte! You mean it? After all you've worked for?"

"You want a dose of reality?" she said. "Here it is. No matter how hard I work my tail off for Kip, he'll always look to a Bernard to solve his problems. Through your cases, my stories got picked up several times by the bigs. Did they want to hire me? No. Toby Duncan is the first person who has seen me, talked to me, and listened to me — besides you and your family — in years. Maybe in my whole life. I would be stupid to put a floundering career ahead of genuine caring."

"If it *is* genuine," I reminded her gently. "We don't know how either of you will feel in a few days."

"That's why I'm getting to know him now. I want to find common ground and build on that. I want to do whatever it takes to be his girlfriend."

"You used to make fun of girls who did that."

"In hindsight, I was only half wrong. It's wrong to reinvent yourself for someone else. I would never do that, but I will nurture the activities we enjoy doing together."

"You don't know what you're getting into," Mayes said. "Dunc lives with his mom and sleeps with his blue tick hounds. He hunts and fishes whenever he isn't working."

Charlotte's chin jutted out and a militant glare radiated from her eyes. "He also reads thrillers, loves cooking shows on TV, and sings like an angel. We have that in common."

I nodded and fought back a smile. Charlotte might have had supernatural help launching her romance, but she would massage that into something real. "Good for you."

Mayes held up a hand. "Enough. We have murders to solve. Don't touch this rock again. Keep your family away from it."

"Gotcha."

"Breakfast, and then we hit the road," Mayes said. "I've got to keep Duncan away from Charlotte today so he can do his job."

We hoofed it back to camp, where breakfast was waiting. Deputy Duncan raced to Charlotte and swept her into a hug. "I missed you."

It was painful to hear his voice cracking with truth, and I hoped for Charlotte's sake that the romantic bubble didn't burst.

Soon we were loaded up and headed in different directions: my family and Charlotte to the farm, Deputy Duncan to the rehab center, and Mayes and I to the cop shop. First up on our to-do list was interviewing Burl Sayer.

Chapter Forty-Four

"Release me. You're violating my constitutional rights," Burl Sayer said, his voice getting louder with each word he uttered.

Sayer seemed to recognize me when I sat down beside Mayes in the interview room, but once the interview got underway, he didn't spare me a second glance. His eyes locked on Mayes, as if Mayes were his sniper target.

I shivered. Burl Sayer still wore his camo garb, though he'd lost the ball cap and boots. They'd given him some white booties to wear instead, which clashed with his macho image. Except there was no mistaking the rigid set of that granite jaw or the menace in his rough voice.

"Where were you three nights ago?" Mayes asked.

Sayer pounded the table with his cuffed hands. "You can't pin that boy's murder on me. I had nothing to do with it."

"Did you know Haney Haynesworth?"

"I'd seen him skulking around. One time I stopped the guy and ordered him off my property. The kid wet himself. He wasn't part of the invasion, but he kept a low profile like me. He cut through my woods regularly. After that first time, I let it slide. He wasn't hurting nobody or nothing."

"Someone took him out."

"But not with a gun. I heard he just lay down and died."

"Who said that?"

Sayer scowled. "Don't rightly remember."

"You ever see Haney with anyone else?"

"Once. A girl with long dark hair."

"And?"

"And nothing. I followed them, but all they did was sit on a rock. That guy sat on the rock any chance he got. He could sit there for hours. He had the stillness of a sniper. I respected that."

Mayes went hunter-still. "Which rock?"

Sayer's cheek twitched. "Over Annabelle's way a piece. Near the lake."

Mayes exchanged a glance with me, then turned back to Sayer. "You ever sit on the rock?"

"Nah. I got too much ground to cover. Can I go now?"

"No. Tell us where you were three nights ago."

Sayer got a wild look in his eyes. "If I'd a-killed that boy, there'd be a bullet hole in him. No hole. I didn't do it."

"Prove it."

"I was out, man. Patrolling, like always. I was nowhere near where he died."

"Did anyone see you?"

Sayer shuddered. "They better not have seen me. I can't fend off the invasion if I give my position away. You got nothing on me. I'm outta here." He stood up.

Mayes stood along with Sayer. "Hold up. You're going to be our guest a little longer. We have three separate incidents in which you brandished your weapon. All are documented on official police reports, and two parties are pressing charges."

"That's against the Constitution," he said. "A man's gotta right to bear arms."

"On his property. Last time I checked, you didn't own the entire mountain. Unless you can account for your whereabouts for Haney's murder and Dana Finley's murder, you are my number one suspect."

Dana Finley? I wracked my brain. The only other murder was White Feather. Oh yeah. Dana Finley was White Feather's legal name.

Sayer smacked the table again. "Never thought I'd say this word, but you drove me to it: lawyer."

"We can work out a deal regarding the charges, if you cooperate. Do you have information about the murders?"

Sayer glared at Mayes and sat down again. "Lawyer."

Mayes swore under his breath. He nodded at me and went to stand beside the door. My turn to gather information.

I started with a soft, soothing voice. "Mr. Sayer, I know we can't continue to ask you questions about the case, but before I go, I want to thank you. I understand your need to keep the land safe. My husband served his country and safety was his top priority."

Sayer didn't say anything. I wasn't sure how I would work into touching him. He seemed to be quite volatile. If I invaded his personal space, those handcuffs might not hold him. The only thing I knew about him for certain was that the war had changed him.

"Like my Roland, you must've seen terrible sights," I said. "There must have been times when you'd rather be home, rather be enfolded in the peace and quiet of the Georgia mountains. But those who are born to serve and protect feel that obligation so strongly that they put themselves in harm's way over and over again."

He seemed to be listening intently, though his gaze was averted. I took a deep breath. Wasn't any point in drawing this out. "Thank you from all of us on the home front." I reached across the table and squeezed his hand lightly.

Instantly, light fractured and percussive booms sounded. I couldn't hear, couldn't breathe for all the acrid smoke and thick dust. I was seeing a vignette through Sayer's eyes, hearing his thoughts. *Neutralize the threat* ran through my mind. More images flashed in my head, all of them pertaining to a soldier's duty.

I released his hand and rose. Outside in the gleaming corridor, Mayes got right to the point. "Well?"

Not wanting to blurt anything out, I took a slow breath to clear my head. "Nothing useful. When I touch a living person, only traumatic incidents are vivid enough to transfer. He's stuck in a warzone mentality. If he'd killed recently, I should've picked it up."

"What about your BS meter? Was he telling the truth in there?"

"He believed everything he said, which isn't saying a lot when it comes to a man living in a different reality. My gut tells me he didn't kill Haney or White Feather. What about you?"

"No point in guessing. I'm holding him as long as I can. I don't need any more bodies piling up."

"Sayer needs counseling for his post-traumatic stress."

Mayes held his silence until an admin staffer walked past us. "Not my job to see to his mental health."

I folded my arms across my chest. Sayer needed an advocate, and apparently it was me. "My sheriff at home would arrange it."

"We do things differently up here."

"So I see."

He took three steps, then he turned back, his eyes cold. "My priority is bringing these killers to justice and getting Twilla Sue back on her feet. My gut tells me it's all connected. I don't need anyone second-guessing me here, not even you."

Denial sprang to my lips. Sayer's troubled mind spoke to a part of me that ached from Roland's mysterious disappearance. I wanted that wounded warrior to have a chance at a normal life. Unless someone intervened, Sayer would surely patrol this mountain until he died.

The rose tattoos on my back and hand

blazed red hot for a second. My breath caught. Tears filled my eyes. Rose was listening. I hoped that's all she was doing.

"I'm committed to this investigation," I said slowly, "but when we catch Jonas Canyon, I plan to revisit this conversation about Sayer's mental health."

His eyes narrowed ever so slightly. I felt the brush of energy across the back of my neck. Was he using his paranormal senses on me? I mentally pushed back, shoving a jolt of energy his way.

Two deputies I didn't know hurried by, startling me into remembering where I was. I dropped my energy level and glared at Mayes. He ceased whatever he was doing, and the corners of his lips twitched.

He was enjoying this way too much.

Chapter Forty-Five

"My turn," Dr. Gail Bergeron said, the click of her heels announcing her rapid approach in the corridor. "From the Meese Park site, I've got five skeletons — three men and two women — and not much else."

"We don't have time for this," Mayes said. "Our killer is still on the loose."

"I need Ms. Powell for a few minutes, fifteen tops. Then you can have her back."

Staring at piles of bones wasn't high on my fun list, but I needed a break from the testosterone level in this hallway. "I don't see why not. I won't be long. Mayes can check for Jonas sightings while I'm in the morgue."

Gail nodded, and I followed her down a series of hallways. To his credit, Mayes didn't protest my abandoning him. Guess the guy knew he was outnumbered.

"Thanks," I said. "I needed a break from Mister I'm-In-Charge."

As we walked, Oliver my ghost dog appeared, ranging in front of us, nose to the floor. He raced ahead and darted back to me several times. I was glad of the company. Despite my need to take a break from Mayes, Gail had her own agenda.

"He's not a bad sort," Gail said. "All the people here are concerned about Twilla Sue. I checked at the hospital. Her vitals are where they should be, but she isn't responsive."

"That's what I heard as well."

"Such a shame. I hope she recovers."

"Any word on the Sandelman case we'd been working? Did you catch that little girl's killer?" I asked.

"Investigators questioned Knox and Tawny separately. Tawny denied knowing anyone named Pug. Then she started crying and wouldn't speak again. Knox identified Pug right away. Because the arrest is pending, I can't release his name. But we're actively looking for that red car and building a case against Pug. Thanks to you, we may catch this child killer."

I blushed. "I didn't contribute much. The hard part will be connecting the dots so that the case is solid in court."

"We have our best people working on the case." Gail cleared her throat. "Meanwhile,

I've got a ginormous puzzle to solve at the Tree of Secrets. My bones are of adults, and we don't have five missing persons in the area."

I switched mental gears to her tree case. I remembered hearing two bodies were found beneath stout roots. "Could this be an older, unmarked graveyard?"

"If so, there's no record of it. Someone used that park as a graveyard, but who? And why? All I have are the bones to give us answers, and a few scraps of fabric. The material is a modern blend of cotton and polyester."

"What about cause of death?"

"Nothing obvious. The skulls are intact. No sign of bullet holes or trauma in the skeletons. Don't know if they had soft tissue damage as it's long gone."

"Is that unusual?"

"Nothing's quite usual with these bodies. Their teeth, for instance, show less wear and tear than you might expect. Almost no dental work either."

"DNA?"

Gail opened the door and ushered me into the darkened room. The air temperature seemed to drop ten degrees at once. "No luck so far. Bone marrow is our best shot for a DNA profile, but even that's not yielding any answers."

"You lack fingerprints, dental work, DNA, and physical ID aids. No wonder you want me to help figure out who these people are."

Oliver busily sniffed around each of the five gurneys, then he sat down in front of one of them.

Gail pointed to the bones of the nearest victim. "I thought we'd start here and work our way down the line. Fire up your psychic consultant skills and see what you get."

I made my way to the first batch of bones. Oliver barked loudly from contestant number four. Since I trusted Oliver's instincts, I went down where he sat and drew back the sheet. Gail had laid out the remains as if they were an intact human. I didn't like this part of my job very much, but bones were solid links to the dead.

"I thought we'd start at the top with Jane Doe #1 and proceed in an orderly fashion," Gail said.

"I'm starting here," I said, pausing to read the name on the ID tag, "with John Doe #2." I wasn't about to tell her a ghost dog told me where to start. "Don't touch me while I'm checking this guy out. If for any reason something goes wrong, call Mayes and my dad."

"Will do. But I need answers."

"Don't we all." I touched my moldavite necklace and was comforted by its good energy. Gritting my teeth, I took hold of one of John's arm bones. The transition from living to dead happened as expected with the usual chill and disorientation from tumbling through the veil of life. Odd to think that these sensations were starting to feel routine. All too soon, I was standing in the thin murk of the Other Side.

Oliver leaned against my leg, and I reached down to pet him. "Good boy. Now why are we here? Why did you want me to start with this guy?"

The faint sound of music drifted my way. This was what we in the investigation business called a clue. I followed it and found a glade of trees and a meadow. A man sat in a chair beside a large musical instrument, a cello by the look of it. Melancholy music poured out of him in a way that made my heart ache.

As his song drew to a close, the man began to weep. "It's no use," he said. "I don't want to go on without her."

He carefully placed his cello in a case, stood, and stretched. Then he turned and headed down a narrow path, directly to a familiar-looking rock. He clambered aboard, sitting still as a statue. I touched the rock and felt the vibrations of the drumbeats I'd heard earlier while in his position.

The Little People again. They were tangled up in this somehow.

John Doe #2 spoke. "I'm ready."

"Ready for what? Spending the day on the rock?" Though I'd spoken aloud, he didn't notice, which often happened during a dreamwalk. I had yet to figure out why at times I could talk to the spirits and at others I was relegated to viewing a scene from their life.

Would I be stuck for hours watching him sit? One minute he was sitting on the rock, the next minute he vanished. I stared at where he wasn't in disbelief. Was this the Little People's version of the Rapture?

"Hello?" I called into the void but got no response. I waited a few more minutes, but John Doe #2 was done with me. I gave Oliver another pat and straightened up. Time to go home.

I pictured myself standing in the morgue and braced for the dizzying tumble of my spirit as I passed from the land of the dead to the land of the living. The large wall clock was the first item I focused on. Only five minutes had passed, though it seemed much longer to me. The ambient light seemed extra bright after that dark place, but my eyes adjusted with a few blinks.

"Well?" Gail asked.

"John #2 spent time with the Little People. I heard him playing a cello, but he was very sad. He chose to go sit on a transition rock, a gateway to the Little People's world. He moved on to live with them."

"John Doe #2 is a human. Nothing about his remains suggests otherwise."

"We know time is different over there. No telling how long he stayed with the Little People. Somehow he made it back." At her look of disbelief, I added, "He came back dead."

"Tell me more about him."

"He didn't speak to me. He was sad about something. A woman. He didn't want to go on without her."

"You have a physical description? Height, weight, hair color, age . . . anything you can remember."

"He was taller than me. Heavier than Mayes, but not by much. He wore jeans and a flannel shirt. And Hush Puppies boots, looked like. That's it." I thought of something else. "I mentioned the cello, right? He placed it in its case before he headed to the rock."

"Hush Puppies footwear became popular in the 1970s."

"They're still around," I said. "Though you don't see as many of them."

"So John Doe #2 could've gone missing anytime in the last, say, forty-five years? That's a lot of records to search."

"Except, he would've gone missing here. And the cello would be a big hint. I wonder if it's in police evidence somewhere."

"Why don't you ask Mayes to help us on that?"

"You heard him. He doesn't want to spend a second on this case. He's got the name of a murderer and a dragnet out to catch him."

The door opened and Mayes strolled in, a scowl riding his angular face. "We have to go. Jonas sighting at the hardware store."

Chapter Forty-Six

Seemed like I was splitting my vacation week between riding in cop cars and taking dreamwalks. Deputy Mayes hurried me into the sheriff's SUV, and we zipped over to the local hardware store. Good thing I had experience being tossed around all willy-nilly. Though I was firmly buckled in, I gripped the armrest again to keep from sliding around in my seat.

"You done with Dr. B?" Mayes said.

"Nope. You won't like this."

He didn't say anything, so I let the silence stretch out as we careened around another corner. He wasn't the only one who could do inscrutable.

"The cases are connected." He said this as if he'd just learned the world was ending.

My stomach had the audacity to growl. Barely ten o'clock and my breakfast had already worn off. This was going to be a long day. "Good chance."

"I'll bite."

"This guy I dreamwalked about sat on that same rock I was on this morning. He heard the drums, and then he wasn't on the rock anymore. He vanished."

Mayes re-gripped the steering wheel. His shoulders rounded. "The rock is a Nunne'hi portal?"

"Certainly seems that way."

"Haney spent time with the Little People. Jonas stole from them. And now those five bodies at the park, people who show no sign of skeletal trauma, may also have been with the Little People?"

"I can't prove it, but you reached the same conclusion I did. What do we do now?"

"Capturing Jonas is still our priority."

"I can't make the timeline work. Jonas appears to be in his early twenties. Based on clothing found with the Tree of Secrets bodies, these five people died over forty years ago. No way could Jonas be that old."

Mayes parked at Dave's Hardware, a one-story building with a green-metal roof. "We'll figure it out. First we have to catch the guy." He radioed in our position, then turned to me. "Ordinarily, I'd ask you to stay in the vehicle, but Jonas Canyon isn't an ordinary killer. If he uses his powers on me, I'll end up like Twilla Sue. Stay behind me in case he has a gun. If he starts in with the mind control, block it."

A glance around the empty lot didn't give me much hope for success. "Doesn't look like anyone is here."

"We're not taking any chances. Let's go."

Out of habit, I checked to make sure both pockets were still full of crystals, then I touched my moldavite pendant for good luck. It also reassured me that Oliver, the ghost dog who'd attached himself to me, was within hailing distance if I needed him.

Yesterday had been jam-packed with events, and today seemed to be tracking on the same frenetic pace. I smiled to myself and followed Mayes into the store. The thrill of the hunt was upon me. Even though Mayes quartered the store with his gun held high, I glanced around to get my bearings.

The store was a relic of a bygone era, with a pitted concrete floor, wooden display shelves, and sparse inventory. We had a place like Dave's Hardware back home, hanging on by its toenails only because the nearest superstore was a twenty-minute drive.

"Over here," a man said.

We followed the sound to the cluttered checkout counter. The voice belonged to a young man. He looked to be in his early twenties with a peach-fuzz face, stringy blond hair, and thick, sun-kissed eyebrows.

"You missed him," the young man said. "He came in the store, grabbed a shovel, and lit out."

Mayes introduced me to Trey Becker. "You get him on film?"

"Yeah," Trey said. "People think we're behind the times, but I got him cold. I want to press charges. My grandpa said Jonas comes in here and takes things regularly. That's why I had the cameras installed last month. Come on back, I'll show you the feed."

"Did he say anything to you?" Mayes asked.

"Nah. He doesn't talk to me, not since high school."

"You know him?"

"He hung out with some of the guys after school a bit, but I never liked him. I couldn't believe kids would do whatever stupid thing he said. Not me."

Interesting. As we walked to the backroom, I tried to piece together what it must have been like growing up with an energy vampire. "Did the guys feel any different after being with Jonas?"

"What do ya mean?" Trey asked.

I shrugged. "Tired or sleepy. Even sick

with the flu."

"The guys that hung out with Jonas cut school a lot. Since I didn't hang out with them, I was relieved not to see any of them."

"What happened to those kids?" I continued. "They still live around here?"

"Two of 'em died in a car accident senior year. I don't know what happened to the other guy. And then Haney. He hung out with them some, and now he's gone too."

"Sounds like hanging out with Jonas wasn't good for anyone's health," I said.

"What was the other boy's name?" Mayes asked. "The one you lost track of."

"Sam Knowles."

Mayes stopped, contacted Dispatch, and ordered a records search for Sam Knowles. He had an answer in less than thirty seconds. "Knowles died the summer after you graduated, two towns over. The pathology report states the cause of death is unknown."

"Yeah, right," I said. "I've got a good idea what happened to him."

"You do?" Trey said.

Mayes shot me a quelling look in the narrow hallway. I shrugged and answered Trey's question. "Obvious to me. Jonas is toxic to his friends. Seems like none of them live very long."

We continued to the small office. Trey pulled up the video feed, and there was Jonas, looking as confident as you please. He picked up a shovel, turned around, and walked out the door with it.

"We gotta stop this guy," Trey said. "He's robbing my grandparents blind. This store is all they've got."

Jonas was a thief and a serial killer. "Did he have a car?"

"Didn't see one. I thought about chasing after him, but that would leave the store unattended. I can't do that. My family is counting on me."

Trey was a good kid. I found it interesting that he hadn't fallen under Jonas' spell. Should I touch him and try for a read?

Mayes called in to request that all units respond to the area and gave Jonas' description. "I'll send someone by for your statement and for a copy of the video for evidence. We'll head out and start the search. He couldn't have gone far on foot."

As I followed Mayes out the door, I couldn't help myself. I turned back to Trey. "This may seem like an off-the-wall question, but do you have moments of strong intuition that turn out to be right?"

"Not sure what you mean by that, but I'm a good guesser. And I can judge if people are good or bad."

"You can? How?"

"Don't tell anyone I said this, but people glow. My mom doesn't believe me, but I'm never wrong about that."

"That's great. Thanks for telling me."

After we got in the car, I turned to Mayes. "You know what this means. Trey is an aura reader, and he's immune to Jonas' mind control. If you need someone else as a Jonas buffer, he's your guy."

He gave a dismissive shrug and powered out of the empty lot. "He's a kid. He probably doesn't know how to do what you do."

"Maybe. But he's a resource. A hole card, so to speak."

We turned a corner and something caught my eye. A dark object lay on the grass beside a bush. Mayes stopped, and we took a closer look. A hoodie sweatshirt like the one Jonas had worn in the hardware store.

"Read it," Mayes said.

Chapter Forty-Seven

I could think of lots of reasons to read the sweatshirt and no reason to stall. So I took the garment from Mayes and stepped away. Whoever had worn this had not done anything horrific, or the negative emotion would've jolted through my fingertips. With a deep breath, I opened my senses to the possibilities.

A grainy image appeared in my head, but it wouldn't sharpen. It felt like I was watching a corrupted video. I had the sense of motion and perhaps a person or two. But the energy, even though it was diluted, definitely felt like Jonas'.

I dampened my senses and turned to the deputy. "Jonas wore this, but I couldn't tell much else. He hasn't killed in this sweatshirt."

Mayes stuffed the item in an evidence bag, labeled it, and stashed it in the SUV. We hit the road again, looking high and low for a furtive white male. "This guy is like a phantom," Mayes said, twenty minutes later. "We get near him, and he vanishes."

"A phantom. Good call. He feeds on the energy of others, so his energy signature varies. That might explain why the images I saw just now wouldn't dial in clearly."

"The guy's flesh and blood, but he seems to have another gear we don't have. I've never run across anyone like him."

A bizarre idea popped in my head. "You think he's nearby but invisible?"

Mayes snorted. "This isn't a science fiction tale. We need help figuring this out. Unfortunately, the person whose knowledge I respect the most, my grandfather, is gone. I could contact him through fasting and rituals, but that would take time we don't have."

Ah. We were finally in my wheelhouse. "If you have something of his, I can find him on the Other Side."

"It might come to that."

We patrolled for another ten minutes, retracing our steps and coming up empty-handed. Mayes cancelled the search, and we grabbed a quick bite of lunch. It annoyed me that he paid for my BLT, but then he made it all right again by claiming it was a business expense.

Our next stop was the rehab center. Mobile units created a blockade in the parking lot, and Mayes flashed his badge several times before we got to speak to the head public health official on site. Dr. Rupert Perrine had the clinical demeanor of a neurosurgeon, the slight build of a dragonfly, and the weight of the world on his thin shoulders. He stood while Mayes explained the situation.

We were not invited to sit down, which I took as a bad sign. The man's cold eyes and stiff posture told me this guy didn't want us in his office. He wanted nothing to do with us. I had news for him. The feeling was mutual.

"No entry," Perrine said. "This place is on lockdown. No one in and no one out."

"The sole survivor of an assault by a serial killer is in there," Mayes said. "We need to talk with her. This is a police matter."

Perrine gave a pained smile. "The meaning of quarantine is that the area is contained. If you waltz in and out, that defeats the purpose, and you become a disease vector. Under no circumstances are you or anyone else allowed inside."

"We were already in there, yesterday, with paper masks on," Mayes explained. "Before you were alerted. We must speak with Ms.

Tice. We have been unable to interview her since she revived. Each minute we delay gives the killer time to hurt more people in our community."

"The answer is still no. Public safety is my concern, and the infectious agent in this building is particularly virulent. According to our records, onset is less than twenty-four hours, possibly less than eight hours."

"We're fine," Mayes said. "We need to get inside to talk with Ms. Tice."

"No can do."

I'd had enough of these men posturing. The clock was ticking on the investigation and on my vacation. We needed a compromise. "How about a video chat? Surely someone in there has a mobile phone or a laptop."

"That sounds reasonable," Perrine grudgingly admitted after a short silence. "Let me contact my staff inside. Give me a minute to set it up."

Perrine left us alone in his office, a sterile place with only the basics — an uncluttered desk and a few chairs. How did he work without a laptop?

Mayes gave me a slight head bob of approval. That miniscule acknowledgment warmed me like high praise. I'd much rather interview the woman in person, but barring a presidential order, this admin wouldn't budge. I respected that they were trying to stop an epidemic, but we had to catch a serial killer.

A brunette wearing khakis and a pale-yellow, button-down blouse and bearing a tablet joined us in a few minutes. She placed the device on Perrine's empty desk and invited us to sit before it. Mayes pulled out a small audio recording device and set it next to the tablet.

"The video chat function is activated. Our staffer went to Ms. Tice's room, but it appears she's in the restroom. We have to wait for her to conclude her business."

I nodded, but my eyes were on the image. Lizella Tice's room was as I remembered it, except that another bed was in the room. "Who's that?" I asked.

"One of the floor nurses came down with the flu last night. They put her in here since Ms. Tice had already been exposed."

"What's her status?" I asked.

"Her treatment plan and health status are confidential, but I assure you, she's getting the best possible medical care."

"Is the treatment helping her?"

"Her health status is confidential," the brunette repeated.

I gritted my teeth, wishing I could be in

that building, in that room, to experience the situation firsthand. A toilet flushed, and a door opened. Wan and skeletal, Ms. Tice walked with the assistance of an aide. I remembered seeing the aide yesterday, a petite young woman with a youthful bounce in her step. She didn't appear peppy today.

The image flickered and crisped.

The aide got Ms. Tice settled in bed, and then crossed the room to move the camera. The field of vision shifted from a view of the bathroom to Tice's bed. I studied her appearance. She seemed no worse today.

Mayes activated his recorder device and leaned in to the camera field. "Ms. Tice, Deputy Chief Mayes. We met yesterday. I am taping our conversation as a matter of record in our police investigation of the death of Haney Haynesworth. Tell me what you remember about Jonas Canyon."

Her expression hardened. "He seemed like such a nice boy."

"Go on."

"He offered me a place to stay," Ms. Tice said. "I was living on the streets. I should've known there was a catch."

"What do you mean?"

"Things changed as soon as I moved in. He had rules about staying in our rooms. He was the only one allowed inside all the bedrooms, and I was always tired after he visited. Eventually, I had no desire or strength to move. I lay there in that bed day after day. If you hadn't come along, I'd be dead. Like the others."

"You met Canyon on the streets?"

"He approached me after a bad thunderstorm. Said he could put a roof over my head, and it wouldn't cost me a thing."

"What about the others?"

"I don't understand."

"Where'd they come from?"

The image wavered a moment, then sharpened. "I don't know."

"Was Haney already at the house when you arrived?"

"Haney was there. He liked to tell me stories and show me his flipbooks."

"Can you remember anything else about Canyon?"

Ms. Tice sagged against her pillow. Her eyes fluttered. "He seemed like such a nice boy."

The aide came back into view. "Ms. Tice needs her rest."

"I have more questions," Mayes insisted.

"Another time," the aide said.

The link ended, and we were shown the door.

"Your thoughts?" Mayes said as we drove away.

"A good piece of theater."

Chapter Forty-Eight

Mayes pulled into the parking lot of an abandoned building, shoved the gearshift into park, and turned to me. "Explain."

"Something is very wrong in that rehab center. Sealing the building may have contained the flu-like outbreak, but more healthy people inside are showing signs of exhaustion."

He shrugged off my remark. "Easily explained by caregivers working around the clock."

My fists clenched tightly, the nails digging into my flesh. I forced my fingers open. "I'm not buying it. They may think the place is sealed, but you and I know it isn't the flu. Jonas must have a way inside. He might even be there now, feeding off all those helpless people. With his talent for mesmerizing, they might not even remember seeing him. We need to get inside."

"Not an easy task, when the state has

jurisdiction. We need compelling proof Jonas is in there."

"Won't happen. He's too good at hiding his tracks."

We sat there in silence for a moment. "Is there a limit to how much energy a body can absorb?" Mayes asked. "Wouldn't Jonas fill up at some point?"

"I don't know. But instead of trying to reach your grandfather in the spirit world, why don't we ask my dad? He did this dreamwalker job for a long time, and he has an extensive network of contacts among the living."

"Good idea."

I called my dad, and he answered on the first ring. "Hey, sunshine. What can I do for you?"

"You're on speaker phone. Mayes and I have some questions for you. Can an energy vampire go past saturation? And one more thing, the video images I see of this energy vampire in my dreamwalk are fragmented and full of static. What's that all about?"

Dad drew a long breath. "I don't know, but Running Bear might. His people stumbled across several energy vampires a few years ago. I can ask him."

Running Bear was my father's best friend and a Native American. I exchanged a hopeful glance with Mayes. "That would be great. Would you also ask him how they handled the situation? We seem to stay three steps behind Jonas Canyon. Our energy vampire must have precognition or something."

"Will do. Can you message me a picture of the man? Odds are it isn't the same person who caused trouble with his tribe, but you never know."

"I'll send the picture right away. How's the craft fair?"

"Your mother's in her element. Larissa and I scouted the exhibits and found rocking chairs we like. They're too large for your porch, but they would look nice in our yard."

Mayes fiddled with his phone. He appeared to have tuned out now that the call had veered into family matters. "We've got room in the campers to carry them home if you decide you want them. By the way, if there's anything Larissa wants, go ahead and buy it for her and I'll reimburse you."

"Okay. Send the picture. I'll forward it to Running Bear and then call him."

"Thanks." I ended the call and turned to Mayes. "I need a picture of Jonas Canyon."

"Just sent it to you."

My phone chimed, and I forwarded the

image to my dad. "Now what? Shall we focus on one of Gail's cases until we have another Jonas sighting?"

"No cold cases, not when we have two active investigations." Mayes shifted gears and off we went, up the mountain. "We have another location to visit related to Haney's case. His father's place was listed in the deed book. No one lives there now, though the property is currently owned by a Janet Smith. We have her permission to look around. After that, we should talk with White Feather's family."

I settled in my seat, trying to release the tension in my shoulder without appearing too twitchy. "I keep forgetting we have two murders because we're spending all of our time searching for Jonas."

"One suspect, two victims. We know by virtue of your dreamwalks that Jonas killed both Haney and White Feather. We still need proof of his guilt for the legal system. The only physical evidence we have against Jonas is that video of him stealing a shovel. Theft doesn't carry the same penalty as a double homicide. And kidnapping the sheriff, of course. He has to be held accountable for his actions."

The drift of his thoughts concerned me. My shoulders lifted almost to my ears. Was he going to screw my guardian angel? "Everyone agreed Jonas was going to Rose for justice's sake. He won't go through our criminal justice system."

"I'd like to do both."

"Rose isn't good at sharing."

"Noted."

The ride got bumpy once he turned off the pavement. I braced myself. "Is this a road?"

"Used to be. Poachers come this way every now and again."

We bumped along until a tree blocked our progress. He parked the car and opened the door. "We walk the rest of the way."

The grass looked to be knee-high. "I wish I had tick repellent."

"Shouldn't be too bad." He flashed me a wolfish grin. "I'll help you check for ticks."

The idea alarmed me, but not as much as it should've. "Charlotte can help me."

"Understood."

His eyes radiated disappointment, but I wouldn't be part of his wish-fulfillment program.

He handed me a water bottle, a mini flashlight, cable ties, and an energy bar. "Take these with you."

"You think it'll be dark before we're return?"

He slung a compact backpack over his shoulder. “I like to be prepared.”

I stashed the light, cable ties, and snack in my pockets, but I had to carry the water bottle. I followed him around the pine and up a meandering trail barely wide enough for a deer. As a precaution, I did a life-signs sweep in our general vicinity. No pingbacks. Just as well. There were too many trees here to be constantly worried about our personal security. I’m sure Mayes hoped we’d get a lead on Jonas out here, but this place seemed so far off the grid. I couldn’t imagine how he would access it.

Soon a faded shanty with a crooked chimney came into view. I stopped. “I recognize this place. From my first Haney dreamwalk. This is where he lived with his family.”

“Ms. Smith said she hadn’t touched anything in the cabin. She bought the property at auction because it connected two other tracts she owned.”

I hurried forward. The door leaned open, half off its hinges. Leaves littered the rough-planked floor. Both front windows were busted out. Inside, a three-legged stool sat by a blackened hearth. Nothing about this place felt cozy or welcoming.

My gaze continued around the small space. A filthy mattress lay shredded to one side of the room. Something had nested in there. A rickety ladder led to a tiny loft overhead.

This place was poverty squared. "Poor Haney," I said. "He lived in the middle of nowhere with nothing."

Mayes finished quartering the space and shrugged. "No electricity, no running water. Hard to believe people lived here in this century."

"With Haney's family situation and his nonstandard mental wiring, he never had a chance."

Mayes prowled around the small dwelling. "Other than the mattress, which I'll check in a minute, there's no place down here to hide anything. I see no books or papers or personal items. Nothing that ties Jonas to Haney."

"When I had the dreamwalk about this place, Haney watched the other kids from above. The loft was probably his space. I'll climb up and take a look."

"Wait. Let me test the ladder first."

A protest lodged in my throat, but I realized Mayes couldn't help it. He was programmed to serve and protect. He pulled on several of the rungs before he pronounced it safe.

Setting my water bottle down on the plank

floor, I guarded my senses before I climbed the ladder. Stray bits of strong emotion could jolt me through my hands if I didn't shield myself, and I wanted no surprises. Upstairs, an intact twin mattress rested on the floor. Unlike below, this area was tidy and free of debris. The rumpled blanket on the mattress looked new. To one side were three dog-eared children's books and a stack of little notebooks.

"Mayes! I got something."

Chapter Forty-Nine

Ignoring the dusty books, I picked up a little notebook. Simple images were drawn on each page. Flipbooks. I remembered them from Haney's first dreamwalk. In this one, a small stick figure waved goodbye to a larger one in a dress. The smaller figure waited for a bit then cried.

"Mayes," I called again. "Come up here. You gotta see this stuff."

From what I knew of Haney's personal history, this flipbook was the story of his mother leaving. I viewed several more, seeing the stories of other boys chasing him, of his father drinking and breaking furniture. Poor Haney.

I heard a muffled noise below. Ignored it. Mayes knew how to climb a ladder. I'd been shielded long enough. Would each flipbook launch me into a different dreamwalk? Or should I examine the blanket with my extra senses fired up to see if Jonas had been staying here?

Decisions.

The house felt oddly quiet. Vacant, somehow. That emptiness scared me. I shrunk into myself and tried to think. Something had happened below, and I'd missed it. With my pulse thrumming in my ears, I crept to the loft's rail and peered below.

The deputy chief lay, face down, on the floor.

"Mayes!" I said in a strangled whisper. A healthy man like Mayes wouldn't collapse on his own. I transitioned to my extra senses and found what I dreaded. Someone was moving away from this place at a dead run. The person was not traveling in the direction of Mayes' vehicle, but up-mountain.

No other life signs were in the area.

Moving quickly, I tossed the flipbooks over the rail and hurried down the ladder. I checked Mayes' pulse. Strong. He was alive. No blood. No obvious sign of injury. I jiggled his shoulders gently and called his name. No response. His respirations were deep, but I couldn't rouse him. He was sleeping, like Twilla Sue.

Certainty slammed into me. Jonas had been here. He'd zapped Mayes and drained a measure of his energy while I was in the loft. My job had been to protect this deputy against Jonas, and I'd failed him. I blinked back tears and tried to formulate a plan of action.

I called Charlotte. "Deputy Duncan with you?" I asked when she answered.

"He is."

"May I speak to him? It's about Mayes."

Deputy Duncan came on the line. "Duncan."

"It's Mayes. Jonas got to him when I wasn't looking, knocked him out. I can't bring him around. He's sleeping like Twilla Sue."

"Does he need an ambulance?"

"He has no external injury I can find. Look, we're a long way in the woods, at the shack where Haney Haynesworth grew up. Dispatch has the GPS coordinates. I can't tell you what to do, but I'm leaving Mayes here while I track Jonas. I'll be back soon as I can."

"Wait!"

I ended the call and muted the ringer. The phone buzzed in my back pocket, but I didn't have time to discuss anything. Before I went after Jonas, however, I could help Mayes with a jolt of energy. That felt right and necessary.

The only way I knew to share my life force was the way Jonas stole the energy from his victims. The image of Jonas straddling White Feather came to mind. He'd placed his palm on her palms before he'd kissed the life out of her.

I would have to kiss Mayes while holding his hands. Except it wouldn't be a real kiss. It would be the breath of life. This wasn't cheating on my missing husband. This was life support for a friend in need.

Carefully, I attempted to roll Mayes onto his back. He didn't so much as grunt or tighten up when I put my hands on him. He didn't roll either. It was like trying to move a refrigerator without wheels. Soon I forgot my qualms about touching him and used my shoulder to push his shoulder over. I positioned his arms by his sides.

Then it was time to straddle his torso. Mayes was lean, but his hips fit mine in a disturbingly intimate way. *Don't think about that,* I cautioned myself. *Do it and get out of here. You have to stop Jonas. You're the only one who can.*

My left palm snugged against his right, my right palm against his left. I interlaced our fingers as I'd seen Jonas do in the dreamwalks. Another disturbing wave of tingles shot through my body. Was intimacy part of the thrill for Jonas? Did he get off on killing people?

Worse, was I like him?

I was nothing like him, and I wasn't stealing anything from Mayes. I focused on the warmth of our palms, willing my energy to flow into him. Our palms heated even more, but his sleep remained deep. I sent him a silent plea, which I knew the physical contact would magnify. *Mayes, wake up!*

No response. I licked my lips, knowing what must come next. I also knew I couldn't block my senses. For this to work, I had to open all of myself to him. I'd never been that open or vulnerable before, not even with my husband. We'd shared living space and hopes and dreams, but not our entire selves.

And Roland was the only man I'd ever kissed.

Not a kiss, I reminded myself. I was not in a relationship with Mayes. I was attempting to revive him, and I needed to get to it before Jonas fled the area.

I could do this. This was nothing more than extrasensory CPR. Holding onto that thought, I leaned forward and touched my lips to his. I squeezed with my fingers, willing more energy into his prone body.

Not working.

I opened my senses to the experience, absorbing the throb of his pulse into mine.

It seemed as if I were in his body and mine at the same time. The sense of intimacy overwhelmed me, and I worked harder at kissing him.

The room wavered, and we plunged together into a dreamwalk. Only it was like no dreamwalk I'd ever taken. Mayes and I were in a waterfall, kissing, and our passion was mutual. I had the sense of coming alive, of my feminine nature surging and demanding release. God help me, I held nothing back, caressing as I was caressed, kissing as I was kissed.

A glimmer of self-awareness flickered. I tried to disentangle myself and gain some objectivity. "Mayes, this isn't real."

"Speak for yourself," he muttered against my neck. "I've wanted to do this ever since I met you. I knew it would be like this between us."

"We shouldn't. We're on a case."

"We're together, as we were meant to be." He stopped touching me, held my gaze. Water flowed around us. "Tell me you want this. Tell me you want me."

"I'm married, and this is a dream. I need you to wake up."

"I like this dream."

He showed me how much he liked the dream.

My body responded in kind, but I pushed away, moving out of the waterfall spray. "Mayes. Jonas did this to you."

He stalked toward me, extending his hand. "Remind me to thank him later. Kiss me again."

"We shared energy. I gave you a boost. You have the power to break free of this dream."

"Why would I want to wake up? You're here with me."

"I have to go. I have to catch Jonas before he hurts someone else."

Mayes' eyes clouded. "Stay. I need you."

"I can't. This," I gestured between us, "this can't be. Our lives run on different paths."

"You are powerful medicine, Walks With Ghosts. I would be honored to call you mine."

Oh, dear. "I'm flattered — more than flattered — and I never intended to lead you on. But this is just a dream. We can't do this in the physical world. Let me be clear. I won't do this in the real world."

"And yet you're here in my dreams."

He was getting closer. If I stayed, I'd be trapped in his pseudo-reality. "Wake up, Mayes. You have the power."

As I transitioned back to reality, I heard

him call for me. "Baxley! Where'd you go?"

I came awake abruptly, as if I'd swum too deep and barely made it back to the surface. The first thing I did was scramble off Mayes. He didn't move so much as an eyelash. He didn't reach for me.

It was all a dream. A crazy mixed-up fantasy concocted by two overworked people. I couldn't possibly have feelings for him. The lightheadedness and pounding heartbeat were side effects of the transfer.

For a split second, I allowed myself to believe the intimacy had been heartfelt. The sensations had felt more than real. They'd been epic. I wouldn't soon forget the intensity of being connected to Mayes in his dream.

Would he?

Chapter Fifty

I summoned my ghost dog, and Oliver appeared beside me. I pointed to the door. "Find Jonas."

Oliver barked happily and darted outside, nose to the ground. I followed, Beretta in hand. Jonas would not get away this time. The path Oliver took snaked and turned back on itself until I didn't know if I was coming or going. At one point, I brushed the cobwebs off my face and wondered how a ghost dog could follow the scent trail of an energy vampire.

But if he'd done it at White Feather's death site, he could do it here.

The grade steadily increased, and my calves strained. We were headed uphill. If I didn't find Jonas, I might be lost in these woods for a very long time. My cellphone stopped buzzing. I pulled it out and checked the display. No signal.

Great. If I got in a jam, I had only my

paranormal defenses to rely upon.

My thoughts veered back to Mayes. Would our virtual kiss present a problem for the real us? Had I cheated on my husband if the kiss happened in the dream world?

My husband. Roland lingered in my mind and my heart. Though the military had declared him dead, I didn't believe it. But each passing day strained that belief.

Stop. Don't invite trouble. Focus on one issue at a time. Right now you're tracking an energy vampire.

Gritting my teeth, I slogged through the underbrush, unable to pass silently, not with all the briars and bushes in my way. Twigs and sticks crackled underfoot and small branches snapped as I followed my ghostly guide. I wished like anything I'd remembered to bring that water bottle on this trek.

How had Jonas gotten through all this foliage without breaking branches? Mayes had called him a phantom, and it seemed Jonas knew things he shouldn't. Could he physically transport himself from one place to another? I couldn't think of any plausible answer to that question. With no reasonable answers, only the bizarre ones remained. His spiriting himself around made sense but it wasn't humanly possible. Which led to another question.

Was Jonas even human? He looked like an ordinary person, but he performed extraordinary feats. He knew we were actively searching for him. If he was so powerful, why didn't he move on? Did something hold him here?

Clearly, Jonas had his own agenda, one that involved staying beneath the radar of law enforcement. Except that I wasn't law enforcement. Perhaps he considered me a threat.

If that was so, why wait until now to come after me?

Ahead, the path abruptly opened into a clearing about the size of half a tennis court. A chunk of mountain stood on the opposite side. Oliver darted ahead in the open space and ran back toward me. Stepping into the open area would make me an easy target. I lowered my guard to search the area for life signs. Someone was hiding directly ahead of me, secreted in the mountain.

The energy signature felt familiar. It wavered slightly like Jonas' had done. I edged behind an oak. The person had to be Jonas, which meant I should be on my toes. From what I'd seen, Jonas was one of a kind, but he might have allies.

I stooped to pet the ghost dog. "Good boy, Oliver."

The Great Dane rubbed against me and faded from sight. He was still with me, but not in the visible spectrum. Time for me to regroup.

Now that I'd stopped moving, my heart raced and my breaths came in ragged gasps. I didn't know what I'd be facing, but I sure as heck wouldn't run away. This was my battle. I used my extra senses to make sure I wasn't outnumbered.

The answer soon became apparent. Except for Jonas, I was alone, with no way to call for backup. Distance-wise, the only possible person I could reach through telepathy was Mayes. I wasn't even sure if he could receive me now that we weren't touching. But I sent the message and a mental image of my surroundings anyway.

I found Jonas. I need your help, Mayes. That dream of us isn't real. The real me is out here on the mountain with a psychic vampire, and I need you. Come to me, Mayes.

That would have to do for now.

I rubbed my pendant. The touchstone centered me and bolstered my confidence. I might be out of my depth here, but my opponent didn't know that.

"Jonas Canyon," I called in a loud, assertive voice from my hiding place. "Come out with your hands up. You are surrounded."

Not even a bird twittered. I heard the loud thump of my heart and that was it. "Jonas. You're done. I'm here to take you in. Surrender and it will go much easier for you."

The late morning sunshine lit up the grassy clearing, lending a surreal feeling to the moment. As matchups went, I hoped the odds favored a Dreamwalker over an energy vampire.

I tried another tack. "I know exactly where you are. You can't hide from me."

A slight breeze stirred the seeded heads of the grasses. No Jonas. He was on the other side of the clearing. He hadn't moved a muscle since I'd locked onto his signal.

I looked at my clenched hands on the gun grip. Could I point this weapon at a person and pull the trigger? I shuddered at the thought. All I needed to do was to secure him. *Let's hope it doesn't come down to making a life or death decision.*

More minutes ticked off my life clock. With each passing second, my options boiled down to one. I had to go over there and get him. I didn't like the idea of walking across the open area. If Jonas had a gun, I'd be easy pickings. I edged around to the left, a somewhat shorter route than the other direction.

I hadn't walked four steps before Jonas

moved. He didn't rush out to fight me. Instead, he retreated inside the mountain. His signal flickered and weakened.

Instinct propelled me forward into the meadow. My strides lengthened to a run. I hadn't come this far to lose track of this guy now. He was mine.

Chapter Fifty-One

The rock Jonas had been hiding behind flared with negative energy. I didn't need to touch it to know a killer had been here. I was winded and wheezed in air as I surveyed the scene. Behind the rock, a person-sized fissure gaped in the mountain.

Oliver materialized again by the crack and barked excitedly. Jonas had passed through the opening, but did I want to follow him? I could wait for him to come out. Except I didn't know if the cave had another outlet, or if the opening itself was a gateway to another realm of existence.

Waiting was not a good option if I expected to capture him. Sealing the opening might work, but I wasn't strong enough to move a boulder. And what if there were another exit?

I had no choice but to go in there after him.

Why hadn't I asked Mayes pointblank if

he was a telepath? We'd just shared energy, so I had to believe an intangible link existed. In truth, Mayes was my only lifeline. I had to try. I shot him another message and a three-sixty panorama of my location. *I don't know if you're reading me, but Jonas is here. I tracked him to this cave in the mountain. Here's where I am. I sure hope you're getting this because I'm going in after him. And thank you for giving me a flashlight. I'll need it.*

Flicking the light on, I positioned it above my gun as I'd seen TV cops do. If the technique worked for them, it would work for me. Oliver barked again and bounded through the crevice.

With another glance around the mountainside for good luck, I slid through the fissure. Between Oliver tracking Jonas and my life sign reading ability, I had no doubt I'd locate Jonas.

The tattoo on my wrist heated appreciably. "Not now, Rose," I muttered. "I'm busy."

A part of me wanted Jonas to be held accountable in human courts, but his fate wasn't up to me. We'd made a deal with my protector on the Other Side. I got Charlotte, Gail, and Deputy Duncan out of the hands of the Little People, Rose would get Jonas, and the Little People would get their deep sleep memory talent back. Once everyone was satisfied, I'd finish up my vacation and go home.

The passageway narrowed. At times I had to walk sideways to get through. I kept my senses locked on Jonas' position. I didn't need any nasty surprises. He was ahead of me but moving slowly. Why was that?

If he had the means to escape, why would he head into a cave? That was the opposite of escaping. He'd proven to be a wily adversary so far, so I had to trust that he had a plan, a plan that wouldn't bode well for me. Even if I caught and secured him with the cable ties Mayes had handed me when we started this hike, how would I march him out of here as a captive?

Don't get ahead of yourself. First, find him. Then get the drop on him. Escorting him out of here won't be a worry for a while.

Oh, joy.

Good thing I was familiar with dark places. Another person might be put off by the dank smell, the jagged abutments, and the treacherous footing. Not that I liked those things, but I'd been in worse situations.

I picked up the pace. Jonas was moving slower and slower. Was he injured? I should be so lucky.

He had to know I was behind him. Despite

my need for stealth, the setting wasn't conducive to sneaking up on my target. Suddenly, Jonas' energy flickered out. He was there, and then he wasn't. The passageway opened up, and I picked up speed, darting along the twisting corridor of rock, feeling the deep chill of the mountain in my marrow.

Another bend and I stood in the center of a cavern. The ceiling vaulted high overhead. Some semblance of twilight filled the empty space. I flashed my light from ceiling to floor all around the area. No one was here, visually or according to my extra senses, but Jonas had tricked me before. Mayes had said the man seemed to be a phantom.

If that was the case, he was still present. I patrolled the space, noting two other openings in the wall, all my senses on high alert. I sent Oliver to the pathway we'd used to get here and told him to stay.

Gun and light raised high, I clung to the edge of the room, watching and listening. "I know you're here, Jonas. Despite your powers, you aren't invincible. I know about your weakness. I know what you've done."

I saw a flicker of movement and whirled to face it. Nothing was there. Was Jonas doing that? I kept moving. I needed to draw him out of hiding. "I saw Haney's flipbooks and figured it out. You wanted Haney from the beginning, so you ruined his family. He was a vulnerable child, and you made him bring you victims. Did he find out you led his mother to the Little People? Or was it White Feather who opened his eyes to what you are?"

Another sparkle of energy fizzed across the room. I headed toward it, weaving fact with fantasy until I struck the right nerve with Jonas. "I spoke to Lizella Tice, Jonas. She told me all about you. There's nowhere you can go now. The cops have your picture. If you don't have Haney to serve as your energy pimp, what will you do? Someone's bound to notice a bunch of people going missing, or another bout of killer flu. You think I don't know what happened at that rehab center? I know everything."

He flashed into solid form before me, malignant energy swirling around him. "You know nothing."

Chapter Fifty-Two

"I knew you were in here," I said, instinctively backing up toward the way I'd entered this chamber. Might as well try my first bluff. "I knew about your invisibility powers."

He shook his head. "You fool. I lured you here. This is my turf, the seat of my power."

"*Your* power? You don't have power. You steal power from others. That makes you a thief and a killer."

"Minor points in the general scheme of things. I'm in need of a new slave, Baxley Powell. You could be my new Haney. People like you."

"I won't be your anything," I said.

"We'll see." He vanished from sight. The room darkened ominously. The hair on the back of my neck electrified. Whatever was coming wouldn't be pleasant.

My flashlight beam flickered then went out. I beat it against the side of my leg, to no avail. "I'm not afraid of the dark. You got the wrong girl."

He didn't respond. It occurred to me that Jonas and I were in the same space. Why not call Rose now? She could secure him with a snap of her fingers.

I sent her a mental text. *Got him. Come now.*

Nothing.

Not even a flash of heat from my rose-shaped tattoos.

How odd. I'd never been out of touch with Rose, not since she'd marked me with her tattoos. She'd said we were connected in the land of the living and the dead. Once she'd come to me while I was trapped between worlds. She'd said we were connected in all realities. Maybe this one didn't count.

I called Oliver for backup, but he didn't come either.

Okay, that was weird. I edged backward some more. I kept the gun held high, ready to shoot Jonas if he laid a finger on me.

My thoughts raced. No Rose. No Oliver. Just me.

Tiny pinpoints of light appeared on the ceiling. I watched them until I realized they were spinning, and I was lightheaded. I sank to my heels, eyes closed. Jonas was manipulating the environment, trying to subdue me. His power was strong here.

I needed to return to the passageway where Oliver the ghost dog waited. The opening should be directly behind me. I stashed the gun in my waistband and crabbed backward until my head bumped the wall. It was a risk to open my eyes, but I did it anyway. Gigantic fish with prehistoric teeth swam through the air.

Quickly, I shut my eyes. The opening had to be one way or the other. I went right first, about ten paces. Nothing. I retraced my path and then headed left. *Bingo.* I eased out into the corridor. Oliver licked my face and hands.

I hugged him tightly and then tried Rose again.

She materialized in a flash of light. For this visit she'd chosen the tough biker girl leathers for her clothing, so her tattoo-covered arms were visible. "What took you so long?"

The scent of burning sulfur would've brought me to my knees if I weren't already sprawled on the floor. "There's some kind of spiritual block in the cavern. I couldn't reach you. Jonas is in there. Somehow he's manipulating how the room looks, and he can go invisible."

"He's not invisible to me," Rose said as she stepped over me. She muttered some words in a language I didn't understand. The cavern reverted to normal in the blink of an eye.

Jonas stood with arms outstretched as if directing a symphony. But one look at Rose and he froze. His eyes stayed overlarge; his arms seemed to be waiting for a chorus that would never come.

I scrambled to my feet, Oliver beside me. "Did you do that?"

"I did." Rose strode toward her prize. "He will bother you no more. Summon the others."

"The Little People? I don't know how to reach them. Mayes showed me how to get to their place."

"Must I do everything? You're trying my patience."

"I didn't know I needed to contact the Little People again. I don't have them on speed dial. My agreement was to find Jonas for you. I found him. Now it's your turn."

"Careful. I'm not in the best of moods today, but having a new soul to torment should go a long way toward getting me into the boss's good graces." Rose scanned the room. "Sweet setup he's got here. I'll have to remember this place. Picture the Little

People portal, worm."

"It's in my head."

Rose glared through me as if she could reach in there and grab the image from my gray matter. To keep her from attempting anything of the sort, I stretched my thoughts. "Got it."

The sense of movement was sudden, abrupt, and disorienting. I fought off a wave of nausea as we landed in another dark passageway. I flicked on my flashlight, relieved at the familiar sight of the wide corridor. I'd been here before. Faint drumming reached my ears, further confirming we were where we were supposed to be.

"I will stay here with the prize. Find their leader and return to me. Do not keep me waiting."

I scrambled to comply, shouting their names as I ran. "Trahearn! Meuric! Arwel!"

Three strapping young men in buckskins and braids met me at the opening. I pointed behind me. "We caught the guy. You can get your memory power back. Please come with me."

They huddled together and talked softly. Trahearn motioned a woman close and sent her away. "We will follow you," Trahearn said to me.

I showed them the way, now fully illuminated. Guess it didn't suit Rose to wait in the dark.

She stood beside Jonas, but she'd transformed into her terrible Medusa-like guise, only her snake-haired head had multiplied to three heads of slithering hair. Her height had increased too, so that she now stood head and shoulders above the rest of us. Jonas was still frozen in conductor mode.

"I'm here to uphold my end of the bargain," Rose said, speaking only from her center head while the other heads rotated to take in the entire room. "Do you have the vessel?"

"It's coming." Trahearn stared at the ground in front of Rose.

Was he frightened of her? Rose probably had more superpowers than the Little People, so that explanation made sense.

"Good. I'm looking forward to having a new apprentice. Who will pay the blood price?"

"I will pay the price," Trahearn said simply, and he moved to flank Rose's right side. She did something to him, and he stood statue still.

"Only one?" Rose tsked. "The afterlife has so many troubles. I could use more assistants. Any volunteers?"

Meuric and Arwel remained mute, their

gazes fixed on solid ground. I didn't look at Rose either, but she summoned me by thought just the same. I took my place at her left side. Rose pointed at Jonas and did something to unfreeze him.

"Where am I?" Jonas asked. He stared everywhere at once. "What happened?"

Flames sprouted from each of Rose's heads. "You have been judged by a council of your peers and found guilty of theft, among other crimes. Do you have anything to say for yourself?"

"I took what was mine."

The air in the corridor crackled and heated until I found it hard to breathe. Rose shot a puff of something at Jonas, and he fell to the floor. "Liar," she said. "You took what did not belong to you, and you did it over and over again. By my count, you've murdered twenty people and injured hundreds more."

Jonas shrugged. "I'm a reaver. This is what I do. Raid and take what I need. My kind has been on this planet for nearly a thousand years. I am following the creation directive."

I struggled to take in his words. *His kind.* Would I have to fight them all? And what the heck was the creation directive?

"We demand justice for his crimes," Arwel said, apparently the new spokesman for his people. “He defiled our land, angered our people, stole our gift of remembrance, and murdered our friend. Do not reward him in your world. He should be stripped.”

An image of Jonas’ too-white body flashed into my head. Hastily, I banished that thought. I did not want to see that man naked.

CHAPTER FIFTY-THREE

"You can't strip me," Jonas countered, his voice going squeaky high. "It will upset the balance of life."

Lightning bolts shot out from Rose's fingertips, zipping down the corridor. "I don't give a flying flip about the balance of life. You caused heartache and mischief, and you made me come here twice to clean up your mess."

I snuck a peek at her. Rose's breastplate was the color of fire and sapphire, overbright and darkly lustrous at the same time. Though she reeked of hellfire, I knew for a fact Rose answered to the Big Boss upstairs, and that she worked undercover in the afterlife. Bottom line, my guardian angel had a day job as a demon.

Two women scurried forward, heads down, bearing a small, jeweled chest. "Give it to my apprentice," Rose directed.

I accepted the item, holding it in both

arms. The chest weighed a ton. I hoped Rose didn't draw this process out. "Open it," she commanded, so I flipped the latch and opened the chest. "Do not under any circumstances let it go."

Rose extended her right hand, and a boom of thunder filled the corridor, echoing throughout the mountain. The Little People fell to their knees. Jonas prostrated himself before her. "Please, no!" he cried.

The air crackled with charged particles and fury. I tried not to breathe in the thick sulfur, but it surrounded me and permeated my body. Jonas arched and moaned. Simultaneously, the chest became so heavy I could not stand. I sank to my knees, resting the chest on the rock floor, but not once did I loosen my grip.

"Seal the chest," Rose said. "Return it to the Nunne'hi."

With trembling fingers, I closed the glowing chest. Drawing deep, I summoned the strength to walk across the corridor and place it before Meuric and Arwel. I edged away from them, returning to Rose's left side.

"Our bargain is fulfilled," Rose decreed.

The warriors and the two women nodded, gathered up the chest, and departed.

Jonas sobbed openly on the floor. "Don't

kill me. Please don't kill me. I obeyed the natural order of things."

"You did not," Rose said. "I'd planned to throw you in the pits of hell, but there is a fate worse than death. You've earned it." She extended her hand to him and made a circular motion. Time froze. Long seconds dragged out. Finally, I could move again.

"What did you do to me?" Jonas scrambled to his feet, screaming.

"I followed the natural order of things, taking what was mine to take," Rose quipped.

"That isn't fair." He launched himself at me, dragging me between him and Rose.

Rose blasted us with a fireball. Somehow the fire flowed around me and landed on Jonas. His hair sparked. His clothes smoked.

He howled in anguish and dropped to his knees.

Rose shoved me aside. "I would erase your memory," she said to her victim, "but I want you to remember what you lost. What you can never be again. I want you to take that to your grave. And your little hideaway inside the mountain? I sealed the entrances. It's mine now. Natural order and all that."

Rose turned to me. "Secure him."

Circuits must have scrambled my brain, because I stood there, staring at Jonas. In what world was this normal? Not mine. How did the fire go around me? Why wasn't I dead? Did I even have hair left on my head?

"Quit touching your hair, worm," Rose said to me. "Use the ties in your pocket."

The ties. The ties that bind. The ties of my life. No, that was wrong. The tides of my life. Was it high tide or low tide? I should know the answer.

Rose poked me. "Snap out of it. Have your nervous breakdown later. Tie the man up."

I shook my head as a jolt of pure energy surged through my body. "Sure." When I'd cinched a cable tie around Jonas' wrists, I tugged him to his feet. I gazed at Rose, who had both hands on the immobile Trahearn. "Now what?"

"Now I'm sending you back to your paramour."

My blood churned at the accusation. "He's not my anything."

"Hold what you've got." Rose smirked and the illuminated corridor faded from view. Light thinned to streaks and exploded into darkness as we moved through the void of time and space. This being my third trip on the Rose Express, I knew not to freak out. But I couldn't help wondering what might be going through Jonas' mind.

He'd said he was a reaver. I'd have to remember that word and ask my dad if he'd ever heard of them.

We touched down none too lightly, sprawling onto the planked floor. Dust billowed in a curtain around us, and I caught a fit of sneezes. All I could think of was "don't let go of Jonas," so I didn't. When I stopped, I looked around the drab but familiar cabin.

Mayes had a pillow under his head and a goofy grin on his face. Deputy Duncan and three other cops had their service weapons drawn and pointed at me.

I stood and yanked Jonas to his feet. "Looky what I found."

Chapter Fifty-Four

Haney might be dead and gone, but his place was a hotbed of activity. I hoped his spirit would finally know peace. Perhaps he and White Feather would finally be together in the spirit world.

"Where'd you come from? What happened to your hair?" Deputy Duncan demanded. He advanced on us, gun centered on Jonas' heart. From the deputy's fierce expression, I had the strong sense he'd shoot first and ask questions later if Jonas so much as moved a muscle. Jonas had the good sense to stay put.

I took the high road and ignored his questions. "Your suspect is in my custody. Do you want him?"

Duncan stared at Jonas like he was a cobra. "What about special precautions? This man is dangerous."

I waved him closer, not sure if the other cops needed to hear the gritty details. "He's a killer all right, but his extra talents were neutralized by my friend on the Other Side. If you lock him behind bars, he'll stay put until the courts decide his fate."

The deputy's mouth tightened. "There's the matter of evidence."

His hesitation annoyed me. Did I have to do everything for these cops? "You have him for robbery and for kidnapping the sheriff. Keep poking around in the lives of your victims. You'll discover that Jonas knew them and met them repeatedly. The bedding in Haney's loft should have Jonas' DNA on it, for starters. Those flipbooks prove Jonas knew Haney."

Duncan motioned for two of the cops to take Jonas away. I crossed the room to Mayes and knelt beside him. "How're you doing?"

He reached for my hand and squeezed it. "Better. Good to see you, Baxley. What happened?"

Since Mayes had a similar aptitude and belief in the paranormal, I didn't mind discussing recent events with him, except that we weren't alone. Even though Duncan had spent part of a day in Little People world, I hesitated to talk freely before him and the other cop, Loggins.

"Oh, a little of this, and a little of that," I hedged.

He pulled me close and whispered in my ear. "Hang on. I'll get rid of the guys. And then you can tell me why your hair changed colors."

I jerked back, wishing like anything I had a mirror. What color was my hair? I drew a strand forward. The ends were singed black and reeked of smoke. Funny Mayes hadn't mentioned that. But the main color was different. Snowy white.

I stared at the altered tresses in mute disbelief.

"Give us a minute," Mayes said to the deputies.

Duncan looked like he thought otherwise, but he and Loggins stepped outside. Privacy came with a searingly intimate sensation. Heat steamed up the collar of my shirt as Mayes stared at me.

"I remember," he said, interlacing his fingers with mine.

From the sexy glint in his eyes, I had no doubt he was talking about The Kiss. I hastened to explain, "After Jonas stole your energy, I gave you a boost using the technique I'd seen him employ in my dreamwalks. What you remember didn't actually happen. It was a dream."

His taciturn face lit up. "The best dream I ever had."

It was good for me, too, but that wasn't the direction this conversation needed to go. Part of me knew I should disengage my hand, but the other part didn't want to let go. "A dream," I repeated gently.

"You saved my life."

"I should've been paying attention when the cabin got too quiet. Instead, I was absorbed in those flipbooks. I'm sorry he got to you. Are you sure you're all right?"

His expression hardened. "I woke up a few minutes before you and Jonas dropped into the room. But before that, I received your messages, only I couldn't find my way out of the dream. Wanting to leave the dream world wasn't enough. I was desperate to get to you. I was afraid Jonas would hurt you."

"He tried, but he failed. I was lucky enough to have someone more powerful than he was on my side. Rose returned the stolen dream churning talent to the Little People. Maybe when Jonas lost that power, his hold over you broke."

He rubbed his thumb over the back of my hand. "Tell me what happened."

I gave him the condensed version of my ghost dog tracking Jonas, of the trap Jonas set, and of the resolution between Rose, the Little People, and Jonas. "My hair. Is it all white?"

He nodded. "Snowy, expect for the tips, which are blackened. That must have been some takedown."

My poor hair. I knew from experience that dye wouldn't work on it. The universe would have another laugh at my expense. I didn't see where white hair was necessary. Why couldn't I just wear a shirt with Dreamwalker printed on the back? Instead, I had to rock the geriatric look.

Railing against the fates wouldn't help. Time to look on the bright side. I'd brought a criminal to justice. That was my take-home message. "I don't fully understand what happened, but I survived and I'm walking around on this side of the dirt and breathing air. I'm glad the ordeal is over." I paused, searching for the right words. "Jonas said he was a reaver. Does that mean anything to you?"

"A reaver. Historically, reavers were Robin Hood–like figures, robbing from the rich to support the poor. Scotland, for one, had reavers on the English border for many years."

"Jonas didn't strike me as a charitable individual. He stole energy from people. A lot of it."

"I can see how reaving would fit with an energy-vampire lifestyle. Stealing is a way of life for them, quite possibly a matter of survival."

"Lifestyle." I shuddered. "I hate to think of what he did in a positive light. He stole people's lives."

My phone rang. Odd. How was that possible? Had Jonas jammed the signal before? I wiggled my fingers free and pulled the phone from my pocket. Dad. "I need to take this call."

"Your mother said I should call," Dad said. "Everything all right with you?"

"Yes. The case is closed. Hang on a second while I put you on speaker. Mayes is here with me, and I want him to hear our conversation." I toggled the phone to speaker. "The police have Jonas Canyon in custody. He's no longer an energy vampire, but he called himself by another name. Have you ever heard of a reaver?"

Silence met my ears. "Dad? You still there?"

"I am. I'm afraid I have bad news for you. About your case."

I was glad he'd qualified his statement. If something happened to Larissa, I'd be a mess. Even so, the phone felt too warm in my hand. “Don’t keep us in suspense.”

“I heard back from Running Bear about the energy vampires he ran across before. There were two of them, a young man and an older woman. He identified Jonas from the photo you messaged to me.”

Mayes and I locked gazes above the phone. A wave of dizziness threatened. “Two of them?” I chirped.

“Yes. He described the woman as being skeletal and extremely dangerous. Apparently there’s a process they go through at the end of their lives where they require enormous amounts of energy.”

There was only one skeletally thin woman in this case. Lizella Tice. The woman at the rehab center. Jonas first identified her as his mother, but we’d dismissed that claim since she appeared to be a victim.

“We know who she is, Dad, and where she is. Thanks.”

“Be careful. Running Bear called the process she’s undergoing a strange name. It sounded like *rémoulade.* I should have asked him to repeat the pronunciation or spell it out. From what he explained, anyone who comes in contact with this woman will be completely drained until she completes the change.”

“What kind of change?” I asked.

"He didn't say."

"Thanks, Dad." I ended the call and sighed. "So much for wrapping up the case. We're not done. We have another energy vampire to catch. You got any fight left in you?"

Mayes nodded. "Feeling stronger by the second."

"Let's go."

Chapter Fifty-Five

On the way to the rehab center, we got a call from Dispatch. Twilla Sue Blair had awakened and wasn't happy about being a hospital patient.

Deputy Mayes grinned when he hung up the phone. "The boss is back to her old self. I predict she'll be making a break for daylight as soon as she figures out what they did with her clothes. She'll want her wheels back."

I nodded at him. We were both in the backseat, with Deputy Duncan driving our vehicle and Loggins following in the cruiser. Another deputy had carted Jonas off to jail. "We'd better capture Lizella Tice fast, then. If she's more dangerous than Jonas, Twilla Sue has no business being part of her take-down."

"You have a plan for getting this energy vampire to abide by our legal system?" Mayes asked.

"I was holding my own against Jonas until he sprang that mind trap on me. It was a lesson I won't soon forget. Energy vampires are dangerous creatures."

"You didn't answer my question. How will we take Lizella Tice into custody?"

I touched my necklace and was dismayed to feel nothing. The ordeal with Jonas had exhausted the energy in the stone. Would the gems in my pocket still be of use? "I don't know how this will end, but I plan to employ the same strategy I used with Jonas. Phone a friend."

"Your special friend?"

"Yes. We're no match for these people. Rose is better equipped to handle them."

"Should you have her meet us there?"

"Don't need to. Once we are in the same room as Lizella, I can summon Rose."

"Are you up for this? You must be at least a quart low on energy by now."

"I can do this. We need to tend to this last bit of business, then I'm crashing for the day. Tomorrow I'm driving home, so I need a good night's rest."

"Speaking of leaving, I'm putting you on notice that I plan to visit you. Soon."

This was a conversation I didn't want to have, but it would be best to clear the air. I met his gaze. "I apologize if I'm giving off mixed signals. You're a kind, attractive, and intriguing man, a man that any woman would be lucky to have, and you deserve someone who can fully commit to you. My situation is complicated. I'm a widow in the eyes of the law, but I think my husband is still alive out there, somewhere."

He inclined his head slightly, then took his sweet time replying. "I value your honesty and loyalty. Those attributes were sorely lacking in most of the women I've dated. Even if we keep our relationship platonic, I would still love to visit, to learn more about your dreamwalking, to spend time with your father and his friend Running Bear. We could all benefit from an exchange of information."

We wouldn't be where we were on this case without exchanging information. I, for one, would like my father to stop feeding me information as needed, piecemeal. I'd like to know the entirety of what we faced.

"You should visit," I said. "There is much we can learn from each other and from my father, who seems to be an endless fount of knowledge."

"We can drive down together," Deputy Duncan said. "I plan to visit the coast as soon as my leave request goes through."

Mayes and I were both startled by Duncan's remark. I'd forgotten Duncan was listening to us. "You and Charlotte?" I asked.

Duncan flashed me a grin. "She's quite something. I want to spend more time with her."

This vacation was panning out beyond Charlotte's wildest dreams. She'd wanted someone who saw *her,* someone who looked beneath the surface. Duncan appeared to get her. I hoped the feeling was mutual.

"I was thinking about doing exactly what they did," Mayes said, his gaze meeting Duncan's in the rearview mirror. "Borrowing a friend's RV and hitting the road."

"You quitting your job?" Deputy Duncan asked. "Twilla Sue won't like that."

"Not quitting anything," Mayes said. "Just need to take some time off. I can't recall the last time I took a vacation."

"That would be never," Duncan said, as he pulled into the rehab center parking lot. "Here we are."

"We'll have to get through the public health gatekeepers first," I warned.

Deputy Loggins joined us, making our party four-strong. Each of us examined our weapons. I tucked mine in my waistband. The deputies kept their weapons at the ready.

I trooped up the metal stairs into the admin trailer. The receptionist was gone. The administrative people were gone. I strode back to the big boss's office. He was gone too.

One thing was certain.

No one was minding the store.

Chapter Fifty-Six

We entered the lobby of the rehab center with me keeping a protective bubble of defensive energy around our party of four. Silence greeted us. If I hadn't seen the command post trailers out front, I wouldn't have known this facility was under quarantine.

I tapped on the glass and called out, "Hello. Anybody here?" Receiving no response, I reached through the receptionist's open window and picked up four fresh cloth masks on the desk. We put them on and entered the building, navigating around the stack of fire extinguishers near the door.

Our footsteps echoed down the empty corridor. The stillness inside the building was oppressive. Air wasn't moving, and it seemed to weigh heavily in my lungs. It reeked too, ripe with the sickly sweetness of death. In an earlier visit, I'd learned this place had beds enough for a hundred residents, and there had been about twenty to thirty staffers on site.

"Did she kill them all?" I wondered aloud.

"We need to find Tice before we count bodies," Mayes said. "We'll get a medical team in here as soon as it's safe for civilians."

Not a soul wandered the halls. It was as if everyone had abandoned ship. The hair on the back of my neck wouldn't settle. Something horrific must have gone down here. I hoped like anything that everyone wasn't dead.

"Ms. Tice?" I called from the hallway outside Room Twelve. "We'd like to talk to you."

No one answered.

No one stirred.

The place felt like a ghost town.

"Is she still here?" Mayes asked.

"Can't say," I answered. "I'm devoting my extra senses to keeping us shielded. I can't scan for life signs at the same time. I say we enter her room. If she's there, I'll contact Rose. If not, we have to keep searching the building for her."

"She could've left the building," Mayes observed.

"Perhaps, but where would she go? If she and Jonas are a pair, she'd want to meet up with him."

"Then she might be on the way to the jail."

"Shh. We don't want to give away any information. Remember, all of you, stay close to me, within arm's length, or risk being compromised. Jonas could mesmerize with a mere glance across the room. If she's more powerful, she could turn you one at a time. Stay vigilant."

"I go in first," Mayes said. "Then Powell, Duncan, and Loggins. The three of us keep Powell in the center at all times."

Duncan and Loggins nodded. I accepted his ordering of our positions because it suited me to be within touching range of everyone. We moved into the dark room. From Mayes' sharp intake of breath, I knew it was bad.

"What?" I asked.

"Ms. Tice's bed. There's blood and something lard-like on the covers."

I edged around him so that I could see for myself. The rumpled bedding was stained crimson and dotted with chunks of white goo. The aroma made my eyes water, as if a skunk had rolled in stinkweed. I strained to see in the twilight.

"What is that stuff?" Mayes asked. "Everybody back up so I can hit the light switch."

Moments later, the room came starkly into focus in a fluorescent glow. Mayes drifted closer to the bed, which meant we all drifted closer. "No bones, just fluids."

Duncan pointed across the room. "Look."

A person lay prone in the other bed, but the floor was littered with bodies. Along the wall, they were stacked three high.

"Good God." I felt as if my heart might leap out of its chest cavity. "Are they dead?"

"One of us should check," Mayes said.

"I'll do it," Loggins said.

"Wait," I said. "We can't do anything for these people because we have no medical training. We need to track Lizella and find out if she's still here."

"How?" Duncan asked.

"I have a helper, a ghost dog, who was able to track Jonas. I'll summon him and have him track Lizella this time."

"A ghost-dog tracker? How is that possible?" Loggins scoffed.

"Many things are possible," Mayes said. "It's a matter of suspending disbelief."

Duncan groaned. "Now you're sounding all mystic again. This is the oddest case. It has been from the start, so why should the finish be any different?"

"Summon him," Mayes said.

So I did, slipping just far enough through the veil to where Oliver dwelt. He was delighted to see me. After the mandatory licks and pets, I indicated what I wanted him to do. Back in the real world, Oliver reared up on his hind legs to sniff Lizella's bed. The deputies muttered uneasily, and then we were off.

"Follow me," I said.

The guys stuck close. Oliver led us all over the building. Bodies were stacked everywhere in the guest rooms. There was no sign of life. Finally, Oliver led us to the receptionist's desk. At a small sob, Mayes stepped in front of me, gun drawn. "Come out with your hands up."

Chapter Fifty-Seven

Deputies Loggins and Duncan pushed in front of me too, brushing past without a care for their safety. "Wait!"

Through my sixth sense, I could hear Oliver barking like he'd treed a possum. The noise echoed in my ears, loud and harsh. I marveled that none of the others heard it.

"Shut up!" a squeaky voice roared.

Ah . . . someone else heard Oliver. Whoever was under that desk had an active sixth sense.

"Be careful, guys," I said. "This person is very dangerous."

Loggins put his gun away and knelt down. "It's a kid. Come out here, little one."

Oliver kept barking. Since the hiding place was near the floor and so was Oliver, I crouched down to take a look. It was all I could do to keep the protective bubble engaged around us and keep track of Oliver.

"I'm scared," the child said.

"You're okay," Loggins said, waving her forward. "What's your name?"

From my vantage point, I could see the child. She was younger than my Larissa. Ash-blonde ringlets cascaded around her pale face. Big brown eyes stared at us with suspicion. An adult-sized T-shirt hung on her small frame.

"Cherry," the child said.

"That's my mother's name." Loggins' voice was sweetness and light. "Come out of there, Cherry. We're the good guys."

"Can't. There are bad people in here."

"How'd you get here?" Loggins asked.

"I don't know," the child said.

Mayes and Duncan crowded behind Loggins. All of them holstered their weapons. Loggins had his hand extended to the young girl. The scene seemed ordinary and in many ways a relief from the horrors in the residents' rooms. How'd a child end up in this place? Was she visiting a relative with a parent?

Oliver suddenly yipped, tucked his tail, and raced back to my side. A whisper of uncertainty flickered through me. At the same time, the air electrified. A nasty metallic taste formed in my mouth.

"Back up!" I shouted, scurrying backward

out of self-preservation. "Step away from the child."

None of the deputies gave the slightest indication they'd heard me. I got a sick feeling in my stomach. My instincts told me to flee the building, but I was here as a paranormal expert. I was supposed to be protecting the deputies.

Cherry poked her head out of her hiding place and touched Loggins. My brain nearly exploded as pure, raw energy shredded my ineffective barrier. Loggins and Duncan crumpled to the ground with two heavy thuds.

Mayes stepped back, reached for his weapon. "Stop right there."

"You won't shoot a child," Cherry said, coming to her feet. "It wouldn't look good on your record. Make the wrong move here, and you'll never be a sheriff."

"Get out of here, Mayes," I said. "She's like Jonas. Don't look at her. Don't listen to her."

"Like Jonas. Ha!" Cherry scoffed. "I'm nothing like that do-gooder. He did the world a favor by removing troubled souls. They should've paid him for his services."

Thoughts raced through my head as I clung to Oliver. Cherry had disabled Loggins and Duncan with a blast of mental power. It was only a matter of seconds until she had Mayes decommissioned. I inched toward the entryway and fired off an SOS to Rose. I also sent Oliver to safety.

Rose, can you hear me? I need you. ASAP. There's a badass energy vampire here. Instead of an answer from Rose, an icy shock wave seared my senses.

"Badass? I love the compliment." Cherry advanced toward me, pushing Mayes out of her way with a flick of her tiny fingers. "You think I didn't know about you? About your little friend on the Other Side? I know exactly who and what you are, Dreamwalker."

It was hard to move. Gossamer threads seemed to be circling me, tightening. My head ached something fierce, and no matter what I tried, my extra senses misfired. Somehow, this child blocked my transmission to Rose.

A glacial pond pooled in my gut. I felt lightheaded and absurdly heavy at the same time. I had to fight back, to save us, but how? This entity had more of everything. She could control people around her with barely any visible effort. She'd shut down my paranormal senses and stopped three police officers at the same time.

The sense of being snared in a sticky

spider web let up for a few seconds, and I scrambled toward the door. I had to get out of this building. Into the sunlight.

In the next breath, I realized why her efforts to control me had temporarily waned. Mayes stood behind her, his gun pointed at me.

"Mayes! Fight it. Don't let her win," I shouted. "Block her with your senses. You're not a robot to be ordered around."

"He can't hear you." Cherry snickered. A new batch of invisible spider webs came my way. These highly charged strands burned and sizzled as they wound around my legs.

I forced my arms to move, bumping into the wall. Something clattered loudly. The fire extinguishers. That burst of raucous sound might as well have been my death knell. I wasn't going to make it.

Think. There had to be something I could do, some source of power I could access. *Power.* I had crystals in my pocket. Could I reach them? Since I knew how to take and share energy, I could zap her if she touched me.

Pulling a reverse psychic vampire move on her was a long shot, but I wouldn't quit without a fight.

"What are you, Cherry?" I asked, somehow finding a way to stuff my left hand into the pocketful of crystals. Simultaneously, the glacial feeling in my stomach spread to my legs. Numbness followed. I couldn't move my toes.

Energy. Cherry was burning a lot of it. How long could she keep this up?

"My name isn't Cherry. I plucked the fake name out of that dimwit's head to make him trust me. I'm Lizella Tice. Not many of my kind left on the planet."

A heavy chilling groan passed through me as the webs cinched around my torso. I couldn't breathe. I jerked and pushed against the bonds. The pressure eased enough for me to gasp in a shallow breath.

"Got your attention," Lizella crowed.

The room spun as the effects of oxygen deprivation came and went. She could crush me in a heartbeat, but she hadn't. What did she want from me?

"You have my complete attention," I managed in a raspy voice.

"In all my centuries of doing this, no one has ever kept coming after me. Why'd you do it? How did you ignore the suggestions I planted in your head to leave me alone?"

What suggestions? "I don't know."

"When the change is upon me, I'm vulnerable, but Jonas made sure I had energy sources to rejuvenate. Then you stumbled upon my nest and moved me to the hospital and then to here. So nice of you to provide me with a surplus of resources."

"*I* didn't provide you with anything. We moved you to increase your chances of survival."

"Semantics. Access to those fresh bodies accelerated the rebirth process. Ordinarily, it takes months to come in contact with so many donors. Thanks to you, I cut the time to nearly nothing. Now I need to tie up a few loose ends, spring my consort from jail, and we'll go our merry way."

Though my fingers were wrapped around a handful of crystals, the arctic chill in my body had spread down my arms. If Lizella didn't touch me soon, I was doomed. "Jonas isn't going anywhere."

"Bars can't hold our kind."

"So he's like you?"

"No one is like me, but I tolerate him." She bared her tiny white teeth. "He's a good provider."

"Not anymore."

Chapter Fifty-Eight

The invisible bonds tightened around my torso, caging me in a breathless void. This time I didn't fight Lizella, didn't waste a drop of my precious energy. I glanced at Mayes. He'd gone still, and his eyes were glazed over.

No help in that direction.

Loggins and Duncan hadn't stirred.

Rose was out of reach, and Oliver was no match for this powerful creature.

I was our last hope. Now I needed a chance to act.

"What?" Lizella shrieked. "What did you do to him?"

"Nothing, but my friend from the Other Side exacted retribution. She stripped him of his powers. He's lost his ability to steal energy."

Raw current slammed into my head, lightning-bolt strong, scattering my thoughts, filling me with excruciating pain.

I closed my eyes and thought of my family. Larissa. I would hold on because of her. I would endure. I wouldn't quit.

As I drew into myself, I mentally reached into the reservoir of crystal energy. *Survive.* That's what I had to do.

The assault ended as abruptly as it started. "Why don't you die?" Lizella shrieked.

"I'm different from your normal prey." I looked beyond her at Mayes. His eyes were blinking, and he gazed around in confusion. A spark of hope flared inside. Perhaps Lizella's powers had limits after all.

"I'm going to kill you with my bare hands." Lizella jumped on me, all forty pounds of her. The shrill noise she made sounded like a stuck pig.

At the last second, I decided not to blast her with energy. I grabbed her with my spare hand and siphoned energy from her as fast as I could. With each second of contact, I grew stronger, snapping those invisible bonds around my body.

"No!" Lizella wailed. "Die! You must die!"

Gunshots rang in the air. Three quick rounds. Lizella jerked around and snarled at Mayes. "You! You dare attack me?"

Lizella dismounted and turned her attention to Mayes. His bullets in her heart hadn't fazed her. If I didn't act, Mayes would die.

I grabbed the nearest fire extinguisher and pulled the pin. I coated her with the foamy repellent. In seconds, she resembled a gloppy, pint-sized statue. When the stream ran out, I grabbed another unit. Mayes joined me, and we drenched her over and over again.

The foam adhered to her short hair, stretching out the ringlets into snowy strands. We circled, coating her from head to toe.

"Is it working?" I asked.

"She isn't moving, and we are, so it's working," Mayes said. "Call for backup."

I fired off a quick message to Rose. This time it felt like the message went through. When the last canister of foam sputtered and quit, Mayes and I retreated, still holding our empty extinguishers.

Loggins and Duncan stirred and sat up. "What happened?" Duncan asked.

Lizella's hand moved up to her face. Mayes shouted in another language and charged her, slamming the canister against her head. There was a loud crack, then Lizella sprawled on the floor.

My heart pounded in my ears. I didn't trust that she was down for the count. Seemed like she'd come back against everything we'd thrown her way. What else could we use as a weapon? The only other idea in my head was fire, which wouldn't work because she was swimming in fire retardant.

A jolt of nausea sent me to my knees and the room spun. I fought for equilibrium, fought like a champion, but I couldn't hold out against this strong current. Lightning flashed. Thunder boomed. Rose appeared in her gleaming armor amidst a cloud of smoke.

"You rang?"

Chapter Fifty-Nine

I dropped the fire extinguisher and stood. My knees trembled, but at least this entity was more friend than foe. Sometimes. I was certain she'd be happy once she knew why I'd summoned her.

"Clean up on aisle three," I said with a rueful smile.

Rose shot me her "I'm not amused" look. She also waved her hand so that every living, breathing person in our vicinity became frozen, out of phase with our reality. Mayes, Loggins, and Duncan were still present, but they weren't privy to our discussion.

"Energy-sucking creature under that goo," I said. "Like Jonas, but with a lot more oomph. She just changed her appearance from that of an old woman to a young child."

Rose leaned forward eagerly once I said "changed her appearance." "Name?"

"Lizella Tice. She's Jonas' mother. We

think. But she called Jonas her consort, so I'm not sure of their relationship." I sighed. "We don't know who or what she is, really, but she can drop grown men with a blast from her fingertips."

"Lizzie?" Rose said, nudging the goopy mess on the floor with her boot. "That you?"

The creature on the floor groaned and sputtered.

The bittersweet look on Rose's face had me worried. "Wait. You know her?"

"Long story."

"This woman — excuse me, this *thing* — nearly killed me, and she may have killed over a hundred people in this building alone. What is she?"

"I'm not exactly sure. At one point she was a selkie."

I tugged on my ear. "Did you say 'selfie'? She's a picture of herself?"

Rose heaved a longsuffering sigh. As we spoke, her appearance changed. Her armor melded into her skin so that she was a normal human height and in her leather biker togs. She knelt down and used her hand to wipe the fire retardant from Lizella's tiny face.

"A selkie. A creature that comes from the sea and can shed its seal skin temporarily to appear as human. They're creatures of Irish mythology."

"Mythology. Stories that aren't real."

"Selkies are very real, and in this day and age, they're quite rare. Four hundred years ago, Lizella made an unfortunate choice of mate and earned the curse of a powerful witch. She's been trapped in human form so long she's become something else."

"Don't tell me you feel sorry for her. This woman is a stone-cold killer. She steals the very spark of life from people. She can blast lightning bolts from her brain and fingertips."

"Like I said, she was a selkie. Now she's something else. An aberration of nature."

"What will you do with her?" I asked. I would not feel sorry for Lizella Tice. She'd hurt so many people. She nearly killed all of us.

"Rose?" Lizella managed in a shocked whisper. She writhed away from my guardian angel. To say she seemed surprised at this outcome was an understatement.

Rose gripped Lizella's foam-covered hand, preventing her retreat. "Not so fast. Last time our paths crossed, you promised to return to the sea. What happened to the grand plan of reuniting with kith and kin?"

"I returned to the sea all right, but it was too late. My species was nearly extinct. The few selkies I found were hiding in remote areas, afraid to be exercise their creation rights. Some of them had even taken seal wives. It was unthinkable." Lizella stopped and coughed repeatedly. "They were ashamed and scared of their own shadows. I couldn't live like that."

"You promised to mend your ways."

"And I did. For a while. Then Jonas came to the sea and cried seven tears. It was a miracle. His tears released me from my prison."

"The sea is your home. Not a prison." Rose's voice had a hard edge that didn't bode well for Lizella. What would Rose do with someone who'd squandered her second chance?

"Turned out to be a prison sentence. I could see people who visited the shore, people I wanted to know, but due to the enchantment, I was locked in the water. Except for seven tears. They have always released us from our skins."

I made a vow to look up the legend of selkies after this holiday. If they were anything like Lizella, I hoped I never ran across another one. Morbid fascination had me following every word of this unusual conversation.

"Jonas set you free, then what?" Rose

prompted.

"We traveled. I was starved for humanity and ended up far from the sea. I had to find ways to sustain the constant energy drain of living as a human. Turned out, my consort had a power I much admired. His ability to transfer energy turned out to be most useful. As you can see, I wore out my last body, and I'm starting fresh."

"Not with Jonas," I said. "He disturbed the natural order and paid the price. A living death."

Lizella shrieked. "No! You can't do that. He's mine to command."

"Not any longer. He's been stripped of his talents."

Lizella tried to slug Rose, but Rose stopped the punch in midair with a twitch of her nose. I held in a gasp. This creature had no chance of surviving this encounter if she antagonized Rose.

Lizella wiped another glob of foam off her round chin. "I've been wronged. Under the treaty, I demand to be compensated." She pointed at me. "That human will do nicely. I'll take her."

"She's not available." Rose's voice hardened. She straightened and stared down at the foamy, child-sized lump with a sneer. "According to the terms of our agreement, you forfeited your protected status when you left the sea."

"But my kind . . . they'll go extinct without me," Lizella whined. "I am the sole surviving female."

"Not my problem. You will be judged by a higher power."

"No, no, no. You can't do this to me. I'll pay you. Anything you want. Please. Don't send me away. Don't punish me for following my natural instincts."

"You lost touch with your natural instincts long ago, Lizzie. Your actions determined your fate. Few are given a second chance. You squandered yours. You're done."

Lizzie screamed and flailed around on the floor. I was reminded of a fish out of water. Guess that wasn't too far from the truth.

"Get used to being helpless," Rose intoned. "It will become your eternal state."

"You can't do this to me. I'll appeal."

"He's aware of your transgressions. Appeal denied." Thunder boomed. Rose said sounds I didn't comprehend, and Lizella floated in the air, encased in a bubble. Before my eyes, the bubble shrank smaller and smaller until it winked out of sight.

I let out the breath I'd been holding. "Remind me never to make you mad."

"I've been fair with you and will continue

to deal with you in that way, as long as you do as you're told."

"I've always been a free spirit."

Rose glanced around the rehab center with disdain. "Not anymore. Your spirit and mine are bound now, through all eternity."

Her stark words clanked around in my head. She expected my obedience — no, she *demanded* my obedience. Best not to dwell on that. "What happened to Lizella?"

"She's earned her place in eternity. Rest assured she will not trouble you or this planet again."

"Good." A wave of relief washed through me, filling me with a sense of normality. Lizella's reign of terror was over. She wouldn't be set free from prison on a technicality. She wouldn't have the opportunity to murder an entire building of people again.

"Follow me," Rose said.

I traipsed after my guardian angel, entering every room in the rehab center. Turned out, only four people were dead. The rest were in stasis. Not trapped in the Little People's memory land, but needing a jump-start to awaken.

If it were only one person, I could help, but so many? It would be impossible. "What can we do? How will I explain this . . . this outage, to the cops?"

Rose stilled for a moment then nodded. "I've been advised to right this wrong. The general public doesn't need to know there are twisted creatures like Lizella in the world."

"How will you do that?"

"The breath of life."

She may as well have spoken ancient Greek. "And that is . . . ?"

"A universal CPR. You must treat me the same as Jonas treated his victims."

Understanding smacked me dead between the eyes. I quaked with terror. "You . . . you . . . you want me to kiss you?"

Chapter Sixty

"No kissing necessary," Rose said. "I believe, if I'm reading your memory correctly, we interlace our fingers, and you blow your human breath in my mouth."

The idea of being so intimately connected to Rose had the hair all over my body standing on end. At the same time, I felt like I'd taken a one-two punch to the gut. "Isn't there another way?"

"Unless you want your police friends to stay in zombie mode longer than would be healthy for them, I suggest you follow my orders. Immediately."

A look at Mayes and his fellow deputies frozen in time had me gulping. Rose had a way to help these people. Would I let a squeamish stomach and my pride get in the way? No. I was a bigger person than that.

Rose's skin felt creepy cold on my hands. When our lips touched, I blew with all my might, filling her with my breath. I broke away to gasp in more air. “Again,” Rose said. Soldier for humanity that I am, I obeyed. Only this time, Rose breathed into me.

Fire burned down my throat, raged in my lungs, and sizzled in my blood. My knees gave way, and I sagged against her. She lowered me to the floor. The room spun, and I stared at her scowling face. It faded in and out of focus like a movie made by a toddler.

“What did you do to me?” I asked.

“I’ve marked you, inside and out.”

It hurt to draw in breath. It hurt to talk, but I had to know. “Why?”

“You know the reason. Excuse me while I fix the mess Lizella made.” Rose strolled down the hall and faded from sight. The room faded too, as darkness overtook me.

“Wake up, sleepyhead,” Mayes said.

His worried face hovered above me. The events of the morning rushed into my head in a terrifying montage. I didn’t recognize the place, couldn’t remember how I got here. “Where am I?”

“At the rehab center. You fell asleep as soon as we started searching for Lizella Tice. Guess I’m working you too hard.”

I hadn’t fallen asleep. Rose knocked me

out on purpose. After she'd marked me again. My mouth felt like it had been on a desert vacation. The chill of the floor seeped into my skin, but other than that, I seemed to be whole.

"Is there water?" I asked.

"You'd drink something here?"

"Not the water I'm worried about," I shot back. Loggins and Duncan peered over Mayes' shoulder. They flashed me quick smiles, then their expressions hardened.

Mayes nodded toward the door. "Loggins, grab Powell a water bottle from my vehicle while Duncan writes a report."

Loggins gave a terse nod and hurried away. I heard the door open and close.

"No sign of her boss," Duncan said. "We've been all over this place twice. No kid. No skinny old lady."

That answered my next question. Rose took what she wanted and left us to whitewash what had happened here. Fluorescent lights hummed faintly overhead. The pillow cushioning my head and the cold floor beneath me were real. I was alive. That was real.

"We have only a minute or two before Loggins returns," Mayes said as he faced me. "Tell us what really happened."

How'd he know? I tried to clear my dry

throat. "You won't find Lizella. My contact from beyond took her. That little kid was Lizella. With all the energy she'd tapped into here, she'd gone through a metamorphosis to a younger version of herself. She planned to spring Jonas from jail and start over elsewhere."

Mayes squeezed my hand. "Figured the threat was gone because nothing else explained why you were out cold when I turned around." He paused long enough to catch my eye. "At some point, I want the whole story."

The pressure from his fingers caused my fingers to curl into his. How had I missed that he was holding my hand again? I shot him a quick glance, and he looked extra smug. At some point, I wanted to know how long he'd been awake and what he'd been doing.

"How will this get spun?" I asked.

"We'll leave that for the health professionals to figure out. From a law enforcement perspective, our person of interest is missing. Except for four dead people, everyone else is sleeping." He shot me a sharp look. "Since the threat has been removed, the rest of these people aren't our problem."

I shrugged. "Not like I could share energy with anyone right now. I could sleep until morning."

The door opened. Loggins returned with four bottles of water. I sipped only a little bit at first, wary of my reaction. I didn't know what Rose-breath had done to me, but I didn't fancy throwing up in front of three men either.

The men drank their water quickly. My body tolerated and made quick work of the water I'd swallowed. The slight headache I had eased, and I felt worlds better with something in my stomach. With everyone looking down on me, I felt at a disadvantage. I struggled to get free of Mayes, but he didn't budge. "Take it easy," he said. "Just a little while longer."

My hand was warm and so was my arm. Was he giving me a boost of his energy now? "I need to sit up."

Mayes nodded and Duncan lifted one side of me while he lifted the other, still keeping our hands connected. "Better?" he asked.

I nodded, not trusting myself to speak. What did the other deputies think of me, of *us*? Had Mayes given them the impression we were a couple? Did I need his energy more than I needed to worry about saving face?

A sigh escaped my lips. I saw a muscle twitch in Mayes' cheek. My mood flashed from hopeful to cautious. Was he reading my thoughts?

"Duncan, put out an APB on Tice," he said, probably for Loggins' benefit. "She's a person of interest in the same crimes we nailed Jonas Canyon for. She's no innocent, but the degree of her guilt is yet to be determined."

What would these cops think if they knew Lizella Tice was a mythical sea creature run amok? Surely they would dismiss that notion as fantasy even though it was the truth. I'd seen some crazy things in this job, but this case was in a league of its own.

"Your color is coming back, Powell," Mayes said. "Bet you're glad this case is wrapping up."

I tried for the same light and breezy tone. "You have no idea. I'm going to need a vacation after this vacation."

"You and me both."

Sirens approached. Mayes ordered everyone to put the cloth masks in place, and he finally allowed me to stand. "You all right?" he asked in a tender voice.

I nodded.

"It's about to get crazy in here. Once we get this sorted out, I'll have Duncan run you back to the campsite." He lifted my chin. "We're going paddleboarding in the morning, right?"

"My last day," I said ruefully. "I promised my daughter."

"I'll get you there. That's a promise you can take to the bank."

CHAPTER SIXTY-ONE

My dreams that night were not my own, but nightmares were to be expected. Haney and White Feather walked hand in hand toward me and my ghost dog through the veil of fog. "You got her?" Haney asked.

I nodded. "We did. Lizella Tice won't hurt anyone again. Neither will Jonas."

"What if she finds us?" White Feather asked.

"I think she will be too busy to chase down everyone they killed."

"Why'd they do it? Why'd they tell us it would be better when we died?" Haney asked.

"You had something they wanted: life. The only way they could take it from you was if you gave it away. My understanding is that they had permission to take little bits here and there from people, but that was supposed to be their extraction limit."

"We were so unhappy," White Feather

said. "My family didn't understand my need for self-expression. Haney is the only one who understood. When Jonas told us he had a way for us to be together for all time, we believed him."

They would be forever young and in love. Not bad, except for the dead part. "I'm glad you found each other up here."

Haney looked guilty. "Your friend helped us. The biker chick."

I smiled. *Good for Rose.* "Anything else I can do for you two?"

"Tell my family I'm happy, really happy," White Feather said. "I don't have to be Native American or white or anything in between. I can just be myself up here."

"Will do." I glanced at Haney. "And you? Any message for a loved one?"

"All I've got is my mom, and she's not anywhere you could find her."

"She's with the Little People, right?"

Haney scrunched up his face. "I thought Jonas was my friend. When I told him about my mom disappearing, he got real interested, and somehow he figured out how to cross into their world. He took me with him, but each time, it cost me. Mom was happy to see me, but nothing I said or did could persuade her to leave. I wanted her to come home and be with me, but she said no, that she'd found her place." His lower lip jutted out. "By the time I figured out I couldn't rescue her, Jonas pretty much owned me. He stole from the Little People, so I couldn't even return to visit her. Once Mom was lost to me, I wanted to die. The only goodness I ever found in life was White Feather. We're together now."

The final pieces fell into place. Jonas took advantage of Haney's loneliness, bartering away bits of his life in exchange for visits to his mother. What child wouldn't give anything to be with a parent? And while he was deciding to suicide, he connected with another lost soul, White Feather, and their needs aligned.

Except this was no Romeo and Juliet who'd died because they couldn't live without each other. This was the reverse. They'd died to be together. Only, if not for Rose, the joke would've been on them. They would have wandered around for several eternities and never crossed paths in the Afterlife. It was that big.

"I wish you well," I added when the silence had gone on too long.

White Feather knelt to pet Oliver, my ghost dog. "I love your dog. Any chance he's looking for a new home?"

"He's his own master these days, and he

likes following me around. I would hate to lose his companionship, but if he wants to stay with you, that's okay with me."

White Feather whispered some words in Oliver's ear. He flapped his head and leaned against me. "He's your dog all right," she said, rising and taking Haney's hand once more.

"We won't keep you, but we needed to say goodbye," Haney added. "We have a job. With your friend."

"A job?" So Rose hadn't done a good deed . . . she'd been thinking of her needs the whole time. My teeth ground together.

"We're greeters now, like in a discount department store," White Feather said. "We welcome spirits to the afterlife and help them understand that they're dead."

I brightened. That seemed like an excellent idea. "Good deal."

"We upset the balance by our actions. We learned our lives weren't ours to end, but we're working to get in His good graces."

"I'm happy for you."

White Feather cocked her head to a silent sound. "We have a customer."

They faded from view. I wondered if Rose would visit, since I was already in her realm. She didn't show, so I figured she was busy elsewhere. I drifted off into a peaceful sleep.

■ ■ ■ ■

I awakened so early, the sky still wore its cloak of night. Larissa cuddled next to me, along with all three dogs. Even Sulay the fat cat and little Ziggy curled against me. I grinned in the darkness. Warmth and love trumped death and dying every time. For a long moment, I listened to the sound of Charlotte's even breathing across the camper. We'd come up here to get away and relax, but this serene setting had been anything but peaceful.

Thanks to Mayes and Rose, we'd stopped a tag team of serial killers. Stopped them cold. The thought made me smile, even as I realized how the trip had changed me. For one thing, I'd learned about energy transfer. I had long known some people would drain energy from people around them, but never in my wildest dreams had I thought I might possess that ability.

Not that I would ever steal energy from another person. That wasn't right. The natural order of things and all that. I was starting to see there was a Big Picture I didn't comprehend. A symphony of actions going on in the world that ensured life wasn't completely random. Except for the fact we humans could mess it up, especially if we ignored our path.

Apparently the natural order for me was to be a dreamwalker, and that designation encompassed a whole lot of territory. The more I knew about Rose, the leerier I was of her, but I needed her, the same as she needed boots on the ground on my side of the veil. That natural order thing again.

And my hair. White as snow, like my grandma's had been. Like my father's was now. I'd seen terrifying sights and been marked by the trauma. The natural order. Funny how my thoughts kept coming back to that phrase.

Where did the Little People fit in the natural order? They weren't of this world or the next. Before this week, I would have scoffed at the notion of the existence of Little People and creatures like Lizella Tice. Not anymore.

Seeing was believing.

Which brought me full circle to Roland. I'd thought my presumed-dead husband was still alive because he hadn't found me in the realm of the living or the dead. He could easily be someplace else, a possibility I'd never considered before this experience. And if he existed elsewhere, was he trapped or there by choice? How would I ever find him in a universe with unlimited possibilities?

At the murmur of voices outside, I leaned across the bed and peered through the thin curtain. My parents were outside, talking with Deputies Mayes and Duncan. My pulse kicked up its heels. I had questions for Mayes, questions I couldn't ask in the presence of my daughter.

I eased from the bed, but the animals and Larissa awakened anyway at my movement.

"Mom! Are you leaving?" my daughter asked, reaching for me.

The fright in her voice triggered a double dose of maternal guilt. "It's early. Go back to sleep."

"Not yet. Cuddles?"

"Cuddles." I hugged her close, reveling in her perfection. She was growing up fast. Seemed like if I blinked, I might miss her teen years altogether. I nuzzled her hair. "Love ya."

"Love ya back. I'm proud of you, Mom. You're the best."

Her praise made my insides hum. "I don't know about that, but I try hard. Has it been fun in the mountains?"

"Yeah, but I'm ready to go home."

I wiggled her nose. "Not before our paddleboarding adventure this morning."

"We don't have to do that."

"Yes, we do. I want to, and I'm sorry your request got delayed. This case was more involved than any of us thought."

"You stopped them. You made it so the bad guys can't hurt anyone."

"This pair definitely won't steal energy ever again. And I didn't do it by myself. I had help. Lots of it."

Larissa pulled back and searched my face in the near darkness. "The cops couldn't have caught them without you."

"I suppose, though I'm sure, given enough time, they'd have found a way to catch this team."

Larissa shook her head. "They found the guy right away and couldn't hold him. Don't be modest. You closed this case. You've got game."

"I can't take credit for justice being served. I couldn't have done it alone either. Please don't glamorize what I do."

"But I want to be just like you. I want to make the world safe."

"It isn't easy, and it takes a huge toll."

Larissa giggled. "Like your hair?"

"My hair. Yep. The universe has a warped sense of humor."

"It's okay, Mom. You totally rock that look. I like the new you."

"The new me is still your mother. Don't you ever forget that."

"I won't."

"I need to talk with Pap and Mama Lacey about the case. They are amazingly closemouthed about Pap's dreamwalker experience, but I hope he can help me process some of what went on this weekend."

"Will you tell me about it?"

"One day."

"Look who's closemouthed now."

The things I'd seen and done did not need to be rattling around in a ten-year-old's head. "You deserve to keep your childhood innocence a little longer. I wish I could shield you even more. At your age, you don't need to know about bad guys. Most kids your age are focused on friends, clothes, or hobbies."

"I'm not most kids."

"Agreed. But I'm doing my best to make sure you enjoy being a kid. I want to do a good job of being your mom." I sat up and tucked the covers around her. "You stay here in this nice, cozy pile with Maddy, Elvis, Muffin, Ziggy, and Sulay. Dream of your favorite things."

" 'Kay."

I dressed in the bathroom and hurried outside.

Mayes heard me right away and stood beside the campfire. His eyes, so shuttered and unreadable when I first met him, now glowed with feeling. The corners of his lips slanted up. I should discourage his interest, but the part of me that had been asleep a long time had awakened. My pulse quickened, my step lightened.

I could've slid into the circle beside my mother, but I walked around to the side by Mayes. He gave up the cushion where he'd been sitting and parked on the ground beside me.

We chatted for a few minutes, with Duncan keeping his gaze on the camper. His continued interest boded well for Charlotte, and I hoped their budding relationship brought them both happiness.

As if he'd conjured her up, Charlotte strolled out of the camper in her PJs with a blanket around her shoulders and declared she wanted to see sunrise over the lake. Duncan took off with her like a shot, and we were alone with my parents.

Mayes took my hand in his. "I want to know what happened. Every detail."

Chapter Sixty-Two

"If you want to know what happened, you'll have to stand in line," I said, enjoying the touch of his hand. "I have questions for my dad."

"Thought you might," my father said.

I took a deep breath. "I get why you didn't tell me everything about this job. It would be overwhelming to take in all that information at once. This case was so different. My eyes were opened to things I'd never seen before. Let's start with energy transfer. Is that why you guys always gather at my place after a case, to share your energy with me?"

My parents exchanged glances. "Partly."

"I know you did it for the sheriff, so I assume you can do it whenever you need to."

They nodded. I turned to Mayes. "You also have a talent for energy transfer. You helped the sheriff and me, twice."

He shrugged. "You needed it."

"But I didn't ask for your help."

"You didn't have to," he said. "I'm on your team."

"My team," I said uneasily. I glanced over at my parents. "Is that why I feel so much better around Stinger? I'm sucking energy from him?"

"Stinger's a generator," my mom said softly, tipping her head toward the camper.

I caught the meaning of her gesture and realized I was talking too loudly. I leaned forward and softened my voice. "What does that mean?"

"It means he radiates energy constantly. With the rate you burn energy dreamwalking, you two are a good fit."

"Who's this Stinger guy?" Mayes said, his face clouding.

"A medium she helped at home. He's also a member of her team," Dad explained. "While I had a few trusted individuals who helped me recover from time to time, Baxley attracts people and animals who help her."

Mayes turned to me. "Like your ghost dog."

"Oliver is free to go off on his own. He is invited to stay with spirits all the time. White Feather even asked him to stay with her and Haney."

"You've seen them again?" Mayes asked.

"They came to me in a dream last night."

I explained their new role as greeters on the Other Side. Then I gave an edited version of what went down between Lizella Tice, the selkie-gone-bad, and Rose. "What I don't understand is the limit of possibilities when it comes to reality."

"The universe is open to possibilities," my father said.

"All my life, I've known there was life and the afterlife." I stared into the flickering flames. "Now I find out about the Little People, people who aren't of this world or the next. Lizella Tice also originated from a category I'd previously thought were folk tales. Myths and folklore have a basis in reality. I'm struggling to believe these facts."

"As well you should," Mom said. "You've opened many new doors of knowledge at the same time."

Her cryptic comment added to my frustration. Words boiled out of my mouth. "Why didn't you clue me in to this stuff before? And how much more is there? Are vampires, werewolves, and Big Foot real?"

"Difficult to say," my father said.

Mayes nodded his agreement. Mom said nothing. It was too much. "Why so many secrets? Why can't I get a straight answer?"

"There isn't one," Mom said. "Dreams span the gamut of imagination across time and space. Reality is subjective."

"You mean objective?"

"I meant what I said," Mom said, going all cryptic again.

An uneasy silence followed. I stared into the fire and tried to wrap my head around what Mom was saying. Each of us knew otherworldly things from firsthand experience. Each of us had a subjective lens through which we viewed the living and the dead.

"So, there's no actual list of what's real and what isn't?" I asked. "No cheat sheet to memorize and prepare myself?"

"No. Every day, every case, is a new world of possibilities," Dad said.

Bottom line, the cast of bad guys I might encounter spanned the length and breadth of time as well as the imagination of all the people who'd ever lived. No wonder there wasn't a manual for this.

"And Roland?" I hated that my voice broke.

"We don't know," Dad said. "Since he doesn't appear to be here or on the Other Side, there's a strong possibility he's elsewhere."

"Where, elsewhere?"

"We don't know," my mother said, gentling her voice again.

I didn't like that answer. It was on the tip of my tongue to tell my parents about my watcher in the woods at home, but I didn't. Guess I was getting the hang of this need-to-know thing, but I didn't really know enough myself, yet, about that mysterious figure to tell them much of anything.

"Did everyone stay up all night?" I asked.

"Only me," Mom said. "Tab slept because he needed to be rested to drive home this afternoon. I stayed up to make sure you got your rest."

I had yet to figure out all my mother's talents. She had an affinity for crystals and natural medicine. I had no doubt she could soothe a splinter out of a bear's paw or accomplish any Herculean feat put before her.

"Thanks. Thanks to each of you here," I said. "I couldn't have done my part in stopping the energy vampires without your help."

"To him whom much has been given, much will be asked," Mayes said.

A movement beyond the campfire caught my eye. Mayes followed my line of sight and vaulted to his feet, his hand hovering over his holstered firearm. "Who goes there?"

My brain kicked into action. Only one person I knew would walk around out here in the first pink of dawn, and that person was heavily armed. Burl Sayer. I shouted, "Blue marmalade," and scrambled to my feet.

Sayer waved a hand in greeting as he trudged toward us with a smaller someone in tow. He wore a rifle on a strap across his shoulder. "You're all right, Red Rooster. No need for code now that I recognize ya. This here's Sunshine. We met at a meeting."

I caught the grateful glance Sayer shot Mayes. Guess Mayes had been successful in getting Sayer some help. I'd thank him later.

Sunshine looked like she'd lived in twilight for years. Her clothes were dirty and dark-colored, her pale face smudged with black. A skullcap covered her head, even though the temperature was in the seventies. But she walked with the same boots-on-the-ground swagger as Burl Sayer, and there was a bright gleam in her shockingly blue eyes.

"Hello, Sunshine." I introduced us, one by one. She nodded but didn't say a word. She seemed a good fit for Sayer. "Where y'all headed?"

"Finishing our rounds on the mountain, then we're getting some shuteye." Sayer glanced around the perimeter and leaned toward me. "You never know when the invasion will start. We have to be prepared."

"Gotcha," I said. "You're welcome to share our fire."

"No can do, but thanks for your hospitality." With that, they waved and continued on toward the lake. I had a moment's heart pang for Charlotte and Duncan, but Charlotte knew the code words if Sayer crossed her path. I had a feeling Charlotte and Duncan weren't paying attention to much besides each other.

"They seem like a good match," Mom said.

"You don't know the half of it," Mayes said. "Sunshine is a group therapy counselor. She helps her clients by literally walking in their shoes for a few days. Sayer may respond to her treatment plan, or it may be a waste of her time, but at least we tried to move him toward reintegration into society."

"Speaking of matches," Mom said with a yawn, "I could use your help in the camper for a few minutes, Tab."

"What?" My father looked up from poking the glowing embers. "Oh. I see. Help. Yes, I will help you."

And just like that I was alone with Mayes. Real subtle, my mom.

Chapter Sixty-Three

"And then there were two," I said to fill the awkward silence.

Mayes reached for my hand, intertwined his fingers in mine. The corners of his lips lifted. "Remind me to thank your brilliant mother later."

I felt like I was in junior high all over again. A boy liked me. I liked him back, but I couldn't actually like him because there was someone else. Or was there? It was too confusing to parse.

I stared at our linked hands. "I can't do this."

"This?"

I couldn't look up. The heat of the fire burned on my already warm cheeks. "Us. I can't do us."

"Have I asked you to turn your back on your family or beliefs?"

"No, but —"

"I am a patient man, Baxley. I wish to be

friends with you."

"Friends?"

"To learn from you. To share knowledge with you. To dreamwalk with you."

My heart was beating much too fast, and I could barely hear for the subsequent rush of blood in my ears. Mayes hadn't mentioned dating or kissing or personal relationships. He wanted to know more about our shared abilities.

"Is that all right with you?" he continued. "Even though you've invited me, will you be angry if I visit?"

A visit. He wanted to come see me. At home. He wasn't calling it a courtship, but that's what it felt like to me. "Uh. Not sure that's wise."

"There are so few of us, Dreamwalker. You would shut me out? After the energy we've shared?"

"I owe you. I know that. It's just that. . . . Well, it's complicated."

"Complicated I understand. We are brothers and sisters in the spirit, right?"

"Yes."

"That's what I'm talking about. Nothing more."

"But our hands."

"That's to remind you."

"Of what?"

"Of the other."

The other. I could pretend not to understand, but I knew exactly what he meant. The synergy between us wasn't solely because of our outside interests and abilities. He wanted more with me. Much more.

"I don't want you to be disappointed," I ventured, finally having the courage to look him straight in the eye. "I'm not looking for a romantic relationship, even though I enjoy your company."

He smiled, a true smile this time. "I also have constraints. My people have certain expectations of me, even though I have non-tribal responsibilities and a law-enforcement career. But I'm not one to blindly follow rules for rules' sake, and neither, I think, are you. Ours will be a professional relationship until we say otherwise. Agreed?"

I liked the sound of that. "Agreed."

"Shall we sit?" he asked. "Or would you rather take a walk?"

I glanced at my leased RV. "Sit. My daughter is sleeping. I won't leave her alone."

He nodded, squeezed my hand gently, then released it. We sat cross-legged in front of the fire. "How's the sheriff?" I asked.

"She checked out of the hospital last night. First thing she did was commandeer her vehicle."

"No more sheriff's SUV for you?"

"Maybe one day. When I've earned it."

"You've earned it already. If not for your efforts, Twilla Sue would have died from her encounter with that psychic vampire."

"If you say so."

"I know so, and so do the other deputies. You stepped up and did her job. The case is closed, and two serial killers are off the street."

He made no effort to respond to that remark. "And Gail?" I asked. "What's the word on her cases this morning?"

The fire crackled and hissed before he answered. "She had the files from the mass gravesite shipped to her Atlanta office. Last I heard, she was leaving town right about now."

I was happy to see her go. "And her other case? The one about the Sandelman child?"

"The GBI rounded up the key players yesterday. Senator Hudson inherited the red car from a cousin and didn't change the registration. They found the car in a storage unit listed under his name. Hudson was arrested."

The red car. My lead had helped solve the case. Maybe I *could* work some of Gail's cold cases. From home. Turned out, I didn't like being on the road very much.

"What about White Feather? Will she have a Native American funeral?"

His face shuttered. "White Feather's ceremony will be private."

My head jerked back at his curt tone. "I expected no less."

"Sorry. I didn't mean to sound rude. Some people try to insert themselves into our ways, and we are wise to their manipulation." He shot me a guilty glance. "I didn't mean to imply you were like them."

"No need to apologize. I understand." Another conversational dead end. "What's the word on the rehab center?"

"Listeria poisoning from caramel apples is suspected. Coincidentally, the illness symptoms ceased once Lizella Tice left the center."

"They can prove the poisoning angle?"

He shrugged. "All I know is that's how the incident is being labeled."

"Are the symptoms the same as being drained by a psychic vampire?"

"Some are similar."

"Huh."

I couldn't think of one single thing to say. We sat together in silence for a while, and it felt comfortable. I liked that I didn't have to entertain Mayes. Roland. . . . No, I wouldn't compare Mayes to Roland. They were very different.

The deputy's stomach rumbled. The very normal sound making me laugh. "I should start breakfast," I said.

Mayes stretched his arms. "I've got a better idea. Let's round up anyone who wants pancakes and take them to the breakfast place in town. My treat."

"Yes. We should do that."

After breakfast, we packed up the campers and headed to the lakeside recreation park, where they rented paddleboards. It suddenly dawned on me what day of the week it was. "Will they be open on Sunday morning? I should've called ahead."

"They'll be open. I checked," Mayes said from the seat beside me, little Elvis nestled in his lap. Deputy Duncan followed our camper caravan in Mayes' car, and Charlotte had opted to ride with him.

"Thank you." I eased around another turn, noting Mayes' death grip on the armrest. "I'm a good driver. Relax," I said.

"We have a lot of weight behind us," he said. "Going slower on the curves would give you more time to correct for errors if something went wrong."

Larissa laughed. "He sounds like Dad,

Mom. Can we keep him?"

Our eyes met in the rearview mirror. My daughter looked so happy with Maddy the lab beside her and Muffin the Shih poo on her lap. Our cats perched on the seatback to oversee everything. Good thing Sulay couldn't talk or else I'm sure we'd get an earful.

"He's not a stray we can take home with us, Rissa-roo. His life is in the mountains. His job and his family are up here."

"Oh. Too bad."

I sent her a private message. *Don't go getting any ideas, young lady. Just because Charlotte is smitten with Deputy Duncan, there's no reason to pair me up with anyone.*

I happened to glance over at Mayes, saw the smirk on his face, and got a sinking feeling in my gut. Had he listened to our nonverbal conversation? We'd had telepathy when we shared energy, but it hadn't happened since. I'd believed the effect would be temporary, but I had no basis for that belief. I didn't begin to know all the skills the deputy chief had. Like my father, Mayes was cagey about what knowledge he shared with others.

"You just never know," Mayes said. "I might be very adoptable." He turned around to look at Larissa. "Is it okay with you if I come for a visit?"

"Yes! That would be so cool. As long as it's okay with my mom."

He nodded at her. "Already cleared it with her, so it's settled. I'll come for a visit."

"When?" Larissa asked.

"Depends." His gaze rested on me, and my face flushed.

"On what?" Larissa asked.

"Schedules, that sort of thing," Mayes said.

"Good. Don't wait too long."

"I won't," Mayes said. "I have a feeling it will be easy to hitch a ride to the coast."

I took the next curve slower. "I have that same feeling. I hope it works out for them."

"They have the same chance as anyone. Nothing's a given in this world. Opportunities are what you make of them."

There was the Mayes I'd come to know. Cryptic and freighted with double meaning. We could be holding hands and singing love songs like Duncan and Charlotte if I accepted Roland wasn't coming back. I wasn't ready to give up on my missing husband — though I had to admit, it was easy to be around Mayes.

When I pulled into the parking lot, the first thing I noticed was the sheriff's SUV. "Is Twilla Sue here?"

Mayes nodded. "She is. Her nephew runs this place, so she got him to open up for you today."

"Is she better?" *Better* wasn't the word I wanted to use, but I didn't want to go into the details of the case with Larissa listening so attentively.

"See for yourself."

We joined my parents, Charlotte, and Duncan outside and walked toward the rental office. Twilla Sue came out on the porch and waved. Her face looked thinner than when I'd met her a few days ago, but the sparkle in her eyes and the pep in her step were unmistakable.

The sheriff was back in the land of the living.

"Morning!" Twilla Sue called. "Come on up here, and let's get this paperwork done. I swan, there's too much paperwork in this world."

Turned out that everyone except Charlotte and Duncan wanted to paddleboard. Charlotte took one look at the paddleboard demo Mayes provided and said she didn't want to ride home in wet clothes. Deputy Duncan rented a jon boat for them, and soon everyone was on the water.

Both my parents were spry and fit for their sixty-something years, and they took to paddleboarding like they'd been doing it all their lives. Larissa also seemed a natural. Mayes spent a good deal of time getting her stance and paddling stroke grooved.

I putzed around in the shallows, learning the ins and outs of paddleboarding from the directions Twilla Sue shouted from the shore. Our dogs flanked her, except for Elvis, who'd managed to get picked up by the sheriff.

A chilly blast struck my legs. I glanced down and there was Oliver, barking his ghost-dog head off. Seemed he approved of paddleboarding too.

He went invisible again, but the chill remained, letting me know he was here with me. The sun blazed on this last day of summer vacation. We'd be home a little after dark, and then the fall schedule would take priority. I welcomed the coming routine, and I'm sure Larissa looked forward to seeing her school friends again.

Not wanting to get overtired before the long drive, I paddled ashore and joined Twilla Sue at the picnic table.

"Thank you, for saving my life," Twilla Sue said. "Without you, I'd be dead right now."

"We did our best to get you back. The important thing is that you recovered, and a serial killer is off your streets."

"We'll be years figuring out who those people are in the mass grave. Of the ones we could obtain DNA for, there were no hits in our database. The dental impressions haven't proved useful either."

"You've got good people here and so does the GBI. You'll figure it out eventually."

She raised her brows. "Any chance we can talk you into relocating?"

"No. My home is on the coast."

"Pity. You ladies have two of my best men stirred up."

"I can't speak for Charlotte, ma'am, but I've done nothing to encourage Deputy Mayes."

"That man is used to women throwing themselves at him. Your lack of interest and your similar talents are the perfect lure for him."

"I'm not looking to replace my husband."

"Be gentle with him, whatever you do. He's one of the few good guys. I've made no secret of the fact he should take over if I'm successful in running for office. We need him to stay here and have his head here."

I was uncomfortable with where this was going. "And you, Twilla Sue? Are you sure you still want to run for public office?

Seems like this kidnapping took a lot out of you."

"I remember you were there, in my dreams, and that you tried to get me to leave that sanctuary. I couldn't for a while, not until I felt like I'd had enough time with my baby. Mayes explained about the energy transfer, that without the four of you sharing your life force with me, I'd be dead same as those seven young men Jonas incapacitated. So, I'm thanking you with all my heart. I won't forget what you and your family did for me. If you ever need anything from me, all you have to do is ask."

I was speechless. That didn't happen too often.

"Plus, I wrote out a check for your services." She handed it to me.

I gawked at the amount. "This is too much for five days of work."

"It's just right. Put it in your daughter's college account, or get yourself a new vehicle, or do something nice for your parents. The consulting fee is yours to spend however you see fit."

My parents paddled to shore and joined us. "Everything all right here?" Mom asked.

"We're good," I said, pocketing the check. "Very good."

■ ■ ■ ■

After the uneventful drive home, I went through the motions of unpacking and getting Larissa ready for school the next day. I was beyond tired, but I was also unable to settle down. Long after bedtime, I wandered the house, checking doors and windows, but even that routine wasn't enough to lull me into bed. I halted in the dark kitchen, sipped a glass of tap water, and stared out into the night.

For some time now, I'd detected an energy signature. My watcher in the woods. In the last month, we'd managed a few telepathic communications. Though the idea of being watched seemed alarm-worthy, my watcher had truly been looking out for me, even hogtying a man who put snakes in my truck.

His life signal was inconsistent, and he rarely responded to my mental queries. I'd always had the sense that it was difficult for him to be here. Part of me hoped it was Roland or one of his military buddies, but there was always the possibility that it was an enemy of Roland's, staking out our place in hopes he'd appear. Sometimes I thought my elderly neighbor, Mr. Luther, knew the watcher's identity.

Now, after my six days in the Georgia mountains, I'd learned life existed along a continuum between the living and the dead. I believed my watcher hailed from this gray zone in between, which would explain why he wasn't always there and why he rarely seemed whole. He probably couldn't abide on Earth full time, but somehow he'd found a way to project his essence here.

That didn't sound like an act of vengeance or greed or enmity. That sounded like an act of love. It had to be Roland. Who else would want to keep track of me and Larissa? Who else would risk everything to protect us?

No one.

I opened the kitchen door and settled on the back steps, Oliver alongside me. I viewed the area through my extra senses and confirmed no one was in our immediate vicinity. I quested farther with my heightened senses, searching for that dampened energy signature belonging to my watcher.

Nothing.

Oliver nudged my hand with his cold nose, and I petted him. For the heck of it, I pulsed a telepathic message to my watcher, even though I didn't believe he was out there.

I'm home. Miss me?

As I waited for the reply that didn't come,

I gradually released the tension in my shoulders. I'd had quite the adventure in the Georgia mountains. It would take time to get back into my routine here, not that *routine* was part of my vocabulary. My medium friend, Stinger, would visit tomorrow, and I had a couple of landscaping jobs to bid. Mayes would visit, and I'd have to take that one day at a time.

Something sparked on the paranormal plane at the far edge of my property. Anticipation made my hands tremble.

Are you there?

I listened so hard for a reply that I forgot to breathe. Oliver gave me a last nudge, then bounded away. As quickly as my hopes had risen, they crashed. Just because I wanted to talk to my watcher, that didn't mean I could summon him at will. Did it?

Might as well assume he could hear me broadcast thoughts, even if I couldn't detect his physical presence. *I'm home from our trip. Larissa learned how to paddleboard, and I solved a couple of murder cases. I learned more about the realms between life and death, and I figure that's where you come in. Somehow you are slipping between realms to keep track of us. You don't have to worry about us anymore. We are safe and happy and able to pay our bills.*

I sat there in the dark, listening intently. Far as I could tell, there was no reply, no flare of energy or life sign anywhere in the vicinity. Something niggled at the corner of my mind. I focused on that slight buzz, dialing in that certain frequency.

You've changed.

My jaw dropped. The watcher was here. I'd summoned him. How was that possible?

Wrestling with a demon and folklore creatures will do that to a person. But I'm fine. Everyone is fine here. You don't need to keep making this long trip to check up on us. I may have seemed incompetent when I first became the Dreamwalker, but I've got this now.

I didn't move a muscle. I listened to the ominous silence, wondering what he thought of all this. Did my words relieve his concern?

No answer unfolded in my head. Had my watcher lost interest? I tried something else, a calculated bluff. *I know who you are.*

The answer roared in loud and clear. *You know nothing.*

Aha. He was listening and paying attention to what I said. Time for me to put him on notice. With Mayes coming to visit soon and with Springer's help, I should have enough juice to access the watcher's realm. *Wait and see.*

ABOUT THE AUTHOR

Formerly a contract scientist for the U.S. Army and a freelance reporter, mystery and suspense author **Maggie Toussaint** has seventeen published books, fourteen as Maggie Toussaint and three as Rigel Carson. Her previous mysteries include *Gone and Done it, Bubba Done It, Doggone It, Death, Island Style* and three titles in her Cleopatra Jones series: *In For A Penny, On the Nickel,* and *Dime If I Know.* Her latest mystery, *Dadgummit,* is Book Four in her Dreamwalker series about a psychic sleuth. Maggie won the Silver Falchion Award for Best Cozy/Traditional mystery in 2014. Additionally, she won a National Readers Choice Award and an EPIC award for Best Romantic Suspense. She lives in coastal Georgia, where secrets, heritage, and ancient oaks cast long shadows.

Visit her at www.maggietoussaint.com.

The employees of Thorndike Press hope you have enjoyed this Large Print book. All our Thorndike, Wheeler, and Kennebec Large Print titles are designed for easy reading, and all our books are made to last. Other Thorndike Press Large Print books are available at your library, through selected bookstores, or directly from us.

For information about titles, please call:
(800) 223-1244

or visit our website at:
gale.com/thorndike

To share your comments, please write:

Publisher
Thorndike Press
10 Water St., Suite 310
Waterville, ME 04901

DISCARD